Until Sage

Aurora Rose Reynolds

Table of Contents

Until Sage

Until Him

Dedication

To Anjelisa

You were beautiful, with dark hair, and a smile that lit up the world around you. You were far too perfect for this world and taken much too soon.

May you always know how much you are loved.

1/10/2002–5/18/2002

To Elizabeth

There are people in this world who show you what strength truly is.

You, my darling, are one of them.

Prologue

Science says it only takes four minutes to fall in love with someone.
I didn't believe that was true, until I met Sage Mayson.

Kim

HEARING A *thump, thump, thump,* the steering wheel in my hands jerks hard to the left, making me squeak as my car swerves into the oncoming traffic lane. Getting the car back under control, I slow down as it bounces, letting me know I have a flat.

"Great! Just flipping great." I pull carefully off the road and onto the shoulder, flipping on my hazards as I put the car in park. Grabbing my cell from my purse sitting in the passenger seat, I curse to myself once more when I see the battery is just about to die. "You should have stayed in bed," I mutter under my breath, but then I think about the baby blue suede bag I scored for seventy percent off from the underground sale I went to and remember instantly why getting out of bed this morning was so totally worth it.

Scanning through the contacts in my cell, I find the number for AAA and press call then put the phone on speaker. "Thank you for calling triple A. Your call may be monitored. Please press one for—"

The phone dies in my hand, and I let out a growl of annoyance. Dropping the now useless piece of crap into the cup holder, I check for traffic and then get out of the car, slamming the door behind me. Checking both tires on the driver's side, I see both are good, so I move around to the back and drop my hands to my sides. The back right tire is not only flat, but shredded. There is no way I can drive on it without doing major damage to my car.

Resting my hands on my hips, I scan the road to see if there's anyone coming, but the street is completely dead. "Looks like you're on your own." I've never changed a tire in my life, so I have no idea what the hell I'm going to do, but hopefully I can figure it out.

Going to the trunk, I open it up and pull out the bottom floorboard, where I locate both a spare and a jack. Taking out the jack, I set it on the ground then spend ten minutes trying to unlock the screws for the tire, which seem impossible to remove. Feeling tears of frustration burn the backs of my eyes, I lean into the trunk, resting my forehead on the edge of the spare tire. "This sucks."

"Need some help?" a voice asks from behind me. Startled, I jump up, bumping my head on trunk lid, and then quickly pull myself up to stand. Holding the top of my head, I spin around feeling lightheaded. "You okay?"

"I…" Blinking, my mouth runs dry. "Um…." I stare at the guy in front of me, trying to get my mouth and brain to work in unison. *Hot* is the only word filtering through my head as I take him in. He's probably six-two, if not taller, long and lean, with broad shoulders, a tapered waist, and skin that shows he's a mixture of something beautiful. Smirking, his full lips tip up ever so slightly, making me realize I'm staring at him and still haven't answered his question.

Shaking away my sudden stupidity, I mutter, "My tire blew."

"You got a spare?" The deep timber of his voice slides over my skin as he steps closer, giving me a full dose of his presence.

I was wrong; hot isn't the right word. I don't think there's one in the English language to properly describe him. Long, thick lashes make his unusual gray-green eyes stand out. His jaw is angled, hard, and his nose crooks a little to the left, but even with that imperfection, nothing could take away from his beauty.

"Yeah, I have a spare, but I can't get it out of the trunk." I give myself a silent pat on the back for putting together a full sentence without stuttering. As he comes even closer to me, I jump as his hand wraps around my hip, and he moves me to the side, away from the road.

"Let me take a look." His head disappears into the trunk, and two seconds later, he stands holding the tire I couldn't get out moments ago.

"How did you do that?"

"You have to push down on the tire while you loosen the bolt."

"They should really print that on the tire or something," I say, feeling my nose scrunch up, and he smiles, showing off a dimple in his right cheek that makes my stomach feel full and melty. Jesus, whoever this guy is, he's dangerous to the world's female population.

Dropping the spare to the ground near the back tire, he grabs the jack and puts it in place. "Do you know how to change a tire?"

"No," I reply distractedly, watching the muscles of his arms flex as he takes a long thingy and starts unscrewing the bolts from the tire.

"What was your plan then?" He pauses, looking up at me, and my eyes move to his.

"What?"

"If you got the tire out of the trunk, what was your plan?"

"I was going to wing it," I tell him truthfully, and his eyes close briefly as his head shakes side-to-side.

"Come over here."

"Why?"

"I'm gonna teach you how to change your tire."

"Oh." I take a step toward him. Apparently not close enough, his big hand wraps around mine, and he tugs, forcing my feet to move until I'm practically standing between his bent knees.

"Now, you always want to loosen the bolts before you get the car off

3

the ground, it makes it easier to remove them once the car's in the air."

"Okay." I nod, and he smiles again, making me feel like a giddy schoolgirl. This is getting ridiculous. I have never been affected by anyone the way he's affecting me.

"All right. I'm going to loosen the bolts then we're gonna raise the car. Got it?" Nodding, I watch the muscles in his arms flex as he loosens each of the bolts. "Then you use this to pump the jack." He takes the long thingy in his hand that he loosened the bolts with and uses the flat end of it, sticking it into the jack that he starts pumping. "Once you get the tire off the ground about two inches, you stop."

"Okay," I agree, watching him pull the long thing back out of the jack once the tire is off the ground.

"After you get the bolts loosened and the car in the air, you remove the bolts completely," he says as he starts to remove them.

"Can I try?"

"Absolutely." He lets go of the handle, and I take over and try with all my might to turn the bolt, but nothing happens. "Let me help." He gets close, too close, placing his hand next to mine on the handle. "Push on three."

"Okay." I bite my lip when his body cocoons mine, and his scent of dark, warm amber seeps into my senses.

"One… two… three." I push with him, and the bolt spins. "Good job. If you're having problems getting them loose, you can always stomp it."

"Stomp it?" I turn my head to look at him, and he grins.

"Step on it. Use your body weight to force it to move."

"Oh, got it." I nod and move away from him to get the next bolt off without help, but the last one isn't as easy. I start to do what he suggested, but he stops me with his hand wrapped around my bicep.

"You have heels on." His eyes drop to my three inch wedged espadrilles. "And I'm here, so you don't need to break your neck." He leans over, and with one flex of his muscles, the bolt spins. Pulling off the tire, he grabs the spare and puts it on then sets all the bolts. "This time, we do the opposite. Tighten them as much as we can then drop the jack and tighten them up the rest of the way," he explains, and I spend the next five minutes watching him tighten all the bolts then drop the jack, allowing the car to lower to the ground before tightening the bolts the rest of the way.

Stepping back when he stands, I notice a thin coating of sweat covering him. The sun has hit its peak, and it's about twenty degrees hotter out than it was this morning when I left my apartment. Lifting the bottom of his shirt, he wipes his face, giving me a glimpse of his abs. That's when I notice the dirt and grime from his hands has transferred to his shirt, a shirt I know by the tiny U on the pocket would probably cost eighty dollars, if not more. "Oh, no."

His eyes drop to where mine are looking. "What?"

"Your shirt, it's ruined," I point out, and he shrugs.

"It's all good. Where are you heading?"

"Just about fifteen minutes down the road into town. I think there's a mechanic there that's not far from my place."

"All right. I'll follow you in." He picks up the jack in one hand and the tire with the other, like it weighs nothing at all, and carries them back toward my trunk. I stare after him, wondering what I should do.

"That's not necessary." I follow after him. "I'm sure you have things to do," I say as I open my door and reach in to grab a twenty from my bag sitting on the passenger seat. Slamming the door, I go to where he's bent over the trunk. As soon as he stands, I hold out the bill toward him. "Thank you so much. I don't know what I would have done if you didn't stop."

His eyes drop to the bill in my hand before meeting mine once more. "I'm not taking your money."

"Please, take it," I push, holding it out farther in his direction.

"No."

"Your shirt is ruined because of me. At least, let me give you this for helping me out."

"I don't need your money." He moves around me and opens the driver's door. "Get in. I'll follow you to town."

Holding his stare for what feels like forever, I finally give in when I see I'm not going to win. Putting a little stomp in my step for not getting my way, I watch his eyes crinkle in the corners and his lips twitch. Sliding behind the wheel, I turn the car on and look up at him when I put my hand on the door handle.

"Don't drive over twenty."

"Has anyone ever told you that you're a little bit bossy?"

"Can't say they have."

"Hm." I tug the door but he doesn't move, and when I look up at him, he's looking at me like he's trying to figure something out. "Um…" God, I just realized I don't even know his name. "Sorry, what's your name?" I ask, and his eyes meet mine.

"Sage. Sage Mayson."

"That's a cool name. I'm Kimberly, um… but my friends call me Kim."

"Kimberly," he repeats, and the way my name dances off his tongue makes my heart double beat in my chest. "Wait for me to pull out before you pull off."

"Aye, aye, captain," I say, and his lips tip up and he shakes his head before pushing my door closed. Watching him out my side mirror as he walks back to his car, I study the way he moves. It's like he's in control of every single muscle in his big body. His shoulders are back, and his stride is long. If I were walking next to him, I would have to double my steps to keep up.

Seeing him open his door, I move my eyes from my side mirror to my rearview mirror and notice his car for the first time. His isn't a car at all; it's a Cadillac SUV, the exact one my dad drives, only Sage's is black. And not a shiny black. No, it's a matte finish, so I know it's custom. Sage doesn't look much older than me, so the ride could be his parents', but if it's not, now I really wonder who the hell he is and how he can afford something like that. I know my dad paid an arm and a leg for his, because I heard my mom bitching nonstop about how much it cost when he came home in it.

Hearing a horn, I snap out of it and pull onto the road, speeding up until I hit the twenty mark on my speedometer then slow down. The normal twenty minutes it would take me to get back to town takes me over thirty, and when I pull up outside the mechanic shop, I shut the car down and watch Sage pull into the spot right next to mine.

Getting out, I grab my purse and the shopping bag from the backseat then head toward one of the open bays. Sage is talking to a guy with dark, almost black hair that is a little long and tattoos covering every inch of skin not hidden by his white shirt, which is spotted with black grease and dirt.

"Gareth, this is Kim," Sage introduces as soon as I get close.

"Hi." I give him a smile, and he lifts his chin a fraction of an inch in greeting.

"You got keys?" he asks.

"Yep." I hand them over, and as soon as I do, his eyes go back to Sage.

"It'll be done in about forty minutes." My teeth snap together, and my hand moves to my hip.

"It's actually my car," I point out.

Gareth looks at me and repeats, "It'll be done in about forty minutes."

"Wow, aren't you just Mr. Wonderful?" I grumble under my breath, and Sage chuckles next to me while Gareth smiles, and if I hadn't experienced Sage Mayson's smile this morning, Gareth's would

7

for sure take my breath away.

"You need to keep this one," Gareth mumbles before walking off, and I wonder what he means by that, but I obviously don't stop him to ask.

"How about coffee?"

My head swings Sage's way at his question, and something strange fills my chest. I would normally say no to any kind of anything with a man who looks like him. A man who looks like he has the ability to break your heart with one smile. But there is something telling me that if I pass up his invitation, I will regret it for the rest of my life.

"Sure."

"Good." He smiles gently then startles me by placing his hand against my lower back, leading me over to his truck. As soon as we're at the passenger side door, he swings it open. Taking my bags from my hand, he waits until I'm inside before handing them back and shutting the door behind me. Letting out the breath I didn't know I was holding, I look around.

The car smells like him, and the inside is just as clean as the outside; there isn't even a little dust on the dash. Turning to look over my shoulder, I see him open the back passenger door then watch him take off his shirt and toss it inside before reaching in and grabbing a new one, putting it on before slamming the door closed.

"Oh my," I breathe, turning to face forward, hoping he didn't see me checking him out.

"So you live around here?" he asks as soon as he opens his door.

"Yeah, just a few blocks over off Lowery in the Hamilton subdivision," I say as he slides his tall, lean frame behind the wheel.

"That's a nice area."

It is nice, and I will never be able to afford a house in that subdivision. The only reason I can afford my one bedroom apartment there is because my landlords, Mr. and Mrs. Dennison, take a huge chunk of my rent off each month so that I can help them out with babysitting when they need a night out or just need a break from their four kids. They're adorable but total hellions.

"Do you live with your parents?"

"No."

"Houses in that subdivision are close to a mill."

"I know," I agree as he studies me like he's trying to figure out how I can afford to live in that area.

"Where do you work?"

"Are you a cop?"

"No."

"You should be," I inform him, and his lips twitch. Letting out a sigh, I roll my eyes when I see he's not going to give it up. "I rent an apartment above a garage from a doctor and his wife who live in the subdivision. I help them out with babysitting, and they give me a break on rent each month," I rattle out quickly then pull in a breath and let it out. "Is there anything else you need to know right now?"

"I want to know everything." He turns away from me to face the windshield. "But I'm thinking that will all come with time."

My breath leaves on a whoosh, and my heart starts to pound against my ribcage as I watch him back out of the parking spot. I don't know if he meant to make that statement sound like we would be spending time together or not, but it did, and the thought of getting to know this man has my stomach filling with butterflies and my palms sweating.

"You okay?"

Turning my head, I find him studying me closely. "Yeah, totally cool." I drop my purse to the floorboard then wipe my hands down the front of my bare thighs. "So, if you're not a cop, what do you do?"

"I work with my cousin."

"Okay..." I wait to see if he will fill me in, but he doesn't. "What kind of work do you do with your cousin?"

"Private security, bounty hunting, PI work, we do it all."

"So you're kind of like a cop, but you're not a cop. Why is that?"

"My dad's a cop. He loves his job but hates that he has to deal with red tape. He can't just go in and get a job done. He has to make sure all the i's are dotted and t's are crossed."

"So you don't like red tape."

"Basically," he concurs as we pull into the drive through line of one of the small coffee huts that sits in a parking lot on Main Street. "Do you know what you'd like?"

"A large iced green tea," I murmur, leaning forward to grab my purse so I can get some cash out. As soon as we pull up in front of the window, he places our order with the girl working inside. "Here." I hold the ten-dollar bill in my hand toward him, and he shakes his head. "Please, let me pay for our drinks," I press, but he ignores me and pulls down his visor, taking down a twenty from the bills he has stacked there. "You know, it's kind of annoying that you won't let me pay," I inform him as he hands me my drink.

"You'll survive." He smiles at me before giving the girl a tip and pulling away from the window. "What's your plans for the day?"

"I have a date with a bookshelf I bought from IKEA that will likely take me a year to put together. What about you?" I ask, taking a sip of my drink.

"My schedule's clear. Do you want some help putting it together?"

"Really?" I ask, stunned, and he brakes at a stop sign then turns to look at me.

"Sure."

Wow, okay.

"That would be really nice," I respond quietly as warmth and something soft and sweet spreads through me.

"Good," he replies just as quietly, heading back to the mechanic shop, where he waits for me to pick up my car and pay before following me back to my place.

As soon as we reach the house, I lead him down the long driveway that curves around the back of the property. My apartment is above the third garage, but the way it's set up makes it feel like I have my own space and I'm not living in someone else's house. Hitting the remote for the garage, I pull inside and watch Sage drive up and park behind me. Grabbing my bags from the passenger seat, I open my door, get out, and head toward the trunk, where I meet him.

"Have you been over here before?" I ask when I see him looking around the neighborhood.

"I've spent my whole life in this town. When I was younger, I wanted to buy a house over here before the developers got a hold of it," he says, taking my bags from me.

"You did?"

"Yeah, years ago, when this was nothing but farms and open land for miles."

"I would have liked to see it then."

"It was beautiful. My parents own a house a few miles down the road from here. Their house used to be in the middle of nowhere. Now, the city has grown up around them. My dad loves it, but my mom hates it and has been talking about moving farther out to get away from everyone."

"This place is growing fast. Since I moved to town a couple months ago, they have built a Starbucks and a Taco Bell. I have never seen buildings go up so fast before," I tell him as I head for the set of stairs inside the garage. With him at my back, I open the door to my apartment and turn on the light.

My apartment is just under six hundred square feet, with a combined kitchen and living room. There's a small bedroom that is just big enough to fit my queen-size bed, two side tables, and a dresser, and a bathroom with a pedestal sink, and standup shower.

"This is nice," he says, looking around, and I smile. I love my place. The dusty blue of the walls sets off the light gray colored wood floors that run through the place, making it seem bigger than it is, which is a bonus for sure.

"Thanks." I take my bags from him. "But you should see the view from my bed," I gush, then realize what I just said when his lips tip up. "Not that you will ever see it," I add quickly, dropping my eyes to the floor as my cheeks get hot. "I just said that because I have a huge skylight over my bed that makes it feel like you're sleeping under the stars," I finish, then turn and head for my room without looking at him muttering, "I'll be right back."

Kicking off my sandals, I dump my bags on the bed then pick up my pillow and hold it to my face, wishing I could just scream. I've had three boyfriends. Two of them were when I was in high school, and one of them was in college. I haven't dated since the last. Not really, anyway. I mean, I've gone out to dinner with a few guys, but nothing serious, and none of them ever came back to my place, so I have no idea what the hell I'm doing. Knowing he will hear me if I scream, I toss the pillow to the bed and head into the living room, where I find him standing over the demolished box my shelf came in.

"Did the box come like this?" he asks, looking at me, and I shake my head.

"No, it was in one piece when I bought it," I say, and he looks from me to the destroyed box then back again. "It *might* have fallen down the stairs when I tried to carry it up here."

"Just once?" he asks, and I let out a breath watching his lips twitch.

"Okay, a few times," I revise, and he smiles.

"You got any tools?"

"Tools?" I repeat, and he presses his lips together like he's trying not to laugh at me. "I obviously know what tools are. I just don't have any. Besides, it came with the little thingy to put it together."

"Thingy?"

"Are you going to make fun of me or help me?" I ask, putting my hands on my hips, and his eyes move over my face then drop to where my hands are resting.

"I'm not making fun of you."

"It feels like you're making fun of me," I point out, and he stands, and now that I don't have my sandals on, he's not just taller than me. He towers over me, making me feel tiny and fragile.

"I would never make fun of you. I think the way you talk is cute."

"Oh."

"I'm gonna go out to my truck to get my tool bag. Can I use that door?" He tips his head toward the sliding door off the kitchen that leads to a deck, which looks over one of the large ponds in the middle of the community.

"Yeah, but you'll have to walk around the back of the building and go through the gate at the side. It's easier if you just go out the garage. Besides, if Burt is out back, you may have to run from him, and I can tell you from experience that's never fun," I inform him, and his eyes have once again filled with humor.

"Who's Burt?"

"My landlord's Chihuahua. He's small but scary as hell."

"I'll go out the garage."

"That's probably smart," I murmur, and he shakes his head then opens the door and leaves. I listen to him head down the steps and hear him open the garage door. Standing here, I wonder what I should do, and then my stomach grumbles, reminding me I didn't eat breakfast, which is something I definitely shouldn't be missing out on. Since I need to take my pills, I really need to eat.

Opening the fridge, I grab the stuff to make myself a sandwich and hear Sage coming back up the steps. As soon as he is in the apartment and closes the door, I turn to watch him drop a huge bag of tools onto the floor near the box.

"Do you always travel with so many tools?"

"Most of the time," he says, pulling out a power drill and a plastic box with attachments inside. "I work on my house when I have time, but I don't leave my tools there since someone could break in and take them when I'm not around."

"Is your house in a bad neighborhood?" I ask, opening the breadbox and pulling out a loaf, dropping it to the counter.

"Do you know Percy Priest Lake?"

"Yeah." My eyes go to him over my shoulder, and I notice he already has the pieces of wood for the shelf separated into piles.

"My house is on the lake. The house is shit. One day it will be beautiful, but right now, it's shit, which means I got it for practically nothing and will probably spend way too much fucking money and the rest of my life fixing it up."

"It will be worth it," I tell him immediately. Even though I haven't seen the house, I know for certain that one day, when he's done, it will be beautiful.

"Waking up to a view of the lake every morning and sitting out on my deck at night, watching the sun set on the water, I know it will be, too," he says quietly, and something in his eyes changes in a way that makes my body feel funny.

Pulling my eyes from his, I turn around to face the counter before I say something stupid, like *"I want to see both those things with you."*

"Do you want a sandwich?" I ask instead, and hear him say, "Sure," behind me right before the power drill starts up.

Once I'm done making a sandwich for him and one for myself, I pull down a box of Cheez-Its from the top cupboard and drop a handful on each of our plates. Then I take both over to the coffee table and set them down. Moving back around where he's working in the middle of the room, I head to the fridge and open it up to see what kind of drinks I have, which isn't a lot, since I don't drink soda or anything else besides water really.

"Is water okay with you?"

Turning off the drill, he nods, and I grab two bottles from the still open fridge. I hand one to him as he stands, and then he follows me to the couch where we both sit.

"Do you read a lot?"

Chewing and swallowing the bite of turkey and Swiss sandwich I just took, I look at him and notice his eyes are on my collection of signed books I have stacked up neatly in the corner of the room.

"Yeah," I reply, folding my feet under me and setting my plate on the tops of my knees. "I love reading. I always have. When I was young, I used to sneak into my parents' room in the mornings before school and read whatever book my mom was reading. Then when I got old enough to buy my own books, I would buy romance novels with guys on the covers with their shirts open and their long hair blowing in the wind." I laugh, watching his eyes fill with humor. "Once, my dad found me in my room reading one of those books, and he lost his mind. He was convinced I was reading porn. Thankfully, my mom came to my defense and told him to back down and that he should be thankful I was reading and not out partying and doing drugs."

"My mom reads a lot, too, and so do my sisters."

"How many sisters do you have?"

"Three, and two brothers."

"I always wanted siblings growing up," I confess, wondering not for the first time what it would have been like if I hadn't been adopted, if I had grown up with my mom and sister. I know my life would have been completely different. My mom shouldn't have had kids at all, and I know that because my sister told me about her childhood. She told me what it felt like to wonder if she would get dinner or where she would sleep.

"So do you think it will take us a year to finish the shelf?" I joke when I feel sadness start to creep over me like it always does when I think about Kelly and what she had to endure growing up alone with our mom.

"Nah, it shouldn't take long at all."

HOLDING THE LAST shelf, I watch Sage screw in the last four shelf guards and fight the urge to laugh at the frustrated look on his face. It's been over five hours since he told me it wouldn't take a year to put the shelf together, and he was right; it shouldn't have taken so long. He had all the right tools, but half the screws and things that came with the shelf had disappeared, which meant we had to go to Home Depot to buy them. And seeing how he just happened to know everyone we came in contact with, our ten-minute run into the hardware store took us forever.

Okay, so I may have spent a little time there wandering down the aisles. Home Depot may be a store dedicated to men, but every female knows they have the best cleaning supplies at the best price you can get anywhere. Plus, Sage took me to the kitchen department so I could see all the stuff he was planning on putting in his place, which included an awesome six-burner gas range with matching fridge, dishwasher, and double oven. He also showed me the cupboards and countertops he had chosen, which were a cool, sandy-colored material with flakes of teal, silver, and gold glass in them.

After he showed me everything, I made him promise that I could see the kitchen in person when he was done with it, and that was when something changed. I don't know exactly what it was, but when I made him promise, his face turned soft and his eyes warm, right before he took my hand and led me to check out, not letting me go until I was back in his truck.

"Are you laughing at me?" he asks, bringing me out of my head, and

I shake it then press my lips together when he starts to grumble under his breath. About what? I don't know, but it's cute seeing him like this. "Fucking finally." He takes the shelf I've been holding and puts it in place before stepping back. "Jesus, this thing was a pain in the ass. I think we'd have been better off building the shit from scratch."

"That would have probably taken us four years," I correct him, and he turns to look at me, smiling.

"You're probably right. Now where do you want it?"

"Back against that wall." I point to the only wall in the room that doesn't have an angle to it, and he picks it up and carefully puts it in place. "Thank you for helping me out. If I had been on my own, I probably would have tossed the whole thing over the deck and had a bonfire with it."

"Good thing I came to the rescue then," he says, then he pulls out his phone and looks at the screen. Knowing what's coming and that he's about to leave, I pick up our plates, which are still sitting on the coffee table, and take them to the sink. "It's late. Do you feel like ordering something?"

My body, which I didn't know was tight, relaxes and I turn to face him.

"Sure." I shrug like it's all the same to me, when it isn't. "I have a few menus." I open one of the drawers in the kitchen, and he shakes his head.

"Nah, I know a place. Do you like Italian?"

"What woman in their right mind doesn't like Italian?" I ask as my answer.

"Right." He puts his phone to his ear, and I listen to him place an order then give my address without having to ask me for it, which I can only imagine must come in handy with his job. As soon as he's done, he puts the phone back in his pocket. "We have about an hour, maybe a little longer, before the food gets here."

"Cool. Do you want to watch a movie or something?" I ask, going to the couch and picking up the remote, and I turn on the TV that hardly ever gets used, since most of the time I'm reading or listening to music if I'm home.

"I actually need to make a few phone calls. Do you mind if I step outside for a bit?"

"Sure." I nod, and he touches my waist with the tips of his fingers as he walks past me to the door.

Stepping out onto the deck, he shuts the door behind him, and I watch him put his phone to his ear. Seeing his phone, my mind goes to Kelly. She hasn't returned any of my phone calls in the last few days, and even though she has a tendency to disappear for days at a time without so much as a text to let me know she's okay, I still worry every time it happens.

Going to my room, I find my cell in my bag, put it on the charger, and wait for the Apple icon to pop up on the screen. Then I wait for the phone to turn on. As soon as it does, I see I have three texts from my mom, all of them asking how my bag hunt went this morning, and one from my dad reminding me that I need to book my ticket to go home to surprise my mom for her birthday, but nothing from Kelly. Sitting down on my bed, I snap a picture of my new purse and text it to Mom with *It went awesome.* Then I send a text to my dad letting him know I already bought my ticket and when I will be arriving. With that done, I toss my phone on the bed and change into one of my lounge-around-the-house outfits before I head to the living room, where I wait for Sage to finish his calls and our food to arrive.

Sage

JESUS FUCKING CHRIST. My chest heaves and I pull in a deep breath, trying to get my breathing under control and my heart rate back to normal. I didn't expect this to happen. Not yet, anyway. But after Kim and I ate, we were sitting there talking and she laughed. It was at that laugh that I leaned in and kissed her without thinking, and then one thing led to another and we were taking off each other's clothes like it was a fucking race to see who could get who naked first. I won, and fuck me, I thought she was beautiful fully clothed, but she was beyond that when she was laid out completely exposed to me.

Lying back, I drag her with me and soak in the feeling of her weight settling against me, her hot, wet pussy pulsing around my cock and her soft hair falling against my chest. Wanting to keep her right where she is, I tighten my hold. Never fucking ever have I had this with any other woman, a connection that defies logic and time, a connection that makes me question every fucking thing in my life.

"I'm too heavy." She tries to move off me, and my grip tightens even more as her words whisper across my damp skin.

"You're not, so don't even think about moving," I growl, feeling her body tense against mine. "Please," I add quietly, running my fingers through her hair, and she relaxes.

Placing a kiss to the top of her head, I wrap my hand around the back of her skull to keep her in place. My whole life, I've been hearing about the boom. When I was younger, I thought it was bullshit, some crazy story my dad and uncles made up to tell me and the boys in my family. But as I got older, I thought that if by some chance that shit was real, it was a good thing I was adopted, so I wouldn't have to deal with it. Now, after meeting Kim, I'm wondering what the hell is going on.

Listening to her breath even out, I feel her body relax against me, letting me know she's fallen asleep. Carefully moving her so I don't wake her, I get up and head for the bathroom to get rid of the condom and grab a washcloth. I walk back into the room and find Kim in the exact position I left her in. After cleaning her up, which is something I have never done for another woman, I toss the rag toward her laundry basket in the corner and get back into bed.

As soon as I'm lying next to her, she turns toward me and cuddles into my side. That's when I notice the stars above me through the skylight over the bed. Lying here with her warm weight against my side and her soft skin under my palm, I fall asleep thinking she's right; it does feel like you're sleeping outside under the stars.

Waking to the sound of soft music playing in the distance and the smell of bacon, my eyes open to a view of gray skies. Getting up on an elbow, I look down and find my jeans and shirt both folded and in a neat pile on the floor. Grabbing my cell out of the front pocket of my jeans, I hit the screen and see it's just after eight.

Once I'm out of bed, I pull on my jeans and head out of the room where I find Kim in the kitchen. Her back is to me, and her mass of hair is tied up in a high ponytail at the top of her head, showing off the elegant slope of her neck. Taking her in, I notice she's wearing a pair of shorts with flowers on them and a tank top to match that she put on at some point when I was making a call before dinner arrived. Without thinking, I head right for her and rest my hand on the side of her waist then curve it around her stomach, pulling her back into me feeling her shiver.

"Hey." Her eyes come to me over her shoulder, and her cheeks turn a pretty shade of pink.

"Morning." I lean down, kissing the exposed skin where her neck and shoulder meet. "You got an extra toothbrush?" I ask, and her eyes go soft in a way that I know I could get used to seeing every day.

"No, but you can use mine. I don't mind." She shrugs.

"All right." Touching my lips to her temple, I give her waist a squeeze then head for the bathroom. Coming out a few minutes later, I find her cracking eggs into the pan she just fried bacon in, and as soon as I'm close, she turns her face toward me.

"I don't know…" She pulls in a breath then lets it out slowly. "I don't know how this works," she says, turning around completely, and I stop a few feet away from her. "I mean…" She lets out another huff of air. "I don't know if you want to eat or if you just want to go."

"I'm not going," I state, watching her tense shoulders relax at my answer.

"Good," she whispers, and I feel that one word wash through me. "Do you want coffee?"

"Yeah." I close the distance between us, and she pulls down a coffee mug from the cupboard, handing it to me.

"Coffee pods are in the drawer under the machine." She nods toward the Keurig on the counter. "Cream is in the fridge, and sugar is there." She points to a canister. "How do you like your eggs?"

"Anyway you want to cook them is good with me."

"Okay." She gives me a smile then cracks two more eggs into the pan before taking toast out of the toaster and buttering it. Leaning back against the counter next to her with a cup of fresh coffee in my hand, I look at the shelf we put together and see that she already stacked her books on it.

"You've been up a while," I observe, and she looks from me to her shelf that is now full of books.

"I can never sleep in. No matter how late I go to bed, I always wake up early." She pulls down two plates before looking at me once more. "Did you sleep okay? I was going to go in and shut the skylight, but I didn't want to wake you by closing it."

"I slept better than I've slept in a long time," I confess, and her eyes soften. "I like the skylight. I might have to put one in the master at the lake house."

"It's pretty awesome. I like lying under it when it rains even more than at night when the skies are clear."

"I'll have to experience that myself sometime," I say, taking her hand and pulling her a step closer to me after she finishes buttering the toast and putting two fresh slices in the toaster. "What's your plans for today?"

"I have a client coming into the salon at ten, so I have to work. What about you?"

"Work tonight, but after that I'm free. You feel like hanging out later?"

"Sure." She leans into me with her weight, and I dip my face, brushing my lips over hers, touching my tongue to her bottom lip. Her mouth opens and I deepen the kiss. "We should eat," she breathes into my mouth as my hands roams down her body and I drag her tighter against me.

"Yeah." Kissing her one last time, I regretfully let her go.

"Here." She hands me a plate loaded with bacon, eggs, and toast. Picking up my cup of coffee, I follow her outside to a colorful round table with two chairs that's on the deck. "I know it's not a lake view, but it's not a bad one." She takes a seat, setting her plate and cup on the table. Folding into the chair across from her, I laugh when she does. The chair might be okay for a chick that's probably five-eight, but at six-four, my knees come up to my chest when I sit. "Oh, God." She covers her face, peeking at me through her fingers. "We can go inside to eat."

"It's all good." I place my hand over hers when she goes to stand. Stretching out my legs, I cross my ankles. "I've always been tall. Even when I was little, I was bigger than everyone else, so I had to make it work."

"How tall were you in high school?"

"When I graduated, I was six-two," I say, and her eyes widen.

"How tall are you now?"

"Six-four."

"I knew you were tall, but sheesh, you're *really* tall!" she says, and I laugh then watch her pick up her toast and take a bite.

"So you do hair?" I ask, thinking it's ridiculous as fuck that I didn't find that out from her yesterday, seeing how we spent the entire day together.

"Yeah, I went to college and did the whole four-year thing to please my parents, but I was never happy. So when I graduated with a degree in business management, I decided to spend two more years doing something I knew I would be happy with. I've always loved makeup and hair, so it seemed like a no-brainer."

"Where are your parents now?"

"Florida, about two hours outside of Miami."

"Why Tennessee?" I ask, and something shifts behind her gaze, but she hides it quickly.

"I just wanted a change." She shrugs then nods to my plate. "You should eat before your food gets too cold."

Picking up my fork, I dig in then spend another hour with her before I leave her with a kiss and a promise to see her later.

Kim

HEARING KNOCKING ON the sliding glass door, I roll out of bed and glance at the clock. It's after 1:00 a.m. Sage sent a text while I was at work and told me he would be over late, since what he was doing was going to keep him a while, but one in the morning is not someone who is interested in you. One in the morning is the time a booty call shows up, and I do not want to be a booty call, no matter how amazing the sex was between us.

Feeling something uncomfortable fill the pit of my stomach, I grab my robe and pull it on quickly while the knocking turns to pounding. Hitting the living room, I turn on the light, and that's when I see Kelly standing outside, looking at me through the glass with her fist up ready to start knocking again.

"Hey," I greet her as soon as I slide the door open.

"I'm leaving," she states, tossing her hair that looks exactly like mine over her shoulder.

"You're leaving," I repeat, and she nods, shouldering past me into my apartment that she hasn't been staying at and she's only used when the guy she's been messing around with kicks her out of his bed, leaving her no choice but to come here to crash. "Why... I thought—"

"I can't do it. I thought I could, but I can't," she cuts me off, going to the closet, grabbing her black duffle bag from the floor, and opening it up.

"I need you," I whisper, watching her pull things off hangers and shove them into the open bag on the floor.

"You need me." She turns around to face me, picking up the bag, and I notice then that her eyes are wild, which means she's gotten high recently—something she told me she would stop doing. "You don't fucking need me. You just want to use me like every fucking other person in my life does."

Rearing back like she slapped me, my body jolts. "That's not true."

"It's not?" She laughs, but her cackle sounds evil and grates across my skin. "You didn't even fucking try to find me until you were out of options."

"You know that's not true."

"I'm sure, bitch!" she shouts, and I take a step back.

I've never seen Kelly like this. I've never seen her so out of control, and I don't have any idea how to fix this or how to defuse the situation. "You know my parents never told me about you or about our mom." And they didn't. I didn't even know I was adopted until the day the test came back and I found out my kidneys were in the beginning stages of shutting down. That's when they told me I had an identical twin.

That's when they told me everything.

"I don't fucking care!" she screams at the top of her lungs, leaning toward me. "I do not fucking care about you." She points in my face, and my heart cracks open. "I don't care about any of this shit. I do not need your kind of fucking drama in my life."

"What happened?" Something had to have happened. Something had to have set her off to make her act like this.

"Nothing happened. I just finally got a fucking clue."

"Kelly, please." I grab onto her arm as she starts to storm past me. "Let's just calm down. Please don't go. Let's just get some sleep and we'll talk about this tomorrow, when you're thinking more clearly."

"Thinking more clearly? Fuck you, Kim. Fuck you and your holier-than-thou attitude. Ask your fucking perfect, rich-ass parents to help you out." She jerks her arm from my grasp and heads for the door.

Running after her down the steps in the garage, I yell, "Kelly, please don't do this!" as she hits the remote for the garage, sending the door up. "Kelly," I beg, but she doesn't stop or even turn around to look at me. She ducks under the door, runs across the pavement, and gets into the car that is parked and running in front of my garage with the lights on, slamming the door once she's inside. Standing here, I watch her back out of the driveway then take off.

"Oh, God." I crumple to my knees, dropping my face to my hands as rain starts to fall. Realizing I'm now soaking wet, I get up and make my way back into my apartment where I call my parents and tell them what happened while I cry until I can't cry anymore.

PULLING UP OUTSIDE the shop that I need to open in the next ten minutes, I put my car in park and pull out my cell to once again check if I've missed a call or a text from Kelly or Sage. I haven't heard from either of them in over a week, and even though I shouldn't be surprised or hurt, I am.

Really, I'm more hurt by what Sage did than by Kelly taking off. I knew she was struggling with not only her decision to help me, but her life in general. I knew there was a chance she would take off, but Sage, I didn't expect him to play me the way he did. Not after the day we spent together or after him seeming so sure he wanted to continue seeing me the morning after. I should have known better, but I stupidly thought he was feeling the same thing I was.

Seeing he hasn't replied to my text of *"Hey"* from two days ago, I shove my phone in my purse and step out of my car. Slamming the door, I turn and stop dead when I see him standing on the sidewalk, sweaty and wearing nothing but a pair of black workout pants, his eyes on me.

"Hey," I say quietly, walking toward him. That's when I notice his eyes are hard and his body is tight.

"You live in this town. Gonna say this once and only once. You pull some shit like you did again, next time, you'll be sitting behind bars," he says harshly, and my feet stop moving while my heart starts to pound. I don't know what he's talking about, but I do know he's pissed.

"Pardon?"

At my question, his eyes travel over my hair and face then down my body, but not in a good way. Not in the same way they did right before he made love to me. No, the way they travel over me makes me feel dirty and cheap, like I need to take a shower to get clean.

"You were good, babe. So good I would have paid you for it if I knew that's what you wanted."

His words are like a punch to the gut, and I take a step back, feeling my throat get tight. "What?" I finally get out, and his eyes harden even more.

"Coming up to me in the bar, playing games, acting like you did, then trying to slip some shit in my drink so you could get my wallet?" He scoffs, and reality hits me in the face. Kelly. She did this. That's why she took off, and that's why he's not spoken to me. He thinks I did those things to him.

"My sister." My eyes slide closed, and my hand tightens on the handle of the purse in my hand.

"Your sister?"

"My…" I pause, opening my eyes and try to pull in a deep breath because my lungs suddenly feel too tight, like they are twisting inside my chest. "My twin… my twin sister. She…" I take a step toward him, and he takes a step back, like he can't stand the idea of me getting close to him. Stopping, I hold out my hand palm up toward him, and my words come out whispered. "Whatever happened, that wasn't me. It was my sister."

"Right." He nods, but I can see he doesn't believe me. But why should he? I never told him about Kelly, because I didn't want to ruin whatever was happening between us. I didn't want him to find out about my problems until I knew he was the kind of guy who could shoulder them.

"I'm sorry. I—"

"Just stay the fuck away from me, bitch." And with that parting blow, he takes off without a backward glance. Standing here with my heart pounding in my chest and my stomach twisting into knots, I watch him until he's out of sight.

Feeling sickness climb up the back of my throat, I run for the door of the salon, unlock it, and get inside. I toss my bag to the couch then move to the bathroom where I fall to my knees in front of the toilet. Throwing up the bagel I had for breakfast, I rest my forehead against the seat of the commode, not caring how gross it is. Not caring about anything.

Tears fill my eyes, and I whisper, "Fuck everyone, and definitely fuck Sage and Kelly."

Chapter 1

Sage

"HERE'S WHAT YOU asked for."

Looking from the envelope that was just tossed on the table, up to the man who has been my dad since I can remember, I feel my chest get tight. I know what's in the envelope without looking at it, and I also know it's too late. The soft check I did on Kim came back as her being an only child, but I know now from a few different sources that she was adopted by a couple in Florida when she was born. I also know she has an identical twin sister who grew up in Alabama with their mom and had a life completely opposite of Kim's. That life has led her to trying to cope with the pain of her childhood by using drugs and men, going so far as prostituting herself out to deal with that hurt.

When I first found out that information, I knew I completely fucked up. I should have trusted my gut when I saw the look on Kim's face as I confronted her. I didn't do what I should have done, and I not only hurt Kim, I messed up beyond repair.

"I know you're a man now. I know you don't need my advice. But I'm gonna give it to you anyway," he warns, taking a seat on one of my folding chairs at the card table set up in my kitchen. I've been using it since I moved into this dump, because I've been saving almost every penny I make and putting it into my house.

"Dad—"

"No, you'll hear me out. Sit." He nods to the chair across from him as he stretches out his legs. "Who's this girl to you?" he questions, nodding to the envelope on the table.

I don't even know how to answer that question. I thought for a moment she could be my future, but then shit went down and I thought she was a liar and just as fake as the rest of the women who've come into my life. *I should have known better*. "I don't know."

"You don't know, or you're afraid to find out?" His eyes search mine, and he shakes his head, running his hand over his cropped hair. "I get that you want to experience life, experience women. I was young once, so I understand that shit. But, son..." He holds my gaze and drops his voice. "You're never going to find someone if you don't give anyone a chance, if you're always searching, never stopping to see what's in front of you."

"I fucked up," I tell him the truth, and he moves, crossing his arms over his chest and leaning back in the chair.

"How?"

Taking a seat across from him, I look at the envelope and tell him what went down. I fill him in about meeting Kim, about the time we spent together, and then I explain about Kim's sister and what happened at the bar. Last, I spill what occurred after, when I corned Kim outside the salon. "I fucked up," I repeat my earlier statement when I finish, and he leans forward, resting his elbows on his knees studying me.

"Did you apologize?"

"Yeah." I did apologize, but I knew the second I did that it was too late. The sadness I left her with had changed into anger, leaving me no shot at fixing what I broke.

"If she's important to you, do it again, and again, and again, until she understands you're sorry. Really fucking sorry," he says, and I lift my chin, letting him know I heard him. But also knowing that ship has sailed, because not only is she still pissed at me, she now has a man, and even though I might be fucked up in a lot of ways, I won't go there with her tied to someone else.

"Now, we need to talk about Nalia," he adds, bringing my attention back to him, and that tightness in my chest changes to something even more uncomfortable. I hate the look on his face right now, hate that he and my mom both have the same expressions every time Nalia is brought up. I love my sister. I love her with all the love I have inside of me. But I'm pissed off at her. "She's your sister, and as much as you and I don't like what she's doing, she still needs us right now."

"I'll be here for her, but I don't want anything to do with Sharon," I state, referring to the woman who gave birth to me.

I don't understand Nalia's reasoning for wanting a relationship with our birth mother. She tried to explain it to me once. Tried to describe how she feels it's the loss of us that turned our mother's life upside down. But as far as I know, her life was shit before she was forced to give us up when we were only two, because she had gone out partying, left us alone, and hadn't come back for two days. No one even knew she was gone until they heard Nalia and me crying, and by that point, we were both in need of medical attention.

"I know you don't, but you still need to be there for your sister. She thinks she can help Sharon. So as much as you and I may not like it, we still need to let her try," he says, and I feel my face go hard and my muscles tense.

"The only person that bitch needs help from is the devil. What she did to me and Nalia..." I shake my head. "What she did to the two of us was wrong. I don't care how she tries to twist it or what reasoning she has for what happened. It was fucked."

"I agree with you."

"Christ, she left us alone for two days, and the only reason she even came back is because she found out the cops were at her place," I growl, feeling pain slice through me at the thought of the woman who was meant to protect us leaving us alone to fend for ourselves when we could barely walk.

"Nalia knows all of that. She doesn't give a fuck," he states quietly.

"I fucked up. I should hav—"

"You didn't fuck up. You didn't do anything wrong. She needs to find her own way and realize for herself that sometimes you can't fix people, no matter how hard you try. And you need to have her back while she does that."

"I get that, but I want not one fucking thing to do with any of that."

"And I understand that, but—"

"No, I know you and Mom have always been about forgiveness and second chances, but no."

"What about your other siblings?"

"We're cool. We talk now and then, but my relationship with them has nothing to do with her."

"All right," he murmurs, and with that, I stand, take the envelope that I will never open over to my desk, and shove it into the top drawer.

"I gotta head out," I state as I turn and head into the kitchen and open the fridge, grabbing a bottle of water for the road. "I'll be out of town for a couple days chasing a skip, but I'll call and check in." I watch my dad unfold from the chair and stand.

"Make sure you call. You know your mom worries."

"I'll call," I agree, picking up my keys before heading for the door. Feeling my dad close, I open the door and grab my bag I dropped next to it earlier.

"Be safe." He pats my shoulder as he moves past me. Lifting my chin, I lock up then move to my ride while he heads for his bike.

Kim

"HARDER, PLEASE," I WHISPER, running my hands up the smooth skin of his back, feeling his muscles bunch at my touch.

"Slow, baby, you feel too fucking good," he murmurs, licking and kissing up the column of my neck.

Nice.

No. More than nice. Perfect.

Pressing my head back into the pillow, I wind my legs around his hips and tip my pelvis, sending him deeper, moaning in my throat when I do.

"Goddamn, you're beautiful."

My face softens and I slide one hand around his waist, up his abs, chest, and neck, stopping at the underside of his jaw to run my fingers along the sculpted edge there.

"No." I shake my head, swallowing over the lump forming in my throat. "You're beautiful." And he is, the most beautiful man I've ever seen.

Waking with tears in my eyes, I roll to my side and wrap my arms around my stomach. He's still torturing me. Months later, the memory of him is still torturing me. "You need to get over this."

I roll to my back and watch the rain beat against the skylight as I blink away the tears in my eyes. A few months ago, Sage came to me and apologized for the way he treated me. I told him I accepted his apology, but I lied. The time that had gone by before his apology had given me a lot of time to think, and the more I thought about what went down, the more upset I got.

Yes, he was wronged, but if he had felt even a fraction for me of what I had felt for him, he would have at least heard me out. He would have at least let me tell him about Kelly, but he didn't do that. He made assumptions and said shit to me that I can't get out of my head. Shit still hurts every time I think about it.

Three weeks after that apology, he asked me to have dinner with him. I didn't say, "Fuck you," like I wanted to. Instead, I lied and told him I was seeing someone—that someone being my best friend, who also happens to be gay. Yes, I lied, but once bitten, twice shy. I may have fallen for the charms of Sage Mayson once, but there's no way in hell I would do it again. But that doesn't mean my heart has given up on the idea of him. Every time I see him, I remember exactly what I felt in those moments we had together.

Letting out a long, deep breath, I sit up. Today would be the perfect day to do nothing but lie in bed and read. Unfortunately, I have a doctor's appointment that I need to get to, and if I don't get up now, I never will. Hearing my cell phone ring in the living room, I sigh. I'm sure it's my mom calling to remind me about the appointment, since she's the one who set it up.

Apparently, the doctor I'm meeting with has helped a lot of people with diet plans and medications, so they can live a somewhat normal life. Putting my feet to the floor, I slowly get out of bed then frown when my cell stops ringing, only to start right back up. My mom can be persistent, but she's never called, hung up, and called again when I didn't answer. Going to the living room, I find my phone where I dropped it last night. I pick it up and see my mom isn't calling. Chris is.

"Hey." I put the cell to my ear as I move to the cupboard and pull down a coffee cup.

"We need to talk," he says, and I feel my brows pull together.

"What's wrong? You sound freaked."

"I saw Sage last night." Pressing my hand to the counter, I drop my chin to my chest.

"Okay," I reply quietly.

"He... fuck. He saw me with Dale and..." I listen to him pull in a breath. "I tried to call you, but you didn't answer."

"What happened?"

"He saw me with Dale," he repeats, but I still don't understand why he sounds so freaked.

"Okay."

"You're not getting it!" he shouts. "He saw *me* with *Dale*. He *saw* me and Dale."

"Oh," I breathe as reality dawns. My hand curves and tightens around the edge of the counter to keep me upright.

"Yeah and…." He goes quiet, and I wait and wait, but he doesn't continue.

"And what?" My stomach twists.

"He gave him a black eye, that's what." I hear Dale say in the background, and my eyes close.

"Shit, I… I'm so sorry. Are you okay?" I knew I shouldn't have lied. I knew I should have come clean, but it was easier to pretend I had a reason to stay clear of him than to deal with the fact he still affected me.

"I'm fine. Don't be sorry. This is good," he tells me, sounding like he's smiling.

"What?"

"I thought he was into you before, but I now know *he. Is. Into. You.* And, baby girl, I'm fucking thrilled this shit is finally done and out in the open." He laughs.

"Uh, did I miss something?" I question. "You just told me he punched you, and you know how he treated me. Why the hell would you be happy right now?"

"No man has that much passion for a woman he doesn't give a fuck about, and you're still hung up on him. Don't you wonder why that is? Don't you wonder why, after so fucking long, a man that you spent less than twenty-four hours with is one you can't stop thinking about? Don't you want to try and figure that out?"

"No." And it's not that I haven't wondered the exact thing. It's that

I refuse to go back there again. I refuse to even allow the idea to enter my head. What we had was a fluke. Yes, he made me feel something for him during those moments, but afterward, he made me feel like shit. So no, I actually don't give a fuck.

"You're a liar, but I still love you, and I hope—I *really* hope—that the next time he asks you out, you say yes," Chris chimes in.

"There isn't going to be a next time," I say, stirring the cream and sugar into my coffee and taking a sip.

"We'll see," he mumbles, and I roll my eyes.

Chris has been Team Sage since the beginning, but Chris is also a hopeless romantic who still believes in fairy tales and happily ever afters. Only, in his fairy tale, he's the damsel in distress waiting for his white knight to show up. He didn't want to go along with my lie, but he did for me as his best friend, something I now wish he wouldn't have done.

"How's your eye? Are you sure you're okay?"

"Yeah, I'm fine. Nothing a little concealer won't cover up," he says.

"I can't believe he hit you." I rub my forehead in an attempt to wipe away the headache that has started pounding there.

"Dale had his tongue down my throat. He thought he was protecting your honor. It was hot. Not the whole me getting punched thing, but the part before, when he tore Dale away from me and growled 'motherfucker,' breathing all hard and shit."

"Oh my god, you're so crazy." I fight back a smile as I head for my room, setting my coffee cup down on my dresser.

"If you're really not interested, I wonder if I could convince him to join my team," he coos, and I hear Dale say something, sounding pissed, which doesn't really surprise me.

Dale and Chris have been dating each other casually for a few years now. When they first started seeing each other, Chris wanted them to get serious, but Dale always had an excuse for why they couldn't. Then, when Kelly left, Chris moved to Tennessee to be closer to me so that I wasn't quote unquote 'alone,' and since then, Dale has had a change of heart. Only now, Chris is the one who isn't exactly sure if he still feels the same way he used to, even though Dale is the only man Chris has ever been serious about. Gah! They are seriously like a soap opera.

"If you can convince him, you can have him," I mutter, then look at the clock and see time has caught up with me, like it normally does when I'm talking to Chris. "Come by the salon tomorrow when you get done dropping Dale at the airport. I need to finish getting ready to leave here in the next twenty."

"Shit, you're meeting your new doctor today," he says quietly, and I pull in a breath through my nose.

"Yeah."

"Do you want me to go with you?"

"No, it's okay. You should spend some time with Dale before he goes home."

"He'll understand if I leave him for a few hours to go with you."

God, I love my best friend. "Seriously, it's okay, and make sure you put some ice on your eye."

"Will do. Call me when you get done with your appointment."

"I will." I hang up and drop my cell to the bed, telling myself that I don't care if Sage knows who Chris really is to me, but royally freaking the hell out that he does.

Chapter 2

Kim

TAKING A BITE from the peach in my hand, I lean against the front counter at the salon and flip through the latest issue of *Cosmo*, not really seeing the words on the pages. My mind is on the appointment I went to yesterday. I didn't know what to expect when I met with Dr. Jayne, but I didn't expect to leave her office feeling as hopeful as I did.

During my appointment, she told me about numerous patients of hers who have had amazing results using the tools she's given them. She also told me that as long as I follow her diet plan and start taking the new meds she prescribed, I should see the same outcome. She explained that I won't *be* better but I should *feel* better, which to me is the most important thing right now. There is nothing worse than feeling like you have the flu everyday and knowing there is no store-bought remedy or any amount of rest to fix it.

Hearing the bell on the door ding, I come out of my head and watch Ellie as she walks in with a smile on her face.

"Hey, honey," she says, holding the door open for Hope, who spots me and runs over, her pigtails bouncing and a huge smile on her adorable face.

"Kimmyyy!" she shouts, holding a black backpack out toward me. "Look what Uncle Sage got me. Isn't it so cool?" she asks, and I look at the bag and notice the words "Detective Kit" scrolled across the front in large yellow writing.

"Wow, that is cool," I agree, getting down on my haunches in front of her and dropping my voice. "Who are you going to spy on?"

"I can't tell you. It's top secret." She sighs like she's disappointed that she can't tell me, and I fight back a smile.

"Well, if you need any help, Detective, let me know." I touch the top of her head then stand to my full height and raise a brow at Ellie. "I thought you were off today?"

"I was, but Selma called and asked if I could come in and do her and Sejla's hair for some big party they have to attend tonight," she explains before she drops her eyes to Hope who is now sitting at my feet, going through all the gadgets and gizmos in her bag.

"Don't pull that all out, honey. Daddy will be here in just a little while to pick you up, and you don't want to lose anything."

"Okay," Hope agrees, shoving everything she has taken out back in and looking up at me. "Can you paint my nails?"

"Of course I can. Go pick out your color," I tell her, and her eyes get big with excitement right before she stands and skips off to the back of the shop, with her new backpack bouncing behind her on her back.

"You spoil her," Ellie mumbles, and I shrug, making her roll her eyes. "Is Frankie in?"

"He's in his office doing a stock order."

"Cool, I'm going to get my stuff set up. You okay out here?"

"You know I am." I give her smile then turn when the bell on the door dings again. The smile on my face slides away as Sage steps inside, looking as beautiful as ever wearing a pair of dark jeans and a long-sleeved dark gray cotton shirt that is molded perfectly to his frame. "Can I help you?"

"We need to talk," he says, taking a step toward the counter I'm still standing behind. Feeling my muscles get tight when he starts to get close, I see his eyes change, and he stops moving as his jaw clenches.

"I know you know I lied and—"

"I don't give a shit about that," he cuts me off, taking another step toward me. "I deserved that after the things I said." He didn't deserve for me to lie to him. I should have just had a backbone and been honest. "We need to talk," he repeats.

"We don't have anything to talk about."

"You know that's not true," he says quietly, and it's at that quiet tone I start to get annoyed. I don't need this right now. I might not need it ever, but I definitely don't need it right now.

"Okay then, I don't want to talk to you," I state, and he opens his mouth to speak, only to close it as Hope yells "Uncle Sage!" while running through the salon at full speed right toward him. Smiling at her, he leans down and scoops her up into his arms.

"What are you doing here?" she asks.

"I came to ask Kim to have dinner with me," he tells her, and my eyes narrow on him right before I put a fake smile on my face for Hope, who swings her head around to look at me.

"You're going out with Uncle Sage?" she breathes with wide eyes that I can see are filled with visions of a fairy tale in the making.

"No, sweetie. I'm not."

"Oh." She frowns, looking at Sage, who is looking at me with a somewhat amused, somewhat annoyed expression on his face. Oh well, he'll have to get over it. Just because I no longer have a fake boyfriend doesn't mean I want to go out with him.

"Yet," Sage rumbles, staring at me.

"Yet?" Hope repeats, tipping her head to the side and studying him.

"She's not going out with me yet," he says, pulling his eyes from me to look at her.

"You have to do something heewowick to win her, don't you?" Hope asks, and I press my lips together to keep from laughing, because I know she means heroic, but the way she says it is way too cute.

"Something like that." He gives her a squeeze before he sets her feet to the floor. The second she's down, she comes over to me.

"Can we paint my nails now?"

"Absolutely. What color did you pick?" I ask, ignoring the fact Sage has now moved closer, causing his scent to fill my lungs.

"This one." She opens the palm of her hand, showing me the color, which is pink, of course.

"Good choice. Go get in the chair, sweetie. I'll be there in just a second," I say gently, touching the top of her head, and she nods at me then turns to face her uncle.

"You should bring her flowers. Mama always says yes when Daddy brings her flowers." And with that bit of advice delivered, she takes off, leaving me alone with Sage once again.

"Would that do it?"

"What?" I pull my eyes from Hope's back to look at him at his question.

"If I brought you flowers, would that make you change your mind?"

"No."

"So what would change your mind about having dinner with me?"

"A million dollars," I snap, and he stares at me for a long time before his lips tip up and he turns for the door.

"All right," he says, right before he pulls it open and steps out, letting the door close behind him.

"Shit." My eyes close and panic fills my stomach, because I know without a doubt I somehow just threw down the gauntlet. With a shake of my head, I move to the back of the salon, put a smile on my face, and paint my favorite girl's nails.

Standing at the front counter after saying bye to Hope and Ellie's husband Jax an hour later, I watch Chris come to the front window and put his forehead to the glass, making a funny face. Laughing, I move to the front door and open it then squeak when he picks me up and swings me around.

"Put me down, you idiot." I smile down at him, hitting his shoulder.

"If I must." He drops me to my feet and follows me into the salon. "Are you off soon?"

"No. Well, kind of, but not really. I have a client who should be here any minute, and then I need to get to the grocery store. And after that, I'm going over to watch the kids for Elizabeth."

"All right, I'll hang with you here then we can go to the store together. I need to get some stuff for my place anyway, so that will give us a little time to chat."

"Sounds like a plan," I agree, right before I turn to watch my client walk in. "Hi, Mrs. Ethel." I smile at her as she picks up her tiny dog and puts him in the bag she's carrying.

"Kim." She doesn't smile, but that doesn't surprise me. Mrs. Ethel never smiles. *Ever.* The only time I've ever seen what could be described as happiness on her face was when she told me that her son was getting a divorce from the 'floozy' he married.

"Are you ready?"

"Would I be here if I wasn't?" she asks, and I press my lips together as Chris turns and heads for the back of the shop, with his shoulders shaking in silent laughter as he goes.

"I guess not." I smile, taking the bag holding her dog. Knowing the drill, I carry him over to my station, set him next to it, open the side pocket, pull out the small collapsible bowl there, go to the sink, and fill it with water. Then I take it back, setting it inside his bag, while Mrs. Ethel removes the scarf around her neck along with her ever-present pearls. Once she's seated, I drape a cape around her then turn her to face the mirror. "Are we doing the usual?" I ask, and she rolls her eyes.

Taking that as a yes, I spend the next two hours trimming her hair, coloring it an off shade of grayish purple, and then teasing and hair spraying the crap out of it. By the time I'm done, she looks the same as she always does, just a little more refreshed.

After paying, she hands me a three-dollar tip, takes her dog out of the bag, and leaves without so much as a thank you. Cleaning up my station so I can leave, I listen with one ear as Chris recounts his run-in with Sage to Ellie, Selma, and Sejla, who ooh and aah over his story. You would think by the way he describes it that it was the most amazing night of his life and that he didn't get punched in the face.

I don't care that he's telling them about what happened, since Ellie knew from the beginning that Chris and I have never been anything more than friends. And Selma and Sejla are cool, but I don't know them enough to feel embarrassed that they know I lied about Chris being my boyfriend.

"So what now?" Selma asks, and I hear a pause in the conversation and turn to find all eyes on me.

"What?"

"What now? What are you going to do now that he knows the truth?" Selma clarifies.

"Nothing," I say, and Sejla frowns.

"Nothing?" she repeats, studying me with a disbelieving and disappointed look in her eyes.

"You need to at least give him a chance!" Selma cries, spinning around in the chair to face me, dislodging Ellie's hands from her hair.

"I agree. You need to at least hear him out," Sejla says, and I know she and her sister mean well, but it's so easy for them to say I need to just give him a chance, because their hearts aren't on the line here. Mine is.

Seeing both Selma and Sejla waiting for my response, I mutter, "I'll talk to him."

"Good," they say in unison, and I smile at the happy and relieved looks on their faces. Pulling my eyes from them, I look at Chris.

"Are you ready?"

"Yep." He stands from the chair that he has been sitting in then goes about giving the girls air kisses and farewells. Saying goodbye to everyone, we leave the salon, and I head to my car while Chris goes to his, telling me he will meet me at the store.

"So how was work?" Chris asks as we grab a cart and walk into the grocery store fifteen minutes later.

"Good."

"Anything happen?" he continues, and I look at him and narrow my eyes.

"Why?"

"Just wondering. Ellie said that Sage stopped by the salon today."

"He did."

"And?"

"And nothing. He came by the salon, asked if we could talk, my answer was no, and he left."

"What?" His eyes grow with surprise. "He didn't demand you change your mind or toss you over his shoulder and speed away with you in his truck to hide you in a secluded cabin, where he could convince you of the mistake you're making by not taking a chance on him?" he asks, and I stare at him, blinking.

"I think you've been reading too many romance novels."

"You can never read too many romance novels," he scoffs, making me smile. Chris is the only guy I've ever met who is more obsessed with romance books than I am. "So what exactly happened? Tell me everything."

"Nothing happened. Like I said, he came in, told me we needed to talk, I said no we didn't, and he left."

"You're lying."

"I'm not."

"You are. I've known you since we were five. I know your tell."

"My tell?"

"Yeah, when you lie, your nose twitches."

"My nose does not twitch," I say, touching my fingers to my nose.

"It does." He smiles, pulling my hand away from my face.

"Whatever," I mutter, picking up a bag of oranges and dropping them in the cart.

"So when are you going to talk to him?"

"Never."

"He apologized. Don't you think you should do the polite thing and at least hear him out?"

"I don't know."

"You don't know, or you're just too scared to find out what will happen if you do?"

"Do we have to do this right now?" I sigh, and he tosses his arm around my shoulders and pulls me into his side.

"We've been doing this for months now. I've seen the way you look at him when you think no one will notice, and I see the way he looks at you, not giving a fuck if everyone sees. Even when he thought you and I were a thing, he still made it perfectly clear to those who were watching that if by some chance he got a shot, you would be his."

"I really think you are reading way too much into this."

"Am I?"

I want to say yes, but that would be a lie. Every time I've seen Sage out, it's taken everything in me to keep my feet from moving in his direction, and when I'm not carefully watching him, I can feel his eyes on me like a physical touch.

"We don't have time to talk about this." I decide to say. "We need to finish shopping, and I have to get to the house. Elizabeth is meeting Jelikai in Nashville for dinner, and you know she can't leave the boys alone for more then ten minutes without someone ending up in the hospital, so I can't be late."

"Fine," he grumbles, but I know Chris. He may have given up for now, but he has not given up forever, and he won't until he gets his way, and I admit there is still something between Sage and me. "Just so you know, I'm reserving the right to tell you 'I told you so' when this is all said and done."

"Fine." I roll my eyes at him then grab the shopping cart from his grasp and finish up my grocery shopping.

"Elizabeth, I'm here!" I shout into the house as I toss my bag on the table near the front door. Hearing no reply over the boys yelling and the sounds of a video game being played, I head up the stairs. Stopping at the door of the theater room, I watch Jimmy, the oldest at fourteen, as he tosses Aiden, who is three, onto the couch, making him laugh, while the other two, Mickey who's six and Hayden who's nine, sit on the floor with headphones on and controllers in their hands.

"Hey, guys!" I shout over the sound of the TV, and all four heads swing toward me.

"Kim." Aiden smiles, running toward me, while the other boys grin and wave before going back to what they were doing.

"Hey, dude." I pick him up, and he wraps his tiny arms around my neck before dropping his head to my shoulder, making something deep inside me wish for a moment just like this with my own baby one day. "Did you eat dinner yet?"

"No." He leans back to look at me. "Can we have pizza?"

"Sure," I agree, and he looks to where Jimmy is now sitting with Mickey and Hayden, who are still playing a video game.

"We get to have pizza!" he shouts. At that announcement, the boys all smile at me. Elizabeth is a health freak, so the kids love when I come over, because they know they will get some form of junk food before the night is over.

"Where's your mom?" I ask, carrying Aiden away from the fighting that has suddenly erupted over the controllers for the video game.

"In her room, getting ready," he says, so I head down the hall toward the master bedroom. Knocking on the door that is open, I smile as Elizabeth pokes her head out of the bathroom and grins.

"Hey, I'm just about ready," she says, putting a long, dangly earring in her ear. "Give me two then I need you to tell me how I look."

"Okay," I reply as she disappears once more. Walking across the room, I take a seat in one of the chairs that are set up in front of the fireplace, with Aiden still clinging to me. As soon as I'm down, he stands on the tops of my thighs and takes hold of my hands.

"Watch what I can do."

I grin right before he jumps and doubles back, flipping over. Narrowly missing getting kicked in the face by his tiny bare feet, I laugh at him as he stands, tossing his hands in the air. "Wow, that was awesome."

"Wanna see me do it again?" he asks with a bright smile as he starts to climb back up onto my lap.

"Aiden, how about we don't give Kim a concussion," Elizabeth suggests as she walks out of the bathroom, putting on her heels. She is beautiful, with long brown hair that flows past her shoulders, skin that subtly announces her Spanish heritage, and hazel eyes that change to green when she's happy, or brown when she's frustrated with her boys.

"What's a concussion?" Aiden asks, climbing up onto the arm of the chair to stand there.

"A head injury, honey," she mutters before looking at me. "So what do you think?" She holds out her hands, spinning in a circle.

"I think you and Jelikai are going to be late getting home," I say truthfully. Jelikai, Elizabeth's husband, is obsessed with her, and I have no doubt that as soon as he sees her, his jaw is going to hit the floor. She looks beautiful in the black heels and red wrap dress she's wearing right now.

"That's exactly the look I was going for."

She grins at me and Aiden laughs, saying, "Mom, you're funny," before jumping off the arm of the chair, landing on the floor with a loud thud, and taking off out of the room.

"I swear one of these days he is going to give me a heart attack," I admit, watching him go.

"I think the three boys before him got all the fear out of me." She laughs, picking up a black clutch that is resting on the bed before turning to look at me. "You okay?"

"Totally, and I already told the boys we are having pizza for dinner, so I will be filling them with lots and lots of processed foods while you're gone."

"Fill them with whatever you like. You can make it up to me by staying late. I'm going to try to convince Jelikai to get us a hotel room in the city."

"I'm thinking that as soon as he sees you in that dress, there won't be much convincing needed," I say, standing. "You guys should stay out. I don't have a client until eleven tomorrow, so I can stay the night if you want."

"I'll keep that in mind," she tells me, walking over and giving me a hug then leaning back. "Are you sure you're okay? How was your appointment yesterday?"

"I swear I'm okay, and my appointment went great. I feel really good about my new plan."

"Good." She touches my cheek before dropping her hand away. "You know where the petty cash is. Use whatever you need, and I'll call you as soon as I know what we're doing."

"Okay." I give her a smile then follow her out of the room and down the hall to where the boys are hanging out. Standing in the doorway, I watch her give each of the boys a kiss goodbye, even the ones that fight her on it. Walking fully into the room, I take a seat on the couch then watch her leave with a wave and a wink in my direction.

After that, the rest of the night goes by in a flash. The boys and I order pizza, watch a movie, and then go to bed after Elizabeth calls to say she and Jelikai won't be back until morning, which means I go to bed with a happy smile on my face for my friend.

Chapter 3

Kim

"WHAT THE HELL?" I glance around before looking back at the briefcase sitting on the passenger seat of my car. The large metal case wasn't there when I went into work this morning, and I know I locked up my car, so I have no idea who it belongs to or how it got in my car.

Feeling my heart pound, I reach over and touch the smooth metal. It looks like something out of a spy movie, like the kind of briefcase someone would deliver money in. "No," I breathe. "No fricking way." With the way this last week has been going, I forgot all about telling Sage I would go out with him for a million dollars. Not that I have forgotten about Sage. He's come into the salon everyday, either bringing me flowers or demanding I talk to him. The flowers I took to the nursing home in town, and I've been working hard at denying his demands. But this—this is something else.

Letting out a breath, I put the keys in the ignition and start up my car. I don't want to open the case where people could see, because if it *is* a million dollars—which I have no idea how Sage could get—someone could see it and then... I don't know... track me down and kill me for it or something.

Reversing out of my parking spot, I head to my house, and as soon as I get there, I head up the stairs with the briefcase held tightly in my grasp. Locking the door behind me, I place the case on the couch and get down on my knees in front of it. I inspect the latches, noticing a button on either side of the handle. Pressing down on them at the same time, the locks click open, sounding horrifically loud in my quiet apartment.

I bite my lip, slowly open the lid, and my heart starts to go wild inside my chest when I see what's inside. Monopoly money, lots of it. Stacks and stacks of it. Some old, and some new and still wrapped in plastic. Picking up a piece of paper that is folded on top of it, I fall to my bottom, unfold it carefully, and then start to read.

Kim,

It's all here, a million dollars that you can count if you want.

It took me a little longer than I thought it would to get all the money together, and some I will have to return to friends and family, since they let me borrow it.

I laugh at that then pull in a sharp breath when I read the next line.

In the twenty-four hours we spent together, you gave me a taste of something beautiful, and the memories of those moments have haunted me since I walked away from you. It's something I have regretted doing since then, something I know I will always regret, because even if by some chance you forgive me, I will never be able to get back the time with you that I missed out on.

If you accept my apology, meet me at my place tonight at seven for dinner.

Xx Sage

Seeing the address to his house scrolled along the bottom, I close my eyes and fall to my back, holding the piece of paper to my chest. I don't know if I'm brave enough to do this with him. I don't know if I'm courageous enough to put myself out there with everything I have going on. Sage doesn't know about my illness, and I don't know what he will do when he finds out. Will he take off on me the same way Kelly did? Will it be too much for him to handle?

The what-ifs are enough to keep me from going to meet him, but it's the idea of regretting something that has me opening my eyes to look at the clock on the stove. If I'm going to do this, I need to get up and get ready to leave now. The urge to call Chris to ask him what he thinks I should do filters through my mind, but I know what he'd say. He'd tell me that I'm an idiot for not already being in my car after seeing the money and reading the letter.

I can't imagine badass Sage Mayson going around borrowing Monopoly money, but he did that, and he did it for me. "Screw it." If I get hurt, if I end up brokenhearted, at least I can say I gave it a shot, that I took a chance. Since the moment I was diagnosed with kidney failure, I have worked on living a life without regrets, and I know I will regret not showing up to meet him if I don't go.

Getting up off the floor, I start to close the briefcase then pause, take a five hundred dollar orange note off one of the stacks, and then pick up my purse, digging through until I find my wallet. Once I have it unzipped, I carefully place the note in the zipper compartment in the middle, and then drop it back in my bag. With that done, I close the briefcase and head for my bedroom, where I hurry up and get ready to leave.

Putting a light pink lip gloss on, I lean back away from the mirror, and then turn my head from side to side. I don't want it to look like I'm trying too hard, so I leave my makeup light, only adding a few more swipes of mascara. My hair is still in the same style I wore to work, which is down with wavy curls that end at the tops of my breasts. Leaving the bathroom, I shut off the light and go to my room, where I change out of the slacks and heels I wore to the salon today, exchanging them for jeans and a pair of ballet flats. Then I take off my blazer and slip on a long, gray, cashmere cardigan over my simple black tank.

Looking at my refection in the mirror on the back of my bedroom door, I put a hand to my stomach that is filled with nervous butterflies since I made my decision to go meet Sage. Knowing I don't have time to debate with myself about going, I head for the living room, grab my bag, my keys, and the briefcase, and then head downstairs to the garage to get in my car.

Driving down a long dirt road, through what can only be described as a forest, I look at the map displayed on my dashboard. The mapping system in my car told me that I arrived at my destination about three minutes ago, but I still haven't seen a house, and I'm starting to freak myself out. It's dark. I'm in the middle of nowhere, or I should say in the middle of the woods, and I'm pretty sure Bigfoot is going to walk out in front of my car at any moment.

Leaning forward to get closer to my windshield, I squint my eyes trying to see through the darkness that has engulfed me, when I notice something move off on the side of the road.

Please don't be Bigfoot. Please don't be Bigfoot, I pray inwardly, and then slam my foot on the brake when two deer run out of the woods and across the road. "Oh my God." I hold my hand to my chest, feeling my heart beat hard against my palm. I pull in a breath then let it out slowly as I take my foot off the brake and start to drive forward, going much slower than I had been before.

It's now seven, which means I'm late. My stomach tightens, and my palms start to sweat then my breath leaves on a whoosh as I come over a slight incline in the road, spotting a house, which is not a house at all, but a cottage. A white stucco cottage with bright blue, red, and yellow trim around the windows, and doors that make it look like it belongs in a fairy tale.

Pulling up slowly, my foot automatically hits the brake when I see Sage standing outside next to his car like he was just about to leave. I don't know how long we stare at each other through the glass of my windshield, but it feels like a lifetime, and before I even realize he's moved, he's at the hood of my car then at my door, opening it up.

"Put it in park and turn it off," he barks, making me jump.

"Sage—"

"Now," he demands, and I fumble with the shifter to put my car in park then hit the button to shut down the engine. As soon as the lights go out, he unhooks my seatbelt and pulls me out of my seat.

"Sa—"

His name ends on a whimper as his hands take hold of my face gently and his mouth crashes down on mine. My toes curl in my ballet flats, and my arms wind around his neck so I don't fly away. I don't know how I did it, but I had forgotten what it's like to have him kiss me. I forgot that it feels like the world around me has disappeared, leaving nothing but him and me. Feeling his tongue touch my bottom lip in a silent request for entrance, my mouth opens and I moan down his throat while digging my fingers into his shoulders, trying to keep myself from falling.

"Goddamn," he growls, dragging his mouth away from mine and tucking my head under his chin. "Fuck me." Hearing his heart beating wildly, I close my eyes and suck in a deep breath before whispering.

"I'm sorry I was late. Bigfoot ran across the road." Pulling my head away from his chest, my eyes open and I find him looking at me curiously.

"Bigfoot?"

"What?" I frown.

"You said Bigfoot ran across the road," he says, and I shake my head, trying to get my brain, which is totally fried from that kiss, to work again.

"A deer ran across the road, not Bigfoot. Though I thought for sure it was going to be Bigfoot. I didn't know your house was in the middle of the woods."

"I should have told you. I… fuck, I didn't even think you'd show."

"You gave me a million dollars in Monopoly money," I reply quietly, feeling a smile lift at the corners of my mouth. I don't know of another man who would put their ego aside and do what Sage did. I don't know of another guy who would care enough to even try to win back someone they barely know.

"You know I'm sorry, right?" he asks, and I force him to let me go so I can take a step back, because he can't be this close when I say what I need to tell him.

"Please." I hold up my hand when he takes a step toward me, and I watch his eyes flash right before he lifts his chin and crosses his arms over his chest. "I should have forgiven you the first time you apologized. It wasn't right of me to tell you I accepted your apology and not actually accept your apology. It also wasn't right of me to lie about who Chris really is to me."

"Who is he to you?" he questions, and I can hear an edge of jealousy in his tone but I ignore it.

"My best friend. He's been my best friend since I was five."

"Is that all he is to you?"

"Yeah, that's all he is to me." I smile weakly, watching his body relax slightly. "What I'm trying to say is I'm sorry, too." I pause, wondering how to tell him how I feel without telling him how I feel. "I just didn't want to get hurt again. I know it's stupid, since we don't really know each other, but you hurt me, and I didn't want to end up hurt again."

"Come here." He opens his arms but doesn't move to reach for me again, and I know this is when I need to go to him. This is me silently letting him know I forgive him—really forgive him.

Stepping into his embrace, I feel his arms wrap around me and his chin drop to the top of my head. Closing my eyes, I wonder how it's possible to feel what I'm feeling right now. I barely know this man, but I feel more connected to him than my college boyfriend, who I dated for three years.

"Thank you for coming to me," he says quietly, and tears burn the back of my throat as my arms tighten around his waist. I'm still scared to death, but there is now hope mixed in with the fear of what could happen.

"Thank you for being persistent," I say, meaning that, and his arms tighten before he loosens his hold slightly.

"Are you hungry?"

"A little."

"I cooked," he tells me, and I tip my head back to look up at him.

"You cooked?"

"Don't sound so surprised. There's a lot about me that you don't know yet."

"Yeah, like the fact you live in a fairy tale cottage," I state, and his brows draw together.

"What?"

"Your house, it looks like a fairy tale cottage right out of a book."

Turning us to the side, he looks at the house. Even though it's dark, the bright colors around the windows are in stark contrast to the white of the stucco. It's all accentuated by the outside lights that are coming down off the edge of the roof and others that are shooting at it from the garden.

"The couple who built it was from London. They wanted to have a little bit of home in the US. When they moved home after their first child was born, they let it sit with plans to come back and visit, only that never happened. Eventually, they realized they would never come back, so they put it on the market."

"That's so sad."

"Sad for them. It worked out for me. Come on." He takes my hand

and begins leading me toward a stone walkway to a heavy-looking wood door that is curved at the top. Pushing the door open, we step right into a small living room with gold and white wallpaper on the walls that has began peeling away. There are plastic drapes all over the floor and a ladder in the middle of the room under one of the many large wooden beams that run across the ceiling.

"I'm in the middle of re-staining all the beams," he explains, pulling me past the living room and down a hall.

Reaching the kitchen, I blink. It's even more beautiful than I imagined it would be when he showed me the things he picked out. The cream cupboards and countertops go perfectly with the light gray walls. The large stove off to the side looks amazing with the huge decorative vent above it that blends in with the cupboards. All the appliances look awesome in the space, and they tie in perfectly with a huge metal-top table that is off to the side with coordinating chairs placed around it.

Taking a step farther into the room, I see a second living room with a large stone fireplace as the centerpiece with a TV mounted above, and one large sectional in front of it that is a dark gray suede material. Fur pillows of different shades are stacked up in the corners, and a few fur throws are tossed over the back. The whole space looks like something out of a high-end magazine ad for housewares. Spinning to face Sage, I shake my head.

"This is…" I look around again, trying to come up with a word that means more than beautiful. "This is spectacular! This could be in a catalog."

"My mom and aunts will be happy to hear that." He smiles.

"They did all of this?"

"Yeah, they love shopping, so I gave them my card and a budget and told them to let loose as long as they didn't show up with anything pink."

"No, this is… this is you."

"If you think this is nice, you should see the view from my bed," he says, and I feel my face go soft.

"You put in a skylight?"

"Yeah." He holds out his hand, and I place mine in it and let him lead me down a short hall that is just off the kitchen. Opening the door to the room, I walk in ahead of him and go to the bed. Climbing in without asking if it's okay, I lie on my back and look up at the night sky that seems to be a hundred times brighter than it does from the skylight over my bed.

"I knew this place would be beautiful when you were finished with it," I say quietly. Then I turn my head when the bed moves and watch Sage crawl up next to me to lie down on his back, just far enough away that we're not touching.

"I still have a lot to do, but it's coming along."

"Have you done it all yourself?" I ask, lifting my head to find him already looking at me.

"You know my uncles own a construction company, so they did some of the work, but my brothers, cousins, and I did the kitchen and floors ourselves."

"You guys have done a great job."

"Thanks," he tells me, and then he rolls toward me, putting an elbow to the bed and looking down at me. Watching him study me with the light through the skylight and the open door of the room, I fight the urge to squirm under his stare. "I've imagined this." He tosses his hand out to encompass everything. "I've imagined sharing all of this with you hundreds of times. I'm glad you're here."

Feeling my lips part, I lift my hand and rest it softly against his cheek. "Me, too," I confess without thinking, and he turns his head and touches his lips to my palm.

"Come on. I made lasagna," he urges, sitting up and getting off the bed, pulling me along with him, and I feel my stomach twist. I can't eat lasagna, and I can't even tell him why not without exposing too much.

"I'm not really hungry anymore," I lie, and he stops at the door to look at me, frowning.

"You're not hungry anymore?"

"I forgot I had a big lunch today."

"Oh." His frown deepens.

"I'll try to eat some, but I don't want you to think I'm being rude if I don't eat much," I say, and he shakes his head.

"It's all good. You can watch me eat and we can catch up," he assures, and so that's exactly what I do. I watch him eat and tell him about Chris, my parents, and even a little about Kelly, before it's time for me to leave. And when I go, he gives me a kiss goodbye that puts his kiss hello to shame.

Chapter 4

Kim

HEARING SOMEONE KNOCKING on my door, my eyes open and I roll to the side to look at the clock. Seeing it's not even five in the morning yet, I sit up and put my feet to the floor then hurry out of bed. I only know one person who would show up at my house at this time, and that person is Kelly, and seeing how my last conversation with her ended, I'm not really looking forward to going through that again.

I put on a long sweatshirt over the top of my nightgown and head for the living room, where the morning sun has just started to light the room. Walking toward the sliding glass door, I see it's not Kelly. It's two men wearing suits, and they both look like they haven't slept in hours. I stop in place when they notice me and watch relief flash through their eyes as they hold up black leather wallets, pressing them to the glass. Seeing both of them say FBI, I hurry across the room, flip the latch, and open the door an inch.

"Kimberly Cullen?" the man who is standing closest to where I am asks, studying me.

"Yes."

"I'm Special Agent Torres, and this is Special Agent Kace. We're with the FBI," he says, and my stomach fills with anxiety.

"How can I help you?"

"Can we come in?" Agent Torres asks, and I check them out. They look legit, but I just don't know.

"We're here about your sister," Agent Kace explains, and my eyes move to him.

"What happened?" I question, and I watch both their eyes change in a way that makes my heart feel suddenly heavy. "What happened?" I repeat, pushing the door open to let them inside.

"Do you have someone you can call to come sit with you?" Agent Torres asks, and I shake my head as I walk across the room to stand on the opposite side, away from them.

"It would really be best if you called someone."

"Just tell me," I whisper, twisting my hands nervously in front of me.

"Your sister's been murdered." My heart stops, and my eyes close as those five words penetrate. Wrapping my arms around my waist, I open my eyes back up, not really seeing anything. "We haven't been able to find her body at this time, but we have men out looking for her."

Oh, God. I move to the couch to take a seat, because my legs feel like they are about to give out from under me. Dead? Kelly's dead? How is that even possible?

"We're very sorry for your loss, Miss Cullen."

"How?" I finally get out through the sudden ache in my throat.

"Unfortunately, we can't discuss that with you at this time, but know we are close to catching her killer."

"Her killer." I drop my eyes to my lap. Kelly isn't just dead; she was murdered. Someone killed her. Someone took her life. "Will I know when you find the person who did this?" I ask, lifting my eyes to look at the two men who have now moved closer to where I'm sitting.

"We will make sure you are given the news as soon as we apprehend him."

"You already have a suspect?" I ask to confirm, needing that information more than my next breath.

"Yes," Agent Torres states, and I drop my eyes to my lap and pull in a few deep breaths, trying to get myself under control.

Nodding, I lift my head then shake it. "Does... does her mom know?" I ask, and they both look at me with confused expressions. "I... I was a-adopted when I was born. I... I don't know my birth mom."

"We were unaware of that," Agent Kace says, and I blink up at him in bewilderment.

"How? How did you find me then?" I don't know my birth mother, but I know she has my number, because Kelly gave it to her along with my address when she first started coming around. She thought her mom—*our* mom—would want to contact me, which she never did.

"An eyewitness believed she was you," Agent Torres explains, getting down on his haunches in front of me. "When we went back to examine who our suspect had been in contact with, we found out it was your sister Kelly."

Pinching my thigh, I try to see if that will wake me up, but it doesn't. This isn't a bad dream I'm going to wake up from any second.

"Please call someone and have them come over. You shouldn't be alone right now, Miss Cullen, and as soon as we are able to give you more information about the case, we will set up a time to meet with you."

Nodding, because I can't talk, I reach out to take a card Agent Kace hands me.

"Call someone," he orders gently, and I nod again. "We'll be in contact soon."

Watching them leave with quiet goodbyes, I sit here hearing their words continue to ring in my ears.

"God," I whimper, dragging my hands down my face and covering my mouth with my shaking fingers. "Oh, God." Looking around the room, everything blurs together while tears fill my eyes, and bile builds in the back of my throat, making it hard to breathe. Squeezing my tear-filled eyes closed, wetness tracks down my cheeks and onto my chest. I get up on shaky legs and head to my room to grab my phone out of my purse where I left it last night. Pulling it out, I see it's dead. Finding my charging cord, I fumble with it until I get it plugged in then wait for it to turn on. I have a few voice mails and a lot of texts but I ignore them, pulling up my mom's phone number in my call log and pressing send.

"Honey," she answers on the second ring, sounding like I just woke her up.

"Mom," I choke out through my tears. I wish she were here. I wish she could wrap her arms around me and tell me everything will be all right like she has done since I was little.

"What's happened? Are you okay?" she questions, sounding more alert than she did moments ago.

"No." I fall back on my bed and squeeze my eyes closed. "Kelly. Kelly's dead, Mom," I get out, right before a loud, painful sob breaks loose.

"What?"

"She was murdered. The FBI was just here. Kelly was murdered."

"Oh, God," Mom breathes, then the phone goes quiet before I hear her talking to my dad, but I can't make out what either of them are saying over the sound of my blood pumping through my ears.

"Baby," Dad says, and my eyes tighten. "Your mom is booking us a flight right now."

"Okay."

"Be strong, honey."

"Okay," I agree on a whisper.

"Be there soon. We love you."

"Love you, too," I say, right before I let the phone fall from my grasp, and then I roll to my side and curl myself into a ball.

Your sister's been murdered.

My eyes burn as those words replay over and over in my head while I watch the ceiling fan spin in circles. I should get up. I should go shower and call my parents back so I can tell them they shouldn't worry about me, but I can't force myself to move. All I can do is think about Kelly, my identical twin. We shared the same hair, the same face, the same everything, down to the freckles across the bridge of our noses, and yet with all of that in common, I hated the person she was.

Hearing pounding on the door, I try to sit up, but I can't.

"Kim, open the door."

Sage. I'd know his voice anywhere.

"Open the goddamn door." He bangs harder, and a new wave of tears fills my eyes. "Kimberly, if you don't open the fucking door, I'm gonna break the motherfucker down," he roars, making me jump.

"I'm fine. Go away." I attempt to yell back, but the words come out in a whisper through my dry throat as my heavy eyes slide closed and I finally give into the darkness surrounding me.

"Jesus, baby?" I hear growled through my subconscious as warm fingers rest against my neck under my ear. My eyes open slowly and I blink. "Baby," Sage whispers, taking a seat on my bed next to my hip, pushing my hair away from my face gently.

"Kelly's dead," I breathe, staring into his seafoam-green eyes resting softly on my blue ones.

"I know." He pulls me against his chest and I sob, clinging to him. Climbing into bed with me, his big body curls around mine.

"I told her I hated her," I say, pressing my face against his chest while my fingers wrap tightly into his shirt. "The last time we talked, I told her she was a coward and that I hated her."

"She knows you didn't hate her."

He's wrong; she didn't know. She died not knowing I cared. Not knowing I only wanted her in my life, that I didn't want to use her, that I didn't want anything from her but to have her in my life.

"Don't think about that right now," he says gently, running his hand down my back. "Don't think about that. Think about the good times you had together."

Good times? I wish I did have good times with her. I wish I had a million happy memories of us together that I could recall right now, but I don't have any of those. Kelly was angry at the world and pissed off at me. She thought I was the one who didn't want anything to do with her or our mom until I was diagnosed with stage-three kidney disease. Until I was left with no choice but to contact her for help. But that wasn't the case at all.

When I first found out about Kelly after I was diagnosed, I had been so upset with my parents for keeping the truth about my adoption from me, for never telling me I had a sister. I know they believed they were protecting me, but having grown up my whole life believing one thing, only to learn it was all a lie, was more devastating than finding out my kidneys were failing in the first place.

Even with the knowledge that my mother had been addicted to crack and had been arrested multiple times for prostitution, I still felt it should have been my choice when I turned eighteen whether or not I had any kind of relationship with my birth family. It took a long time for me to understand why they didn't tell me the truth.

It had been Kelly who had made me understand unknowingly what my parents had been trying to protect me from. They didn't want me to see the ugly side of drug addiction or feel what neglect was like firsthand. They didn't want me to experience the disappointment Kelly had experienced her whole life growing up with our mother.

Where I grew up surrounded with love, Kelly grew up fighting just to survive. Our childhoods couldn't have been more opposite, which made us both different people. Where I have always looked at the world with hope, Kelly looked at the world, wondering when it would knock her back down.

"I should have tried harder," I whisper through my dry throat as more tears fall.

"Stop." His lips press to my forehead and he doesn't remove them. He keeps them right there while he whispers soothingly to me, until my eyes get too heavy to keep open any longer and I fall asleep held tightly in his grasp.

Hearing Sage's voice and two others that sound like my parents off in the distance talking quietly, I wake slowly, blinking my eyes open. Finding the room dark with the only light coming in from the skylight and the moon overhead, I roll to my side, dislodging the blankets that have been carefully tucked around me.

"God." I press my hand to my forehead as I sit up. I haven't eaten today, and after crying for so long, my head is pounding, making me feel nauseous and dizzy. Blinking when the door is cracked open and light spills into the room, I watch Sage's shadow step inside before he closes the door behind him.

"I thought I heard you get up," he says quietly as he walks to the bed, taking a seat next to me and flipping on the lamp on the table. It takes a second for my eyes to adjust to the light, and when they do, I watch him take my hand and place two pills against my palm before grabbing my ever-present water bottle off the bedside table, handing it to me. "Your parents are here."

"How long have they been here?" I ask, downing the pills before resting my suddenly heavy head against his shoulder and closing my eyes to keep out the light.

"About an hour," he says as he moves his arms around me and tucks my head under his chin. "They came in to check on you when they arrived but wanted to let you sleep," he explains, and I nod. "How are you feeling?"

"My head is pounding and I'm hungry," I answer truthfully, leaving out the part about feeling like a part of me is suddenly missing.

"What do you feel like eating?" he asks, and I feel his chin move against the top of my head.

"Soup."

"Do you want me to bring it in here to you, or do you feel like getting up?"

"I'll get up."

"All right." He touches his lips to my hair right before he stands us both up. Moving to the door, he stops me with his hand, taking mine, and I turn to look at him.

"Are you okay?" I ask when I see the worried look in his eyes.

"How much do you know about what happened with Kelly?" he asks suddenly, and I frown.

"Two agents from the FBI told me that she was murdered, but they couldn't tell me much other than that."

"I thought so." He shakes his head while running his hand down his mouth in agitation. That's when I realize there would be no way of him knowing that unless something else happened. I didn't even think about the fact he had shown up here out of the blue, threatening to break down the door until now.

"What happened?" I ask, feeling my heart start to beat hard against my ribcage.

"Ashlyn was kidnapped in the middle of the night. She and Dillon had both been drugged. Dillon woke up when Ashlyn was being taken, but he couldn't do anything to stop it from happening, since he had been given some sort of muscle relaxer," he explains, referring to his cousin, who is my close friend, and her new husband.

"What?" I press my hand to my mouth, and he pulls me against his chest. "Please tell me she's okay," I whisper against my fingers as my stomach turns, and a fresh wave of tears begins to fill my eyes.

"She's fine. She's in the hospital recovering. She got away, but not before she saw who she thought was you at the time, dead. That's why the FBI was here this morning," he says, right before his hand wraps around my jaw and he pulls me back to search my face. Staring blankly at him, his words settle over me, and I watch his eyes close as he shakes his head, muttering a quiet "Fuck."

"Did she…" My eyes close, and then I open them back up slowly. "Did she talk to Kelly… before?"

"I don't know, baby." Dislodging his hand still holding my chin, I drop my forehead to his chest. "I'm sorry," he whispers, and I do the only thing I can do, which is nod.

"Honey," my mom calls as she knocks on my door a second later.

"Mom," I cry, and Sage releases me. Rushing across the small space to her, I wrap my arms around her waist and tuck my face against her chest, where I start to cry again.

"Oh, honey," she whispers, holding on to me. Then I feel myself being transferred and I smell the familiar scent of my dad's cologne as I'm tucked into his chest.

"It's going to be okay," he says, rocking me from side-to-side, and I do the only thing I can do once again. I hold on.

Sage

TAKING OFF MY shirt and shoes, I drop my jeans to the floor and grab my sleep pants, putting them on before taking a seat on the edge of the couch. Rubbing my hands down my face, I yawn. It's been a long few days, and it's all starting to catch up with me. I rest my elbows on my knees and stare at the floor.

Six days ago, I convinced Kim to come stay with me. Since her parents arc in town and she doesn't have the extra room, she agreed, and since then, I've been sleeping on the couch, having given up my room to her and the only other furnished room to her parents.

Sensing movement behind me, I look over my shoulder and watch Kim start toward me. I love everything about having her here, but I wish the circumstances were different.

"You okay?" I ask when she finally makes it across the room and crawls onto my lap. Her parents went to bed about an hour ago, and she had said she was doing the same.

"I can't sleep," she whispers, tucking herself closer to my chest, and I lean back against the couch, wrapping my arms around her.

"Are you worried about tomorrow?" I question, and she stiffens slightly before relaxing once more.

"I'm relieved that Kelly will be put to rest," she replies quietly, and my eyes close as the pain in her voice grates against my skin. Six days ago, the FBI and the police were still looking for Kelly's body. Three days ago, they found her remains after apprehending the man responsible for Kelly's murder and my cousin's abduction. Two days ago, Kelly's mom called Kim's phone for the first time, asking Kim to help out with the cremation expenses—meaning she asked Kim to pay for the whole thing.

I found out after that phone call that it was the first time Kim had ever even had a conversation with her birth mom. She hadn't returned any of Kim's calls since Kelly's death, and it wasn't until she needed money that she reached out. During that call, I could see the hurt and disappointment on her face, but I could also see her strength and resilience as well.

"I don't even know what I will say to her when I meet her. What was it like when you met your birth mom?" she asks, and my jaw tightens. I told her and her parents one night over dinner about my sister and me being adopted. Kim had already known from our mutual friends about my history, but she had never heard it from me, and I knew it was important to tell her, because it was one more thing that bound us together.

"I never met her. I never wanted to meet her," I confess, and she pulls back to look at me.

"But Nalia?"

"She flew out on her own to meet her. I never had the urge to connect with Sharon."

"You weren't even curious about her?"

"I've seen pictures, read about her background. There's nothing else I want to know."

"Oh." She goes quiet for a moment then drops her eyes to her fingers that are twiddling with the cross between my pecs. "I thought when I first found out about my adoption that I was missing out on family."

"You have a family."

"I know I have my parents, but I thought I was missing out on having my blood family. When I met Kelly, I learned quickly that I hadn't missed out on anything," she whispers, and I know this is something she's been struggling with the last few days.

She and her sister didn't have a good relationship, and now that Kelly is gone, she will never have the chance to build one with her. "I know I shouldn't think it, but I'm grateful that my mom chose to give me up. I don't know how she chose which one of us she would put up for adoption, but I'm glad it was me," she says as tears start to fall slowly down her cheeks and onto my abs. "I got lucky. I just wish I could have shown Kelly what love is. I wish I could have convinced her that I cared about her, that I didn't want to use her, that I didn't want to hurt her, and that I just wanted her to be in my life. I hate knowing I will never get to do that."

"Shhhh," I hush her, tucking her face back against my chest.

"How can I face the woman who made Kelly the person she was, a person who didn't think she deserved a good life and love?" she begs. Christ, my throat gets tight, and I wrap my hand around her skull as she sobs, wishing I could change that for her and for Kelly, wishing there was something I could do to make this better or easier for her. "I hate her. I know it's wrong, but I still hate her."

"You have a right to feel the way you feel about your birth mom. No one understands more than you what Kelly missed out on by growing up the way she did," I assure, and she nods then wraps her arms around my middle.

"Thank you."

Kissing the top of her hair, I run my hands soothingly down her back and under the tee she has on then feel her body relax completely against me. Knowing she's asleep and there isn't room on the couch for the two of us, I stand with her tucked against me. Seeing her dad looking out through a crack in my guest room door as I head down the hall with her asleep in my arms, I lift my chin and he does the same in return as I move past him.

Kim's parents both had questions about our relationship when they showed up at her place to find me there, so I explained to them that Kim and I were seeing each other but taking it slow, leaving out the "for now" part of that statement. They don't need to know the depth of my feelings for their daughter until she knows herself how I feel. I had already known I cared about her before, but when I heard she was dead, my heart stopped beating, making me realize even though we hardly know each other, my heart had at some point claimed her as its own.

Gritting my teeth, I look down at the woman in my arms. It's too soon for me to make my intentions clear, especially with everything that has happened, but she is mine, and will be until the day I die if I get my way.

Reaching my room, I put my shoulder to the door and push it open before turning slightly to kick it almost closed so the light doesn't wake her. Heading across the room to the bed, I start to lay her down, only to have her arms shoot out around my neck and tighten.

"Please don't go. Please stay," she whispers, and I don't even have to think about it. I put one knee into the bed and then the other and lay her down on the mattress, settling in behind her. Taking my hand at her waist, she twines our fingers together. "Thank you," she murmurs, bringing our combined hands up to rest between her breasts.

Kissing the back of her head, I toss my leg over her and pin her to the bed, where I expect to stay awake. But lying here, with the woman I'm pretty sure was made for me in my arms, I fall asleep.

Chapter 5

Kim

HOLDING ONTO SAGE'S hand tightly, we walk with my parents and Chris trailing behind us toward the funeral home. The closer we get to the doors, the more my grasp on his hand squeezes and my stomach twists with anxiety.

"You okay?" Sage asks, and I turn my head to look up at him, noticing the concern in his eyes that has been there since we woke up in his bed this morning. Not sure how to answer that question right now, I shrug and he suddenly pulls me to a stop. Turning me to face him, his hands cup my face and his dips toward mine. "You don't have to do this. Your parents, Chris, and I can go in and get everything sorted."

God, this is the guy I instinctively knew I could easily fall in love with. This is the Sage I missed.

"I'll be okay," I reply quietly, and his eyes search mine for a long time before he drops his head, brushes his lips over mine, and then leans back.

"All you have to do is say the words and I'll get you out of there."

Yes, this is the man I'm falling for, and that scares the crap out of me. I nod at him, and as he takes my hand in his, we resume walking toward a set of double doors at the end of the sidewalk.

Reaching the doors, Sage keeps me with him while he holds one open for my parents and Chris to precede us before leading me inside. It takes a moment for my eyes to adjust to the dim light, and when they do, I notice the woman standing just inside the front room. Studying her from where my feet have suddenly gotten too heavy to move, I squeeze Sage's hand.

I saw a picture of Ginny Mavis once when Kelly showed it to me on her cell phone, but where that picture had been bad, showing a frail woman who smoked too much, drank too much, and wore too little clothes, the woman standing before me is in even worse shape. Since that picture was taken, she has lost twenty pounds she couldn't afford to lose. Her dyed black hair has grown out three inches, leaving a stripe of almost white down the center of her scalp. Her skin is wrinkled and pale, almost yellow from lack of nutrition, and obviously, her smoking and drinking has gotten even worse.

"Kimberly?" she prompts like she has no idea who I am, and the twisting in my stomach moves to my heart.

"Ginny."

She lifts her chin an inch then moves her eyes over me before they land on my family that's gathered close.

"I didn't know you were bringing people with you."

"Sorry," I say, not really sorry at all. I wouldn't have been able to make it through these last few days without these people, and I'm not sure if I would have found the courage to come without their support.

"I guess it don't matter now," she mutters, and I fight the urge to yell at her, to scream and ask, *How?* How can she stand a few feet away from the daughter she gave away after losing the daughter she raised? How can she stand there and act like this moment isn't an important one? "We should get this done. I need to be on my way. I got things to do."

"Get this done?" I breathe as my throat starts to tighten around a lump forming there.

"Yeah, I ain't got all day," she clarifies before she moves her eyes to my parents, who I can feel bristling at my side. "I got work. Ain't no one givin' me any handouts."

"Jesus fuck," Sage growls, and she looks at him.

"You're right. We do need to get this over with," Chris says, stepping in front of us and blocking her from view. "Have you spoken to anyone since you arrived?"

"No, ain't no one been out here since I got here."

"All right, why don't you come with me and we'll go find someone to help us?" he offers, taking her arm like a gentleman and leading her away.

"Di... did that just happen?" I ask, and Sage gives my hand a squeeze while my mom takes my other hand in hers, holding it tightly.

"This will all be done soon," Dad mutters, and I pull in a much-needed breath then let it out slowly.

"What do you mean you divided the ashes?" I hear shouted, and I force my mom and Sage to release me so I can take off toward the sound of Ginny yelling. Walking quickly past a row of caskets, I make it to an open door at the end of a long hall, where I find Ginny, Chris, and an older gentleman, who must be the funeral director, arguing.

"You told him to divide her ashes?" Ginny yells, looking at me as I step into the room, and I nod.

"Ma'am, please keep it down," the director urges quietly, while Chris takes a step back from Ginny when she tries to take a second, much smaller box from him.

"Who gave you the right to do that? Who do you think you are?"

"I...." My hands ball into fists, and my jaw clenches so hard I'm surprised I don't break any teeth. "I'm no one, and no one gave me the right to do it, but I did it anyway."

"You have no fucking right to any part of her," she seethes, and my throat burns as I try to swallow down the tears climbing up the back of it.

"I asked them to put a little of my sister's ashes in a separate box for

74

me so I could have them blown into two glass balls. One I was keeping for myself and one I planned on giving to you."

"I don't want anything from you," she hisses, and my eyes slide closed as I feel Sage get close to my back—offering support, giving me what I need, him not having any idea he's even doing it or how much I need it.

"Please give her both boxes." I open my eyes, and Chris, who is holding the smaller box in his hand, shakes his head. "Please," I plea, and he reluctantly hands it over while the older gentleman gives her the larger box. "Thank you," I say quietly, and then I turn around, not giving Ginny another glance. I let Sage lead me out of the room and down the hall. Stopping before we reach the door, I turn back around, realizing this isn't over yet. "I still need to pay for the cremation. I—"

"We've got it, honey," Mom murmurs, reaching out to give my arm a squeeze. "Why don't you let Sage take you out to his car, we'll be out in a few minutes."

"Thank you," I whisper, fighting back tears I refuse to let fall. I won't cry here. I won't do it where there is a chance Ginny could see me break down. She doesn't get to know she hurt me.

"Come on," Sage urges gently, gathering me against his side. As I'm tucked under the protective strength of his arm, he leads me out of the building and back down the sidewalk toward where we parked when we arrived. As soon as we reach his car, he opens the passenger side door, moves us around so that, even though we are still out in the open, we are blocked by the door and tinted window.

Wrapping one arm around my back and his other hand around my skull, he tucks my face against his chest then drops his head until his mouth is near my ear. "You can cry now."

Clinging to him, the tears I've been holding back begin to fall. I wish I could say I was only crying for my sister, but in truth, I'm crying over the woman who gave birth to me. But I promise myself these will be the only tears I ever shed over Ginny Mavis.

"You okay, honey?" Mom asks, and I turn to look at her over my shoulder from where I'm sitting in the front seat. As soon as my parents and Chris came out of the funeral home, Sage told me they were approaching, so I quickly wiped away the tears on my face and got in the car. Once he slammed my door, I expected him to walk around to the driver's side, but he surprised me by stopping my parents and Chris to talk to them. It gave me some much-needed time to get myself under control before they all got in the car.

I know my parents understand I'm upset, but I don't want them to worry any more than they have. They already feel guilty they have to leave tomorrow to get back to work, and I don't want to add to that remorse. "Honey?" Mom prompts, and I come out of my head and nod.

"I'm okay," I assure her, seeing the worry and anger in her eyes. "Promise." Sage reaches over to take my hand and pulls it to his lap.

"That woman isn't worthy of the air she's taking up by being alive," Dad grumbles, and I turn around to look at him. Those words were not only harsh but also full of pain, and that statement coming from my dad means he's upset.

"Dad—"

"No, don't try to make me feel bad for feeling that way. She was a horrible woman when we met her at the hospital when we adopted you, and she hasn't changed. The only thing I wish was different is that she would have let us have Kelly, too."

"Me, too." I bite the inside of my cheek to keep from crying, and Sage's hand squeezes mine.

"Sage," Chris interjects a minute later, and I look at him to find his eyes on Sage's in the rearview mirror.

"Yeah?" Sage answers.

"You know how to get into someone's house unnoticed, don't you?"

he asks, and I wonder where the hell he's going with this.

"Why?" Sage questions, instead of answering with the fact he has no idea of how to get into someone's house unnoticed, making me raise a brow.

"I want to break into Ginny's house and get that box," Chris explains casually, like he's talking about what color the sky is and not about breaking and entering then robbing someone.

"Chris, that is not happening." I shake my head at him.

"Why not? She probably wouldn't even notice it's missing. Hell, I can just get some of the ashes from the bigger box and leave the smaller one, and then she will never know."

"It's not happening," I repeat firmly, noticing Sage hasn't told Chris that his idea is absolutely ridiculous and he won't be a part of it. "You won't do that, right?" I ask Sage just to confirm, but he doesn't answer me. He just gives my hand a squeeze, which makes a chorus of quiet laughter breakout in the back of the car.

Great.

HEARING THE FOREIGN sound of a house phone ringing, I pull my eyes from the book I'm reading. I look into the house through the glass doors that lead inside from the sun porch, where I've been sitting with my mom since we got back to Sage's house. Seeing Sage move across his living room and into the kitchen, I watch him grab a slim black phone from its hanger on the wall and put it to his ear.

"I really wish we didn't have to leave tomorrow," Mom says, and I pull my attention from Sage to look at her. When we arrived out here, I took up one of the long padded benches lining the wall and she made herself at home in one of the three rope hammocks hanging from the ceiling. "Maybe I should stay. I'm sure your dad could handle stuff for a few days without me."

"I have to get back to work, too," I remind her. Even though Frankie told me to take as much time as I need, I can't afford any more. After forcing my parents to take the money back for Kelly's cremation, I don't have much savings left, which means I need to get back to work. "And I need to get out of Sage's house. He's been really nice letting us stay here, but I don't want to take advantage of him and overstay my welcome."

"You think you could overstay your welcome?"

"Yeah." I shrug, and she studies me for a long moment before breaking out into a fit of laughter.

"What's so funny?" I frown at her, and it takes a second but she gets herself under control.

"That man wouldn't care if you moved in and redecorated everything pink. But he will care if you tell him you feel like you're taking advantage of him and overstaying your welcome."

"Mom—"

"Chris told me." She cuts me off, and my eyes widen.

"What?" I breathe as she swings her legs around and sits up, putting her feet to the floor.

"He told me what happened. He told me about what Kelly did to Sage and what happened between you two. I get why you made up the lie about you and Chris being an item, and I even get why you were so cautious about letting anything happen between you two again, but I don't understand why you can't see he feels what you feel."

"God." I tip my head back. "Chris totally got you on Team Sage, didn't he?"

"No." She shakes her head. "Sage got me on his team by being sweet to my girl, by holding her when she needed to be held, by staying with her while we couldn't be with her. He got me when he stopped you outside the funeral home to tell you that he would take care of everything, if that's what you wanted. He got me when he offered your father and me a place to stay, not knowing us from Adam. That's how he got me. What kind of mother would I be if I didn't want the best for my baby? You deserve a man like him in your life. You deserve a man who looks like he would take on the world if it was to protect you."

"He doesn't know about my illness," I confess, and she leans closer to me, resting her hand on my knee.

"I know he doesn't. You told us not to bring it up around him, which we haven't because you are a woman—a grown woman who needs to make her own decisions about these kinds of things," she says quietly before leaning in and moving her hand up to rest against my cheek. "But with all of that, honey, you need to tell him so he can show you that he is exactly the man he's shown you he is, the kind who will stick by you when you need him."

"But what if he's not that guy? What if he finds out and decides he can't handle it? What then?" I ask, voicing my biggest fear.

"I think you need to ask yourself what you will be missing out on if you don't give him the chance to prove you wrong." She leans back, and I pull my eyes from her and look out over the lake through the glass windows behind me. Even knowing she's right, fear has my hands balling into fists. I want to cling to him; when he's close, I find myself going to him without thought, but I don't know if I can trust him. I don't know if I trust myself right now.

"Sorry, ladies," Sage says, and I swing my head around to find him standing in the open doorway with his eyes on me. "Can you come in for a sec? I need to talk to you."

"Um… sure." I start to stand, but my mom gets up, putting a hand to my shoulder to keep me down.

"I'm going to go check on the boys' progress." She gives my shoulder a squeeze before moving past Sage, who gives her a small smile as she pats him on the abs and moves past him into the house. Once she's inside, he slides the door closed behind her and walks to where I am, taking a seat. Dropping his eyes to the floor, he runs his hands over his head in a move that screams he's frustrated about something, and that puts me instantly on guard.

"Is everything okay?"

"I gotta leave town for a few days," he says, turning to look at me. "Jax just called. He got a call on a skip, and I can't afford to pass this one up. If I could, I wouldn't take the job."

My muscles relax, and I let out a quiet, relieved breath. "Please don't worry about me," I beg, reaching over and taking his hand. "I know you have to work. I'll be fine."

"Your parents are leaving tomorrow," he reminds me quietly, and I nod.

"I know, and I have to get back to work, too. This…" I shake my head, trying to find the words to express how much everything he's done has meant to me. "I really appreciate everything you've done, for letting me cry on your shoulder and giving my parents a place to stay. For being so cool around Chris… when he's Chris and could annoy the Pope. I appreciate it all more than you know. You've been a really great friend," I finish, and he studies me for a second before he shakes his head, leans forward, and places his mouth over mine. The kiss is deep, hard, wet, and over way too soon, so when he pulls his mouth away, my eyes are still closed and my hands are wound into his shirt to pull him back for more.

"There is nothing friendly about the things I want to do to you Kimberly," he growls. My eyes pop open and I find his face an inch from mine. "We're not friends, If you haven't figured that out by now, I've still got work to do. It's my job to take care of you. I didn't do any of that shit out of kindness. I did it because I look out for mine. And make no mistake about it, baby, you are mine."

And with that, he leans in, pressing his mouth to mine once more while untangling my hands from his shirt before he stands. "I gotta pack. I'll be out to say goodbye to everyone before I go. You're welcome to stay here as long as you want. I already put a key on your key ring."

Sitting here blinking at his retreating back, I watch him go into the house, wondering what the hell just happened. A few minutes later, I still have no answer to that question when he reappears and kisses me goodbye.

Chapter 6

Kim

"HOW ARE YOU?" Ellie asks as we start to clean up our stations at the salon. From the moment we opened the doors to the shop this morning, we've been slammed with clients and walk-ins, so we haven't had a chance to really talk.

"I'm all right," I murmur, seeing the concern in her eyes. "It doesn't feel real yet, you know?" I grab the broom and start to sweep the little bits of stray hair that have gotten away from us throughout the day.

"I know what you mean. When my brother and Bonnie died, it took a while for the reality of them being gone, really gone, to sink in. I guess it still kind of happens even now. There's still days that I expect them to call or walk through the door," she says, and I notice that her eyes are getting wet. "It gets easier to deal with the loss, but it never goes away."

"I'm sorry, Ellie." I lean over and give her a hug, hating that talking about this has brought up the memories of her brother and his girlfriend, who died in a car accident. When they both died suddenly, the care of their daughter, Hope, who was just a few months old at the time, was left to Ellie, and since then she has raised Hope as her own child. Hope knows about her parents, but Ellie and Jax are the only real parents she knows.

"Honey, you just lost your sister. I should be the one comforting you, not the other way around."

"I wasn't as close to Kelly as you were to your brother and Bonnie," I remind her quietly, and she presses her lips together. Ellie didn't care much for Kelly. Not that she knew her personally, but she did know of the things Kelly had done to me, and being the kind of friend she is, she's been angry at Kelly on my behalf for a long time. "I wish things had been different between us, but they weren't, and now they never will be."

"I'm sorry."

"Me, too," I agree.

"You know I'm here anytime you want to talk about anything, right?" she asks, wrapping her arms around my waist to give me a tight hug.

"I know." I hug her back just as tightly.

"I love you. We all love you," she whispers against my ear, and I pull in a breath.

"I love you, too," I whisper back, vowing then and there to be a better friend to her and the friends I've made since moving here. Over the last few months, I've gotten so caught up in my own personal drama that I've neglected my friends and family, but that is going to change. Life is too short to live the way I've been living, and losing Kelly reminded me of that. Giving me one last squeeze, she pulls away and I wipe my wet cheeks, praying I'll soon stop crying all the damn time.

"How are things between you and Sage?"

This is a subject I don't really know how to go about discussing. Everyone who knows the two of us saw Sage coming around, trying to get me to talk to him before Kelly was murdered. Now they all know I stayed with him while my parents were in town, since he's related to most of the people I consider friends. "We... I... we're..." I sigh then roll my eyes when she starts to smile. "I honestly have no idea, but I do know we are not friends."

"You're not friends?" she repeats, and her brows draw together tightly.

"He told me before he left that we're not friends and he did every-thing he did for me because I'm apparently his."

"Ahh," she breathes, and then mutters, "I see."

"Do you? Because I don't see, and I've been wracking my brain since he left yesterday, trying to figure it out."

"It really is simple, honey. You're his. He's obviously claimed you."

"Claimed me?" My nose scrunches up at that, and she giggles.

"Is it really that bad, being claimed by Sage Mayson?"

"Put like that, I guess the answer is no," I reply as my lips twitch, and she laughs loudly.

"I didn't think so," she says right as the bell over the door goes off. Watching a woman walk up to the front counter carrying a huge bouquet of flowers, I follow behind Ellie toward the front of the salon, where Frankie's been going over the appointment book since the last client left.

"How can I help you?" Frankie asks as the woman sets the bouquet down and steps out from behind it and into view.

"These are for Kimberly Cullen," she answers, and Frankie turns to look at me.

"You got flowers, girl."

"I see that." I smile at him then turn my smile on the delivery wom-an. "Thank you."

"You're welcome." She grins back before she turns and leaves through the door.

"Did Sage send you flowers?" Ellie asks as soon as the door is closed, and I shrug while searching for the card. Finding it a second later, I pull it off and open it up. Reading it, I blink and then turn and hold it out to Ellie and Frankie.

"Mrs. Ethel? Sheesh! Who knew the cheap, mean old goat had it in her to be sweet?" Ellie mutters, and I laugh.

"I can't believe she sent me flowers." I smile, leaning in to sniff one of the huge pink roses, and Frankie shakes his head.

"That woman adores you. You're the only person she talks to when she comes in, and since you started here, she's been a regular of yours. I'm not surprised at all that she sent you these," he states matter-of-factly, and I blink at him, realizing he must not know she doesn't really talk to me. Honestly, I don't think she's even said more than a dozen words to me since she's been my client.

"Well, they are beautiful. I should give her a call and say thank you." I decide, pulling the appointment book toward me so I can retrieve her number. Scanning through the pages, I finally come across it and then reach for the salon phone to dial her number. Putting the phone to my ear, I listen to it ring three times before a woman answers.

"Duesaw residence. How can I help you?"

"Is Mrs. Ethel available?"

"Yes?" she replies, and I wait for her to say more then realize if I do, I'll likely wait a year. Knowing it's Mrs. Ethel, I continue on, forgoing normal phone etiquette. "It's Kim. I just wanted to call and say thank you. I got the flowers and they are beautiful."

"Of course they're beautiful. They cost me fifty dollars," she mutters, right before I hear a loud click.

Frowning, I pull the phone from my ear, look at it, and then put it back to my ear. "Hello?" I call, but get nothing. Taking the phone from my ear once again, I stare at it in disbelief.

"What did she say?" Frankie asks, and I look from him to Ellie and back again.

"She said of course I like them, because they cost her fifty dollars, and then she hung up on me," I respond, feeling my lips tip up as Frankie and Ellie both start to laugh. "I'm thinking you might be wrong about her adoring me," I add, and Frankie cackles harder as Ellie doubles over, snorting in amusement when she does.

"I don't know about that," Ellie says, wiping away the tears in her eyes. "The one time I had to do her hair when you were out of town, she gave me a twenty-five cent tip after complaining I was doing it all wrong, which I didn't. She looked exactly the same way you make her look."

"She's very set in her ways." I smile, smelling the flowers again, not being able to help myself.

"You could say that." Frankie smiles at me then his eyes turn serious. "I know this isn't exactly the best time to talk to you girls about this, but I've been putting off this conversation for a few weeks now and Alex is starting to fret."

"What's wrong?" I ask, watching him go to flip over the "Open" sign and lock the door.

"Come have a seat." He sits on the purple couch in front of the window, and Ellie and I look at each other before going over to take a seat across from him. Folding my hands in my lap, I wait to see what he will say while my stomach fills with worry.

When I moved to town, Frankie took a chance on me and gave me a job. I didn't have much hands-on experience before I started, but he didn't care. He hired me anyway and, with his help and guidance, I've gotten really good at what I do. I don't know what I will do if he tells me that he's getting rid of the salon, or worse, getting rid of me.

"I know both of you have a lot going on," he starts, looking at Ellie and I both softly, making me worry even more. "Alex and I are moving to Florida."

"What?" Ellie and I ask at the same time.

"This hasn't been an easy decision for us to make, but Alex's mom is getting older and needs us closer, so we have decided to put the shop up for sale," he says, and my chest starts to get tight with anxiety as my hands ball into fists. "Before we do that, we wanted to offer it to one or both of you for a little off the asking price. I know this is unexpected, so you have a little time to think about it before you give me your answer. But I hope you both really think about saying yes." He smiles at us, and his face softens. "You girls have worked your asses off for this salon. The clients love you, and I know if you two do decide that you want to buy it, you could do some amazing things with this place."

"You would really sell it to us for less?" I ask, wondering exactly how much it costs to own a salon. I've always had it in the back of my head that one day I would open my own shop, but I figured that would happen in a few years, not now.

"For you two?" He looks between both of us. "Absolutely. You girls have made me so proud. You are both amazing young women. This place has been my baby for ten years, and there is no one I trust it with more than the two of you."

"That would... God, that would be amazing," Ellie whispers, reaching over to take my hand, and I wrap my fingers around hers. "I mean, we will have to talk about it, of course, and see what you're asking. But it would be amazing!"

"What about you?" Frankie asks me softly, and Ellie's fingers squeeze mine.

"Like Ellie said, we need to talk about it, but if we can get things worked out, I think you know we would both be honored to have this place."

"That's what I was hoping." He smiles. "I'll have the real-estate broker come in and talk to you two so that you know exactly what the details are before we move forward. But everything can stay unless you feel like you don't want some of the stuff, and then I'll have those things moved out, sell them, and take that off the list price I give you."

"Kimellie Salon," Ellie says, and I turn to her and raise a brow. "Just testing it out." She smiles, and I return it while rolling my eyes at her.

"All right, Alex will be happy I've finally talked to you." Frankie smiles as he stands. "Now, let's get this bitch cleaned up. I need a drink."

"On it." I stand with Ellie, and we go to the back and finish getting things cleaned up while talking quietly about the prospect of the shop being ours. I can't help but be a little more than excited over the idea, and I can't wait to tell Sage about it. I just hope it all works out.

"WHAT DO YOU think?" I ask Sage when the phone in my hand goes quiet. I just told him about Frankie's offer to Ellie and me, but he's been quiet, and I don't know him well enough to understand what that means.

"I think you should do it."

"Really?"

"Yeah, baby," he replies gently, and my stomach melts at the endearment. He doesn't call me baby all the time, but when he does, it always has an effect on me. "You and Ellie know how to run the shop. You've done it in the past when Frankie's been out of town. I'm sure there'll be a lot to learn, but with the two of you together, I have no doubt you'll figure it out and make it a success."

"I hope so. The idea of owning a business freaks me out a little, but I'm also very excited to see what will happen."

"Don't focus on the freaking out part," he says, and I hear the smile in his voice.

"I'll try." I grin, watching the night sky twinkle above me.

"What are you doing tomorrow?" he asks, and I hold the phone a little tighter in my hand, wishing he were close instead of all the way in Kentucky. I didn't think I would miss him as much as I do, but after spending so many days with him, I miss him a lot—maybe even too much.

The only good thing to come out of him being so far away is we've gotten to know each other a little more, since every night before I fall asleep, I give him a call and we talk. Or I talk, and he breaks in every once in a while to add something about himself or something he did when he was younger that fits in with whatever I'm blabbering on about.

"Kimberly?"

"Sorry."

"It's all good. I thought you fell asleep," he tells me quietly as I roll to my side and get more comfortable in my bed.

"No, just thinking," I murmur. "Tomorrow, I have work in the morning then..." I pull in a breath. "Ashlyn's called again, so I think I'm going to visit with her for a little while after that."

"Are you ready for that?" he asks, sounding concerned, and my eyes close. Knowing Kelly's killer is behind bars has helped me feel more at peace but I still need to hear what took place firsthand from Ashlyn. I need to learn what happened so I can hopefully let it all go.

"I..." I pause when I realize I'm going to say I will be okay, instead of being honest. "I don't know, but I want to know what happened."

"I get that," he mutters, and I hear a car door slam on his end of the phone.

"Are you still working?"

"Yeah, I have to stop in at the bondsman before I can head back to the hotel for the night."

"I'm guessing you still haven't found the guy yet?" I prompt while covering my mouth so he doesn't hear me yawning, since the last time I yawned with him on the phone he ended our call, telling me that I needed to get some rest.

"Not yet, but I'm close. His people are on edge and tired of me knocking on their doors looking for him. Eventually, one of them is gonna give him up. Me being around is taking money out of their pockets, since they can't go on selling dope or bitches while I'm watching them."

"I hope you get him soon. I miss you," I confess, ignoring the part about the drugs and bitches, since it's liable to freak me out. The phone goes quiet except for the sound of his breathing, and I wonder why I didn't just keep my mouth closed. "I—"

"Don't make plans for tomorrow night," he growls, cutting me off before I can finish whatever it was I was going to say.

"What?"

"You just gave me the incentive to get this done."

"Oh," I breathe as warmth fills my body from the top of my head to the tips of my toes.

"Get some sleep. I'll see you tomorrow."

"Night, Sage," I get out, right before the phone goes dead. Placing my cell on the bedside table, I don't fall asleep right away. I lie here for a long time looking at the night sky while thinking about Sage Mayson.

WALKING INTO THE shop the next morning with a cup of hot tea in my hand, I give Ellie and Jax a smile when I see them standing at the front desk.

"Hey, guys," I say, then feel my eyes widen when Jax comes forward, grabbing me up in a hug that squeezes the breath right out of me. Hearing Ellie laugh, I hug him back awkwardly while trying to keep hold of my purse and tea without damaging us both.

"Been worried about you," he states, letting me go, and I give him what I hope is a reassuring smile.

"I'm okay, or getting to where I *will* be okay," I state, and he nods at me then moves back over to stand close to Ellie, wrapping his arm around her waist.

"I told Jax last night about Frankie's offer. He thinks we should go for it. Well… that is, if you want to?" she urges, suddenly sounding nervous.

"I do," I reply, setting my purse and tea on the counter. "I talked to

Sage about it a little, and he agrees we should figure out how to move forward."

"You talked to Sage?" Jax questions, sounding surprised, and I look at him and find his eyes studying me closely.

"Yeah."

"He never calls anyone when he's working."

"Oh," I mutter, wondering what it means that he's called me every night since he's been gone, and he's also sent texts checking in during the day.

"I told you he claimed her," Ellie says dryly, and I turn my eyes to her and narrow them. "What? He did." She shrugs, smiling.

"Anyway." I roll my eyes at her, and her smile turns into a knowing grin. "I guess we just need to wait and talk to the agent to see exactly what Frankie is asking. Then we need to figure out how to do this, how to get financing and all that. And I know there are some things we've said we would change about this place if given the chance, so now that it's a real possibility, we need to figure out what of those things are a priority and how much it will all cost."

"I'm so excited," Ellie whispers, and I see a wide smile on her face that I know mirrors my own. Feeling guilt instantly wash over me for being as happy as I am, I drop my eyes from hers as my muscles start to get tight.

"Kim?"

"Yeah?" I answer, keeping my eyes down, but that still doesn't stop me from hearing the concern in her voice.

"You okay?"

"Totally," I lie, trying to shake off the sudden sadness that has settled over me. I know I'm alive and I have a life to live, but shouldn't I feel something more than I've been feeling? Shouldn't I be in bed crying my eyes out over my sister?

"Have you talked to anyone?" Jax asks, and I pick up my cup of tea and hold it between my suddenly cold hands as I look at him.

"About what?" I question, and he tips his head to the side.

"About Kelly?"

"I've talked to my parents, Chris, and Sage," I fib, and he shakes his head like that answer disappoints him in some way.

"Would you be willing to talk to someone else?" he inquires, and I frown.

"Do you mean a shrink?"

"Not necessarily a shrink, but someone who has experience dealing with this kind of thing."

"I don't need help. I'm fine. I promise. It's just a lot, and I really don't know how I should be feeling," I confess, setting the cup down with my hands still clasped around it.

"Feel whatever you want to feel. Whether it's happiness or sadness, there is not a right way to deal with grief," Ellie interjects quietly before reaching over to take my hands from my cup of tea and hold them between us. "I know you may feel guilty at times over the fact your life is moving forward when your sister's has come to an abrupt end, and that's okay. But you are still alive." She squeezes my hands. "You are still moving on. Your life didn't end when hers did."

"Thank you." I blink away the tears that have gathered in my eyes. I didn't know how much I needed to hear those words until this exact moment, but I did need them.

"Ashlyn would really like to talk to you. She's been worried and thinks you're avoiding her," Jax says, and I can see that almost losing Ashlyn, who is not only his sister but also his close friend, has affected him more than even he has let on.

"I know, and I haven't been avoiding her," I lie. I *have* been avoiding her. When I found out Ashlyn got away from the man who killed Kelly, I was thankful. Then, over the next twenty-four hours, I went through a range of emotions that left me off-balance. I would never want my friend dead, but knowing my sister was gone and Ashlyn survived made it hard to understand. And all the emotions I was feeling overwhelmed me with guilt. So much guilt that I couldn't talk to Ashlyn, not until I got my head sorted out. "I'm going to go see her after work," I say, and Jax relaxes while Ellie lets out an audible breath.

"Good," Jax states, and I pick up my bag.

"We should get set up. We need to open in just a few minutes," I say to Ellie, and she turns to look at the clock behind her then her eyes widen.

"Shit," she mutters before leaning up to peck Jax on the lips. "You need to go. I gotta get to work."

"You know just how to kill a man's ego." He smiles at her, and she smacks his shoulder then pushes him toward the door and out with one more kiss. Laughing at them, I head to the back of the salon, where I get stuff set up before worrying the entire day away about what will happen when I see Ashlyn.

Chapter 7

Kim

PARKING NEAR THE large fountain in the driveway at Dillon and Ashlyn's house, I shut down my car, slip off my seatbelt, and open the door, grabbing the bouquet of flowers I got her from the passenger seat. Getting out, I push the door closed with my hip and head around the hood of my car and up the large front steps toward the double front doors. I've never been to this house, but before Ashlyn and Dillon were a thing, Ashlyn would complain about how obnoxious Dillon's place was. So it's pretty damn funny, seeing how it's now the place she calls home.

Pressing the doorbell, I wait for someone to answer then put my face to the glass on the side of the door to see if anyone is moving around inside. Ashlyn told me that she and Dillon would be hanging out at home most of the day and to just show up when I got off work, so I did. Now I'm wondering if I should've sent a text or called to make sure they'd be around. Hearing the door being unlocked, I pull myself from the glass, wondering how I didn't spot anyone, and then smile at Dillon when I see it's him.

"Hey," he greets with a warm smile as he opens the door. "Ash has been waiting on pins and needles for you to get here."

"I should have called to tell her that I was going to be a little longer than I thought. The shop was busy all day," I say quietly as I step into the house.

"It's all right," he assures as he closes the door and guides me through a large foyer with two sets of stairs that lead to the second level and down a hallway. "She'll be back in a second. She ran up to see if she could find her damn cat. He's been in hiding all day." We step into a large room that has bookshelves lining the walls and a fireplace in the middle of the room, with a comfy looking couch and two chairs surrounding it. "Do you want something to drink?"

"Water would be good," I reply as I spot Ashlyn standing in the doorway with her ugly, angry-looking cat hissing in her arms. Staring at me, her eyes fill with tears, and I hear Dillon curse right before she disappears behind his large frame as he wraps his arms around her. Watching the hairless cat drop to the floor and run out of sight, I stand here not sure what to do with myself. I've been friends with Ashlyn for a long time now, and I've never felt awkward around her before, but suddenly, it feels like she's a stranger.

"I'm okay," I hear her say, and it takes a second, but Dillon lets her go only to take hold of her face between his hands.

"You sure?"

"Yeah," she replies with a nod, and he leans down, pressing a kiss to her forehead before letting her go and turning to look at me.

"I'll get you some water."

"Thanks," I say as he turns to leave. Looking at Ashlyn, I hold the flowers out awkwardly toward her. "These—"

I don't have a chance to finish my sentence. Before I can do little more than open my arms to prepare myself, she rushes across the room, engulfing me in a hug that takes me back a step.

"I'm so sorry, Kim, so, so sorry," she whispers, and tears instantly fill my eyes as her words rush through me, leaving me off-balance once more.

"You have nothing to be sorry about," I murmur, closing my eyes. "None of this was your fault."

"I just know you must hate me for not doing more, for not—"

"You were drugged and kidnapped from your bed in the middle of the night," I cut her off, reminding both of us of what took place. Kelly had gone to that crazy man willingly. Ashlyn had not. She was an innocent victim. She didn't deserve anything that happened. Not that Kelly deserved to be murdered by someone, but my sister's lifestyle was full of careless acts that constantly got her into trouble.

"I just... I... I wish I could have done more," she confides, pulling away, and I shake my head at her as she accepts the flowers from me. Setting the bouquet on the coffee table, she takes my hand and pulls me to the couch that is just as comfortable as it looks. Wiping away the wetness from my cheeks, I lift my head as Dillon comes back into the room offering us each a bottle of water before picking up the bouquet and leaving without a word.

Spinning off the top of the bottle, I take a sip before setting it down and looking at her. "Please don't cry," I plea quietly when I see tears falling from her eyes and down her cheeks in waves.

"I'm just glad you're here." She takes my hands and squeezes them tightly. "I thought you were dead. You don't know how relieved I was when I found out that it was..." She pauses as the same guilt I've been feeling fills her eyes. Pulling in a breath, she moves her eyes past me and closes them. "I didn't know her. I knew you had a twin, but I didn't know it was her. I thought—"

"I know." I squeeze her hands. "Did... did she say anything? Did you talk to her?" I ask, and her sorrowful eyes come back to me.

"No, when..." Her eyes close again before she opens them back up. "When I woke up, I heard her... I heard her..." She cuts off her own words and shakes her head like she wants to get rid of whatever memory she's having. "He tossed her into the room with me. I was so out of it," she whispers, and I hold on to her now shaking hands tighter. "I was asleep in bed with Dillon, then I was there. I couldn't remember anything happening before that moment. I thought I was drunk. It felt like I was drunk. My head was pounding and everything was blurry. I didn't know where I was. I thought I was dreaming."

"Ash," I whisper.

"I saw her. She was barely alive. I thought she was you, and I knew I needed to get free to get us both out of there, but he came back," she explains, and my own hands start to shake from the fear I hear in her voice. "He..." Her eyes fill with distress, and she visibly shivers. "I passed out, and when I woke up, I was free. I..." She forces me to let her hands go then pulls me in for a hug. "I checked on her, but she was already gone. I was too late. She was already gone. She freed me before she—" Her voice cracks as she sobs, and my chest aches with her unspoken words. "She saved me," she whispers. "Because of her, I was able to get away from him."

I drop my face to her shoulder as I absently hear the sound of the doorbell ring through the house.

"I'm sorry, Kim," she says, and I squeeze my eyes closed as a sob I can't hold in any longer rips painfully from my chest.

Suddenly, Ashlyn is gone and the familiar scent of Sage is cocooning me. Burying my face in his shirt, I hold on to him and cry while his hands smooth over my hair and he whispers soothingly into my ear. It takes a long time to stop crying, and when I'm finally able to pull myself together, I'm exhausted and a headache has started to pound behind my closed eyelids.

"I shouldn't have told her," I hear Ashlyn say from close by, and I pull my face away from Sage's now soaked shirt and open my eyes to look at my friend, who is standing under her husband's arm, nervously wringing her hands together.

"I need...," I croak out then rest my hand against my dry throat. "I—"

"Drink," Sage commands, cutting me off by taking my free hand

and pressing my bottle of water into it. His worried eyes scan my face as my hand holding the bottle shakes. Wrapping his hand around mine, he holds the bottle steady, repeating, "Drink," as he tips it toward my mouth.

Taking a sip with his help, I sit up. Wiping at my cheeks, I pull in a much-needed, deep breath before looking at Ashlyn once more. "I needed to know," I tell her, thankful my voice no longer cracks, even though it still feels raw from the tears I've cried. "I needed to know," I repeat, and she nods, biting her lip as tears fill her eyes again.

"She saved me. I owe her everything," she whispers, and I let those words wash through me and clean away the anger I've been holding on to.

No one knows why things happen the way they do. I just hope my sister is resting in peace. This life wasn't always fair to Kelly. Yes, a lot of what happened to her was her own doing, but having been raised the way she was, it's sadly understandable why she acted out the way she did. Why she couldn't just accept good things when they came into her life, and why she was always waiting for the floor to crumble from beneath her feet.

Fighting back the new wave of tears I feel creeping up on me, I dig my nails into the palm of my hand until they're gone, then stand, and go to my friend on shaky legs. I hate that she had to go through what she went through, but I'm glad Kelly was able to save her before she died.

"I love you," she whispers as we embrace in the middle of the room.

"I love you, too. Thank you for telling me what happened, and thank you for giving me a little bit of closure," I say, and her arms tighten before she releases a shaky breath and lets me go. Pulling in a breath of my own, I wipe at my face once more, having no doubt I look a mess. I'm sure my makeup is now all over my face and Sage's shirt.

Sage.

I turn to look at him and blink. I knew he was here, since I cried all over him, but it didn't really hit me until right now that he is *here*. He's back. I want to run across the room to him and throw myself against his chest in happiness and relief, but I don't do that. I stare at him like an idiot then mutter, "You're back."

"Yeah."

"I...."

"We'll be in the kitchen," Dillon mumbles behind me, and I look over my shoulder and watch him lead Ashlyn out of the room.

"Kim." My head swings toward Sage and I lick my lips in sudden nervousness. "Come here." He pats the seat next to him, and I look at the couch then him.

"Did you get the guy?" I ask, and he frowns.

"Yeah, why are you looking at me like that?"

"Like what?"

"Like you wanna run away."

"I don't look like that," I lie, knowing I do look like that, because there is a part of me that does want to run from him. The part of me that just realized he's back and my parents are gone. I have no excuse to use when things between the two of us start to get too intense, and things between us tend to get intense when we're just standing in the same room breathing the same air. It's not about his hands or his mouth on me. It's his presence that affects me. He has the ability to become the sun I so desperately need in order to survive, and I'm afraid if I allow myself to feel all that warmth, when he's gone, I won't be able to live in the shadows.

"Kimberly," he says, snapping me out of my thoughts, and I realize he's no longer sitting on the couch but standing in front of me with a concerned frown on his face.

"Sorry, I...."

"It's all right," he assures gently, stepping closer and resting his hand on my hip. Then his lips touch my forehead before he leans back, gripping the underside of my jaw in his free hand. "You gonna be okay?"

"I'm getting there," I tell him, and his face softens. I know then just like I knew the moment I met him that I will regret it if I don't take a chance and see what could happen between us.

"You here with me?" he questions as his thumb sweeps sweetly across my chin.

"Yes, I'm here with you."

"Good." He smiles then leans down to brush his lips softly over mine. "Come on." Taking my hand, he leads me out of the room and down the hall toward the sound of Dillon and Ashlyn talking. As soon as we enter a huge kitchen, Ashlyn stands and comes around the large island in the middle of the room.

"You're coming tomorrow, right?" she asks as soon as she's standing in front of me, and I shake my head in confusion.

"Going where?"

"All of us are going out to dinner at Madison's. I thought he told you already," she says, nodding toward Sage, who drops my hand and slides his arm around my waist tucking me close to his side.

"I don't know anything about dinner," I state, and she frowns at me then looks at Sage.

"I thought Aunt Sophie said Kim was coming."

"She is," he replies, and I look at him, finding his eyes already on me. "I told my mom we would be there."

"You did?" I ask, feeling my eyes turn squinty at his assumption.

Scanning my face, his lips twitch before he mutters, "You can yell at me later, but we're going. My family's been worried about you, and they want to see for themselves that you're okay."

"You could have asked me if I wanted to go," I grumble, and he shrugs.

"Sage's right. Everyone has been worried about you," Ashlyn confirms quietly, breaking into my stare down with her cousin, and I look at her. "Everyone knew your parents were in town, so they didn't want to bombard you, but they all want to see you."

"Who's all going to be there?"

"Everyone. The whole family is supposed to show up," she says, and anxiety fills the pit of my stomach, because I know everyone also includes Sage's parents, Nico and Sophie. "You have nothing to worry about. I promise it's just dinner. No one is getting married," she mutters, and I smile at that. We had told her just weeks ago that we were all having dinner, when in truth Dillon had planned a surprise vow renewal ceremony for her, since they had eloped in Vegas without anyone around. "Please say you'll come."

"We'll be there," I agree, reminding myself of my promise to be a better friend. "Are you sure it's okay that I come?" I confirm, and Dillon chuckles.

"I don't think you got much choice in this. I think these two bringing it up now is just a warning of what will happen tomorrow," he says with a smile, and I smile back then look at Ashlyn.

"Thank you for having me over."

"You're welcome anytime," she urges, giving me a hug before wrapping her arm around mine and leading me toward the front of the house, with Sage and Dillon following us. As soon as we reach the door, she opens it, giving me one last hug with a quiet goodbye before moving to stand under Dillon's arm.

Sage takes my hand in his and leads me outside then down the steps to my car. "I'll follow you to your place," he tells me, opening my door, and I tip my head back to look up at him then shake it.

"That's okay. I'm sure you want to get home after being gone."

"I do, but we'll go to my place after we stop at yours to pick you up some clothes."

Blinking at him, I open and close my mouth like a fish out of water, trying to get my brain and mouth to work. "I'm not staying at your place," I finally get out, while taking a seat behind the wheel and hitting the button to turn on my car. He doesn't reply to my comment, and I wonder if he heard me, but I don't have a chance to ask if he did before he shuts my door.

Watching him in the side mirror as he heads for his ride that is parked behind mine, I let out a breath, thinking I may be in way over my head this time.

And that's proven true an hour later when I'm getting into his car and heading to his place with the bag I packed.

Sage

LOOKING OVER AT Kim sitting in my passenger seat, I smile at the windshield when I notice the scowl she's still wearing. "You still pissed?" I ask, hiding my grin, and she turns her narrowed eyes on me.

"I think you cheated," she states, and I start to chuckle but fight it back. "I don't know how you did it, but I'm pretty sure you cheated."

"You can't cheat at Rock, Paper, Scissors, babe. It's a game of chance," I correct, and she gives a little huff that's way too fucking cute.

I purposely ignored her statement about not staying with me when we were out in front of Ash and Dillon's place and followed her home, figuring I could convince her to stay with me when I got her alone. It didn't work. She had dug in her heels and refused to come with me, so I did the only thing I could: I challenged her.

Chris and her parents all said on more than one occasion that Kim was stubborn and would never turn down a challenge. Knowing that, I used that weakness against her. I told her that if she won a game of Rock, Paper, Scissors against me, I'd let the idea of her staying with me go and head home, but if I won, she had to pack a bag. She lost, even after demanding a rematch two more times.

"Well, somehow you found a way around that rule," she grumbles as we turn into my driveway, and I smile at that comment.

It's not hard to know someone's next move in Rock, Paper, Scissors. People tend to use the move you used before them, and Kim did just that every time, not even realizing she was giving herself up.

Reaching my house, I shut down the engine and turn to look at her. "Are you always a sore loser?"

"Yes," she admits, and I lean over, sliding my fingers over her cheek, then down her throat, and around the back of her neck to pull her toward me over the center console.

"I'll teach you how I did it sometime, if it makes you feel better."

"You did cheat." Her eyes widen, and I grin right before I touch my lips to hers.

The second I feel the softness of her mouth under mine, I nip her bottom lip and she opens her mouth on a gasp, giving me exactly what I wanted, what I've been missing. Sliding my hand up into her hair, I use my grip to deepen the kiss then groan when she whimpers against my tongue. Her hand moves to my chest then up to my shoulders, where her nails dig in. Pulling back, I slow the kiss and rest my forehead against hers.

"I'm not having sex with you," she says suddenly, and I chuckle, tip her head down, and press a kiss to the top of her head.

"I'm not having sex with you either," I confirm, letting her go. It's not that I don't want to. There is nothing I want more than to feel her heat around my cock, to hear the little whimpers and pleas she makes when she's under me or over me, but we need to take things slower this time. The last time we were together, it was sudden and spur of the moment, and I'm not willing to let us burn bright only to fizzle out.

"I said it first," she gripes, and I laugh as I open the door and get out. Pulling open the rear door, I reach in, grab her bag and mine, and then meet her at the sidewalk.

Leading her into the house, I flip on the light, and then shut the door. Turning around, I stop mid-step and scan the room. The beams have all been re-stained, and the plastic that had been covering the floors is all folded and stacked in the corner with the ladder and paint cans. "What the fuck?"

"My dad and Chris got all but two of the beams done before my parents went back to Florida, so I decided to finish them while you were gone," she says, sounding nervous, and I pull my eyes from the room to look at her as she slips off her jacket. "I'm sorry. I should have asked if it was okay to keep going." Her eyes drop from mine.

Shaking my head, I let both bags fall to the floor, grab her jacket from her, and toss it toward the coatrack near the front door. Then I turn and pick her up, listening to her squeak as her arms fly around my neck.

"What are you doing?" she asks breathlessly as I head toward the sitting room off the kitchen.

"Thanking you," I reply. As soon as I reach the couch, I bend at the waist and lay her down, covering her body with mine.

"Sage."

"Right here." Dropping my mouth to hers, I move my knee between her legs so she's straddling my thigh. Roaming my hand down the back of her calf, I pull her ankle around my hip. Her head tips to the side, and her mouth opens on a quiet whimper. Hearing that sound and tasting her on my tongue, I press my already hard cock into her hip as her hands slide up the back of my shirt and her nails dig into my skin.

Jesus.

I move my hand over the top of her thigh, her hip, and then her stomach. Biting her lip, I cup her breast and roll my thumb over her hard nipple through her shirt, hearing her moan as I move my mouth down her chin and the column of her throat.

"Please," she whispers, and I pick her up without thinking and take a seat on the couch with her straddling my waist. Wrapping one hand around her hip, I slide the other up her back and into her hair at the back of her head. Dragging her mouth back to mine, I feel her heat through the fabric between us as my hips lift into hers and my balls draw tight. "Please," she repeats, rocking into me, making my teeth ache as my jaw clenches.

Ripping my mouth from hers, I fight myself for control, when every instinct is telling me to take what's mine. With a frustrated groan, I drop my forehead to her chest.

"Um...?" She pants, and I pull in a breath through my nose and tip my head back to look at her. Her hair is wild, her eyes are glazed with lust, and her lips are swollen from my kisses. She looks beautiful. "You stopped," she says, and I don't smile at the disappointment in her voice, even though I want to. I'm glad I'm not the only one affected in this situation.

"You said you're not having sex with me," I remind her quietly as my hands smooth over her soft skin.

"Right." She nods, looking uncertain.

Moving my hands to her hips, I rock her against my cock, letting her feel what she's doing to me. "I want you, Kimberly."

"Sure," she agrees as she tries to stand, but I don't let her. In one quick motion, I flip her to her back and nip her neck. Once I have her attention, I move my face above hers.

"Your mouth is sweet." I lick across her lips, smiling when she gasps. "But I know for a fact your pussy's sweeter. So until I can have all of you, I need us to slow down. You almost had me coming in my jeans like a fourteen-year-old kid who just got his first taste of pussy."

"What?" She blinks up at me in surprise.

"Since you, there's been—"

"Don't," she cuts me off, trying to push me away, almost succeeding since the move was sudden.

"Calm down."

"Get off me!" she yells, pushing harder while using her knees to try to shove me off.

"Listen to me," I bark close to her face, and she stills for a moment as her chest heaves against mine.

"There's been no one since you."

"I'm sure," she cries, pushing against my chest once more.

Taking her hands, I hold them above her head and press them down into the couch, waiting until she stops struggling to continue. "Since the moment we met, I wanted you. And when I walked away from you, I knew. As pissed as I was for what I thought you did to me, I still wanted you and knew no piece of random pussy would change that."

"You…." She shakes her head, and I release her hands and frame her face.

"It was you. You ruined me for anyone else. You didn't even know you were doing it, but did it all the same."

"But—"

"No buts," I interrupt, taking her mouth in a soft kiss before pulling away. "I have no reason to lie to you. Even when I thought you and Chris were together, I still held out hope you'd realize I was waiting for you," I say, watching tears fill her eyes. Then she leans up, shoving her face into my chest.

Letting out a breath, I pull her up with me and hold her against my chest, hoping my confession has brought us a little closer to my end goal.

Chapter 8

Kim

GETTING MYSELF UNDER control, I pull my face from Sage's chest and lean back. I knew Sage wasn't the kind of guy you could easily forget, but I had no idea he felt that same thing for me. It didn't seem possible that he could, but I heard the truth in his words when he told me that he hasn't been with anyone since we were together.

"You okay?" he questions, running his fingers along my jaw, and I nod. "You sure?"

"Yeah, I just feel like an idiot," I confess, and his eyes soften.

"You're not an idiot."

"Tell that to the woman who's had a pretend boyfriend for months because she was too afraid to face the fact she had fallen for a guy she barely knew," I grumble, and he tucks a piece of hair behind my ear.

"You were protecting yourself. I get it."

"You weren't mad?"

"Mad about what?" he asks, and I stare at him in disbelief.

"That I pretended to have a boyfriend," I supply, and his eyes change in a way that makes my skin tingle.

"You pretending to have a boyfriend didn't only protect you. It protected me. You were off the market. Anytime anyone asked you out, you told them the same thing—you had a man—so they would back off. I'm not mad, because in the end, your lie also helped me out."

"You're serious?" I breathe, studying him, and his hand moves to wrap around my jaw.

"You could have taken a chance on someone else, fallen in love, and moved on. So yeah, I'm serious."

Swallowing at the sudden intensity in his eyes, I look over his shoulder. That could have happened, but he also could have met someone else and fallen in love. I would've had to witness the whole thing while knowing I messed up my shot with him because I was too afraid to face my fears. Feeling his thumb move over my bottom lip draws my attention back to him.

"None of that matters now. Right now, we just focus on getting to know each other."

I don't agree with him verbally or by nodding. Instead, I lean up and touch my mouth to his—because I can, because I want to, and because as much as this whole thing scares me, I know I want it more than my next breath. If I end up heartbroken, I will have the memories of my time with Sage to look back on. And if this by some chance works out, I will have something amazing for the rest of my life.

"I'm hungry," I say when the kiss starts to go from a soft touch of my lips on his to him rocking his hard length into me, with me moaning against his mouth.

"Me, too," he agrees, and I can't help but to laugh. Resting my forehead against his, I move my fingers along his strong jaw.

"Please feed me."

His eyes close and his chest presses against mine as he pulls in a breath. Standing us both up, he kisses my forehead before leaving me standing in the living room. Watching him go, I wonder what I should do, and then he's back a minute later with my bag in his hand. I follow him down the hall to his room, where he flips on the light and carries my bag to his bed, dropping it there.

"We'll go out to get something to eat, since I don't have anything here and need to do some shopping."

"Sounds good," I agree.

"I'll stay in the guest room tonight, so you can get ready in here."

"No," I deny, shaking my head and trying to move around him to grab my bag.

"Yes."

"No." I plant my hands on my hips. "You should be sleeping in your bed," I say, and he mutters something before walking toward the closet. Knowing he's doing his whole ignore me thing to get his way, I start to get annoyed. "I'm not staying in here, Sage Mayson," I state, picking up my bag and heading for the door, only to let out a squeal when I'm picked up off the floor before I make it there. Dropping the bag to the floor halfway across the room, I let out a whoosh of air a second later as my back hits the bed and Sage comes down on top of me.

"You're sleeping in here."

"I'm not," I huff out, trying to push him away, only managing to somehow flip him to his back. Looking down at him, I don't know what comes over me. One second, I'm getting ready to hop off the bed and make a run for the door, and the next, my mouth is colliding with his. Our teeth gnash together and I pull back a second before going back for more, thrusting my tongue into his mouth.

A whimper slides up my throat as he pulls his mouth from mine long enough to rip my shirt over my head. It's then I lose what little self-control I have. I remember what it felt like the first time we were together. I remember how it felt when his mouth was on my breast against my skin and between my legs. I remember it like it was yesterday, and I want that again. I want to feel his mouth and hands on me, and I definitely want to put my mouth and hands on him.

Pulling at his shirt, he does a half ab crunch and we yank his shirt off and toss it to the bed. Then his hands slide up my back, and I feel his fingers as they work the clasp of my bra. When that's gone, he drops it on top of his shirt. Pressing my chest into his, my nipples scrape against the light smattering of hair on his chest, and my tongue flicks against his, earning me a growl of approval that I feel tingle between my thighs.

He rolls me to my back, his mouth leaving mine, and his head dips so he can lick over one of my nipples while his fingers tweak and pull the neglected one. Back arching, I wrap my legs around his hips, seeking the friction I so desperately need between my legs. My body is buzzing. I never knew it was possible to have an orgasm from just my nipples being sucked and a little bit of clit stimulation, but I feel the pull of arousal in my lower belly, the telltale sign that if I move my hips just right, I might come.

"Sage," I pant, and his hand and mouth leave my breast.

Leaning back, he looks down at me. I think he's going to stop again, so I do the only thing I can think of. I lean up and press my mouth to his while rubbing my palm over his huge erection through his jeans. Groaning, he pushes my hand away. I want to pout, but before I can, his fingers move to the button of my jeans, and in one flick of his fingers, he has them undone and his fingers are sliding over my pubic bone. Down they go, zeroing in on my clit with an accuracy that has me thrusting my hips up into his fingers.

"So goddamn wet. How did I forget how wet you get for me?" he asks against my lips, and I moan, digging my nails into his back. I'm close, so *close*. Thrusting my hips up, my breath catches when his fingers thrust into me, first one then two, both curving up and hitting that spot deep inside of me that has me seeing stars. "Jesus, your pussy is squeezing the fuck out of my fingers," he rumbles, taking my bottom lip into his mouth and pulling it between his teeth.

"Sage!" I cry out as my orgasm explodes through me, leaving me lightheaded and limp. I'm panting as my eyes open and I find him staring down at me.

"So fucking beautiful. Better than I remember," he whispers, and I lick my lips then sit up. Forced to pull his fingers from me, he puts them in his mouth and his eyes fall closed. "Definitely better than I remember." His eyes open, and I push him to his back.

"Please," I whisper when he tries to stop me from unhooking his jeans. Studying me for a moment, he gives in with a shake of his head and lies back. Releasing him, I watch his long, thick cock flex up toward me and my mouth waters. He's perfect everywhere; even his cock is perfect, long, smooth, and hard with thick veins that run the length of it.

I wrap my fingers around him and my pussy contracts when they don't meet. I remember what it felt like to have him inside me, the stretch and slow burn of pleasure he brought on with each thrust. Looking up at him, I place my lips around the head of his cock and slowly sink down on it, taking him as far as I can go without gagging. Keeping my hand at the base, I twist and pull while I suck and lick, watching his expression as I drive him closer to the edge.

"Fuck, baby." His fingers slide into my hair, and his abs tighten as he leans up to watch me take him into my mouth. "Jesus, I'm gonna fucking come," he warns.

Taking him even deeper, I work my hand in faster strokes. I want him on my tongue and down my throat. I want him to come in my mouth. I want to taste the pleasure I've given him.

"Fuck, fuck, fuck," he chants as his eyes close and his hips lift off the bed, sending him down my throat as he comes.

Swallowing down every last drop, I lick him clean, wondering what the hell came over me. I've never swallowed before... or enjoyed giving a blowjob, for that matter. But I did enjoy giving one to him. No, I didn't enjoy it; I *loved* it.

"Christ." He pulls me up under my arms onto his chest then kisses me deep and wet before pulling back, studying me. "Now I'm even more pissed at myself for walking away," he mutters.

I can't help it. The comment is sincere and so funny that I laugh loudly and drop my forehead to his pec. Hearing my stomach growl a second later, I lean back to look at him. "I think I'm still hungry," I tell him, and he smiles then leans up, kissing me softly before dragging me from the bed, handing me my bra once I'm standing.

"Meet me in the kitchen when you're done getting ready," he says right before he disappears into the closet, coming out a minute later with a shirt in his hand. He doesn't say anything as he walks by me to leave the room, but his fingers graze across my stomach the way they did the first day we met. It leaves something warm sitting in the pit of my stomach as I put on my bra.

Pulling my shirt on, I head for his bathroom, noticing the tooth-brush I bought when I was staying with him is still in the holder. I use it quickly before taking a brush to my hair and putting on some ChapStick. I didn't really dress up for work today, so I figure my outfit of dark jeans, a red, long-sleeved, scoop-neck shirt, and my black, leather booties that match my jacket is casual enough for whatever we end up doing.

As soon as I'm done straightening myself out, I head to the kitchen, where Sage is already waiting with his back to me and his head bent as he flips through a stack of mail in front of him. Standing unnoticed, I take a second to enjoy the view of his ass in the jeans he has on and the way the dark green Henley he changed into fits him like a second skin, showing off the muscles in his arms and back. When he turns to face me, I realize that the back view may be good, but the front is even better. His shirt is molded to his wide chest, and the deep green of his shirt makes his eyes even more phenomenal, if that's even possible.

"Ready?" he asks, and I nod, letting him lead me with his hand against my lower back to the front of the house. Grabbing my jacket at the front door, I put it on then take his hand when he offers it. He closes the door behind us and locks up, then takes me to the passenger side door and helps me in.

I buckle up while he walks around the hood and slides in behind the wheel. "Where are we going?" I ask as he turns on the car and reverses out of the yard.

"There's a few places nearby. Do you feel like having Mexican, Italian, or American?" he inquires, and I wonder which one of those will have the best menu for my new diet. Deciding on Mexican, he drives us to a small strip mall that has a nail place, a donut shop, and a Mexican restaurant in it. He parks near the front door and shuts down the engine, unhooking his belt before opening his door.

Getting out, I meet him at the hood where he takes my hand. The smell of spices and meat hits me when we walk through the door, and my stomach growls again. "Holy cow, look at that," I say, pointing out a picture of the guy from *Diners, Drive-ins, and Dives* standing with a very pretty petite Mexican woman. "Now I'm even more hungry," I admit, and he laughs, tucking me under his arm. I'm not lying; every time I watch that show, my mouth waters and I wish I could be there eating the food, so I'm super excited to experience something from the show firsthand.

"Sit anywhere, you two. Someone will be with you in a moment," a woman says, and Sage nods before leading me to a booth in the back of the small restaurant.

Sliding across the leather seat, I smile at him as he takes a seat across from me and scans the room—my guess, looking for danger. "Anyone suspicious?" I whisper, and his eyes come to me.

"Habit." He laughs, and I grin at him.

"Hello, my friends. What can I get you two to drink?" a man asks, coming up to the table and placing menus in front of us.

"Water, with lemon please," I request, and he nods at me before looking at Sage.

"Beer, whatever you got in a bottle that's cold."

"All right, I'll be back." He half bows at us before taking off toward the back of the restaurant, coming back a second later with a basket of chips and a bowl of salsa, setting them on the table before leaving again. Picking up a chip, I dunk it in the salsa and take a bite, and my eyes widen.

"Hot?"

"God, yes." I fan my mouth then grab my water when the waiter sets it down in front of me. I don't even care how bad I look chugging from the glass. My mouth is on fire.

"Did I give you the hot one?" the waiter asks, and I blink away the tears leaking from my eyes. I don't know if it's the hot one, but it *is* hot.

Watching Sage dunk his own chip in the salsa and pop it in his mouth, I laugh when he has the same reaction I just had. His mouth opens and his eyes water as he puts his beer to his lips and chugs.

"I'm sorry. I'll get you a new one." The waiter picks up the salsa and leaves only to appear out of thin air as he sets a new salsa between us. "It should be okay now." He smiles.

"Thank you." I smile at him before he walks off.

"It *should* be okay?" Sage repeats, and I smile as I bite into another chip without dunking it in the salsa.

"You heard that, too?" I grin, shaking my head. "I don't think I'm brave enough to be the guinea pig. You test it out and tell me if it's safe," I urge, batting my lashes at him, and he picks up another chip, touches just the edge into the salsa, and then places it against his tongue.

"It's good," he mutters.

Laughing at him, I pick up my own chip, scoop up some salsa, and take a bite. It's good, better than good. It's delicious... or I'm starving. Whatever the case may be, by the time our waiter comes back for our orders, I've eaten almost all the chips and salsa.

"Do you know what you'd like to eat?" he asks.

"The salmon taco salad and another water please," I reply, and he nods then looks at Sage.

"Another beer, the biggest burrito you've got on the menu, and a side of guacamole," Sage orders, and the waiter nods before walking off. "So what's going on with the shop? Have you and Ellie had a chance to discuss it again?" he asks me.

I pick up another chip and dunk it in the salsa, but then drop it into the basket. I don't want to ruin my dinner, but at the rate I'm going, it's liable to happen. "We have a meeting at the bank on Monday to see about the loan. Frankie is asking two hundred and fifty thousand for the salon, and that price includes everything—the chairs and supplies—already there. It's a good deal. We just have to make sure we can get the loan, along with the extra money we need to do the renovations we want."

"Is there a lot of changes that need to be made?"

I shake my head. "No, not necessarily. But right now, it's Frankie's shop, and as much as we love it, we want to make it our own. We want to do some upgrades and add a couple more chairs that we can either rent out each month or hire a couple more girls to work. We are always slammed, so the extra staff would mean more income in the long run."

"That's smart," he agrees, reaching over to take my hand. "Have you told your parents?"

Blinking, I realize I haven't told them or Chris about the shop, and they are normally the first people I tell everything to. "I haven't. I've only talked to you, Ellie, and Jax about it."

"Might be smart to keep it on the down low until you have a better idea of what's going to happen. Or at least until you have a chance to talk to the bank about the loan you need."

"You're probably right. I love my parents, but I know if I tell them, they will want to jump in and throw money at me," I mumble.

"Having money thrown at you isn't a bad thing, babe."

"No, it's not, but I want to do this on my own. I want to prove to them and myself that I'm capable of doing something on my own. My parents are the best, but they can be a little overbearing at times."

"They just want you to know they love you and that they support you," he says quietly, giving my fingers a squeeze. "I think sometimes parents try to overcompensate. They never want us to feel like we are missing out on something."

"Do your parents do that with you?" I ask, and his face softens.

"My dad is too cool for that, but my mom is a coddler. I love her for it. I've never worried about the depth of her love for me. So yeah, she throws love at me the way your parents try to throw money at you." He smiles then leans back, letting go of my hand as our food arrives.

Looking down at my salad, my mouth waters. Then I look across to his plate and my eyes get big.

"Jesus," Sage mutters, staring at the plate in front of him. It isn't a normal size plate. No, it's something you would serve a turkey on at Thanksgiving, and the burrito sitting on it takes up the whole surface.

"Do you two need anything else?" our waiter asks.

I pull my eyes from Sage's meal and shake my head then mutter, "Unless you have another stomach somewhere. I think my man might need it."

Smiling big, he shakes his head then walks off.

"Your man, huh?" Sage asks, and my eyes go back to his and my stomach dips when I see the look there. "I like that."

"You do?"

"Been waiting a long time to hear you call me that," he admits, and that warmth I've been feeling in the pit of my stomach spreads through my chest.

"Thank you," I blurt, and his focus on me changes. "For waiting for me, I mean."

The focus in his gaze changes to heat. "You better eat before I say fuck it to the food and carry your pretty little ass out of here over my shoulder so I can take you home and show you my gratitude in a different way."

"Right," I breathe, picking up my fork and shoving it into my salad, taking a huge bite before I tell him I wouldn't mind him doing just that.

"I'm not even sure where to start," he says, and I chew and swallow my bite while watching him look at his plate.

"The middle," I supply helpfully, and he grins at me then digs into his food. Surprisingly, I eat all of my salad and he finishes more than half of his burrito. When the check arrives, I try to pay, but like always, he doesn't let me. After arguing for a few minutes, I give in to him and he pays the bill.

After that he tucks me into his car and we head back to his place, where he leaves me with a soft kiss outside his bedroom door. I stand here watching him after that kiss as he moves to the spare room. I think about joining him there, but the part of me that knows we still need to work on getting to know each other keeps me in his bed, where I fall asleep surrounded by his scent.

Chapter 9

Kim

STRETCHING MY ARMS above my head, I blink my eyes open to a view of crystal-blue skies overhead through the skylight. I don't know what woke me, but something did, since I was sleeping better than I have in forever. I roll to my side and press my face into the pillow, breathing in the scent of Sage that kept me company all night.

Hearing a *shuffle, thump, thump, shuffle, thump, thump* coming from somewhere in the house, I frown and sit up. Tipping my head toward the door, I try to make out what the noise could possibly be. It doesn't sound like the normal hammer to wood that greeted me the first few days I stayed with Sage; it's different.

Curiosity has me getting out of bed and slipping on my sweater to go in search of the sound. Moving past the kitchen and down the hall on the opposite side of the house, I finally locate the noise and pause in the doorway, resting my shoulder against the doorjamb. The room isn't bare like the other two rooms in the house that haven't been renovated. This room has gym equipment shoved into the space, including a weight machine, a stair climber, and a treadmill.

Sage, in all his shirtless glory, is on the treadmill in the middle of the room with a pair of large headphones covering his ears, wearing nothing but basketball shorts and sneakers. His profile is to me, so I can't see all of him, but from my vantage point, I can make out the muscles in his arm that is cocked at the elbow. The side of his chest and back flex as he runs at full speed, hitting the treadmill hard every time his feet find purchase.

"Lord." My mouth goes dry, and the space between my legs starts to tingle as sweat makes every single one of his muscles glisten. Reaching forward, he hits the button on the machine, and I jump when the sound startles me out of my perusal. He must see me jump, because his eyes come to me and a small smile spreads across his mouth. Pulling off his headphones, he drops them to the holder on top of the machine then hits the button that brings the treadmill to a complete stop.

"Morning," he says, walking toward me while wiping his face and chest with the towel he grabs off the weight bench.

"Morning," I reply, licking my lips and letting my eyes slide over him, feeling his do the same in return.

"Did you sleep in that?" he asks, and I look down at what I have on, feeling my eyes widen when I notice he can see all of me through the thin, white lace fabric covering my private bits. I didn't put on my sleep shorts last night when I put on my tank top and got into bed, and I didn't even think about pulling them on this morning when I got up. And the sweater I dragged on barely reaches the top of my panties.

"Shit," I mutter, turning quickly. I start to run down the hall toward his room, but I don't get very far. His strong arm circles my waist and I'm pulled back against his warm, hard chest. Squeaking when I'm captured, I feel him kiss my neck then nibble below my ear. It turns that tingle I felt between my legs earlier into an ache.

"Don't change on my account." His words whisper across my ear, making me shiver, while his fingers slide along my stomach where my tank has risen up. My muscles tense in preparation, and my eyes slide closed as his fingers sneak into my panties and touch my bare skin. Moving my arms up over my head, I hold on to his neck as his free hand moves to cup my breast.

"Oh," I whimper when he flicks my clit. My knees start to give out from under me then the doorbell rings, causing every inch of me to go solid as I freeze.

"Fuck me," he mutters, pulling his fingers from my panties and turning me in his arms. Cupping my jaw, his eyes search my face for a second before he grumbles "Fuck" again and shakes his head. "You may want to get something on. I can only think of two people who'd show up here this time of the morning."

"Who?" I ask, trying to shake the arousal that's still coursing hot and heavy through my system.

"Willow and Harmony."

"Right, I'll jus—" The doorbell goes off again, and I fight back the laugh I feel building up inside me from the frustrated look on his face. "I'll go get dressed," I say, getting up on my tiptoes and pressing a quick kiss to his cheek.

Hearing him groan, I look at him and watch his hungry eyes drag across my skin as he adjusts his hard-on in his shorts. My pussy clenches, and I debate going back and attacking him. "Go," he growls, making my stomach clench.

Nodding, I hurry to his room and right to the bathroom, where I strip out of my clothes, turn the shower to cold, and hop in. The freezing water does almost nothing to cool my overheated libido, but I do feel like I can breathe a little easier. After washing up quickly, I get out and dry off then put on the jeans I had on yesterday, one of my simple black tanks, and my sweater back over it.

I try to get ready quickly, since I don't want Sage to think I'm being rude, but it still must have been longer than I thought, because when I walk into the kitchen while tying up my hair, the smell of bacon is in the air. There are pancakes on the griddle on the counter, along with two beautiful girls sitting on the stools in front of Sage, who is cooking shirtless. I know Willow and Harmony well. We've hung out a lot. We have the same friends—or I should say I'm friends with their cousins—

but I've never been around them since Sage and I... well, whatever we are right now. Feeling uneasy all of a sudden, I pause just outside the kitchen, not sure what to do with myself. Do I pretend like nothing is going on, or do I—

"Kim!" The shout of my name and two women running toward me cuts off my wayward thoughts, and before I can prepare myself, I'm engulfed in a tight hug that cleans all of my worries away.

"Hey, guys," I get out, and then they both attack me with question after question in rapid succession.

"Are you okay? How are you feeling? Do you need anything? We wanted to come see you, but Sage wouldn't let us." That last statement makes me shake my head.

"What?" I ask, and both Willow and Harmony pull back to look at me before looking at their glaring brother.

"He told us we weren't allowed to bother you."

"I did not say bother her. I said you guys needed to give her some space. Jesus, there's too many people in our family. If everyone started showing up, she would have been overwhelmed, and you know her family was here."

"You just wanted her to yourself." Willow rolls her eyes.

Sage shrugs. "Sue me."

"Whatever," Harmony grumbles, taking my arm and pulling me toward one of the barstools. "The point is we don't want you to think we don't care, because we do."

"I know that," I assure her, and I do know they care. After Kelly's death, I must have gotten a million texts and a dozen bouquets of flowers delivered to Sage's house from his family, my friends. It was all really sweet, and I tried to reply to everyone, but sometimes I just couldn't.

"How's Sage treating you? Is he being nice? Mom said to make sure he's being nice, 'cause if he's not, she promised to cut off his balls,"

Willow states, and I flinch.

"Christ," Sage mutters, looking at me. "I knew I shouldn't have opened the fucking door."

"He's being very nice," I promise, watching Sage's eyes darken. Seeing that, my nipples get hard and my clit throbs. I don't think I'll be able to keep myself from jumping him the first chance I get. There is too much heat between us, and I'm pretty sure that if we don't find a way to burn some of it off, we're likely to explode.

"Sheesh! Do you two need me and Willow to leave?" Harmony asks, and I say "no" as Sage says "yes," which makes me smile.

"I'm listening to Kim on this one. Sorry, brother," Harmony says, picking up a cup of coffee from the counter to take a sip.

"So, you two are really together then?" Willow inquires, and I look at Sage and wait to see how he will answer that question.

"We're really together," he confirms.

I let out the breath I didn't even know I was holding then get up and head around the island to get a mug and make myself some tea, but Sage stops me with a hand to my waist before I make it to the cupboard.

"I made you tea," he informs, reaching over and handing me a cup of tea.

I take a sip, realizing it's just how I like it—dark English Breakfast tea with a little bit of honey. "Thanks."

"You're welcome." He presses his lips to my temple then turns me in his arms, walking me two steps forward. Pressing his side into my back, he wraps his hand around my waist while he uses his free hand to remove the pancakes off the griddle.

"Do you two want to go out on the lake with me and Kim?" he asks Willow and Harmony.

I tip my head back to look at him, wondering what he's talking about. He never told me anything about going on the lake. "The lake?"

I question.

His head dips down as his eyes drop to meet mine. "I figure we have a while before dinner tonight. I already pulled the kayaks out of the garage this morning. The lake's calm and the sky's clear, so it's a good day to go out." He shrugs, adding more batter to the griddle while Harmony moves to the oven, opening it up and pulling out a pan full of bacon.

"I've never kayaked before," I tell him, and he looks at me once more with a smile that's almost wicked curving his lips.

"Really?" he asks, and I shrug.

"I'm not really an outdoor-activity kind of girl. I'm more of a sit on the edge of the lake or in the sand at the beach and read a book kind of a girl," I admit.

"You'll love it." He kisses the top of my head while his fingers run along my hip under my tank.

"I don't think you understand. I'm not the most athletic person in the world," I add, and he laughs.

"It's all good. You don't need to be athletic."

"I'm guessing you've made up your mind and no matter what I say I will be going out on the lake," I deduce, and the girls, who are watching me and Sage like they would a Ping-Pong match, both laugh.

"You'd be right. You'll like it."

"If you say so," I mutter, taking a sip of tea, knowing he has no idea what he's getting himself into.

"THIS WAS A bad idea," I grumble, and Harmony and Willow laugh as I take Sage's hand and put one foot in the kayak then the other, hissing "Oh, God" when the boat wobbles side-to-side.

"I've got you. You'll be fine," Sage assures.

I roll my eyes. I don't think he understands how uncoordinated I am. We are both likely to end up in the water if I'm on this damn thing. "What are you doing? I thought you were coming with me." I panic as Sage starts to push me and the boat out into the water.

"I need to get us out a bit before I climb in so we don't bottom out," he replies calmly before climbing into the seat behind me. The boat tips again, and I grab both sides, holding on for dear life as I screech at the top of my lungs. Hearing him chuckle behind me, I turn around to look at him and narrow my eyes.

"It's not funny."

"Baby," he says gently, smiling at me. "Take a breath and look around. Tell me this isn't beautiful."

With a huff, I turn around to face the front of the kayak then pull in a sharp breath. He's wrong. It's not beautiful; it's breathtaking. The trees surrounding the lake are in varying shades of greens, golds, and browns, and the lake itself looks like smooth dark glass that the sky and trees are reflecting off of.

"It's amazing," I whisper as we move smoothly over the water. Turning to look at Sage once more, I see he has the paddle in his hand and is using it on first one side and then the other in an almost circular motion. "Thank you," I mouth to him, and his face softens. Hearing Willow and Harmony laughing, I glance across the lake and watch them as they speed over the smooth surface, paddling in sync.

Seeing them, I pick up my own paddle. "How do I do this?" I ask, and the boat glides to a stop.

"First one side and then the other. You start us off and I'll fall into rhythm with you," he says, and I nod then take the long paddle and begin to put one side into the water. It takes me a few minutes for me to stop going in circles and to get the hang of it, but when I finally catch on, Sage starts paddling with me and we fly over the top of the lake, chasing after Willow and Harmony.

I laugh harder than I have in a long time and smile so much my face hurts. I know my happiness isn't because of what I'm doing, even though kayaking is a total blast. I'm happy because of who I am with. Sage is one of those people who is just easy to hang out with. He puts you at ease, takes the stress away, and makes you smile, even when you don't think it's possible to.

And he is also the guy I'm pretty sure I'm already falling in love with. I just hope with time he can feel the same way about me.

Sage

SLIPPING ON MY dress shirt, I do up the buttons then the cuffs and grab my watch, putting it on before walking out of the closet. Listening to the sound of Kim singing behind the door of my master bath, I smile then laugh. She sounds horrible, but it's still cute to hear her so happy. I head toward the door and grab my shoes, leaving for the living room, where I take a seat on the edge of the couch to put them on.

We were out on the lake longer than I expected us to be, so by the time we got back in and put away the kayaks, Willow and Harmony left to get ready for dinner, which reminded Kim about our plans for the evening. I know she's nervous about being around everyone tonight, but I'm relieved. For a long time, I've hated going to family functions or get-togethers knowing Kim could be there with one of my cousins. If she were there, I would've had to be in the same room with her and not touch her, not talk to her. Fuck, I could barely look at her. It was like torture every time.

But tonight, tonight is different. There are no rules anymore. I can touch her whenever the fuck I want.

Standing from the couch, I head for the kitchen but stop dead when Kim walks out of my room and down the hall toward me. Her hair is half down and pulled away from her face, making her eyes and cheekbones stand out. The dark burgundy turtleneck dress she's wearing looks amazing with her complexion and skims her body like a second skin, ending just above a pair of knee high black leather boots.

"Fuck." Seeing those boots, I know going slow just went out the fucking window. I want her. No… want is too tame a word. I fucking *need* her.

"Is this too much?" she asks, stopping before me and holding her arms out to her sides. "I don't want to look slutty. I didn't even think about the fact this kind of screams 'slut' with the boots."

Jesus, my woman is crazy.

"You don't look slutty, but I'm definitely thinking about you in those boots and nothing else."

"Sage," she snaps, and I lean in, wrapping my hand around her hip, feeling the soft material of the dress under my palm.

"Never mind, the sweater's hot, too. The first time I fuck you," I lean down, nipping her earlobe while grabbing her ass, "it will be up around your waist, your boots around my hips, and your ass on the counter in the kitchen."

"You're not helping me feel better," she growls.

I lean back to look at her then move my hands to hold her face gently. "You look beautiful."

"Are you sure? Your mom and dad—"

"They couldn't give a fuck less what you wear. They already know you and like you. You have nothing to be nervous about. This is my family and the people you've been hanging out with for a long time."

"I guess you're right. It just feels different," she says quietly, dropping her eyes from mine.

Giving her jaw a squeeze, I wait until she looks at me once more before I speak. "The only difference is you're mine now, and everyone knows it. Nothing else has changed. Everyone is still going to be loud and inappropriate. My mom will probably ask about what our plans are, and my aunts will probably hem and haw about planning another wedding. But it will be all good."

"Wedding?" Her eyes widen, and she visibly swallows.

I laugh. "You know July, June, and Ash, babe. So you know exactly what happens when the women in my family get together. They all start plotting."

"Maybe I shouldn't go."

"Oh no, you're coming. Even if I have to carry you over my shoulder. I have plans for your ass tonight when we get back."

"You have plans for my ass when we get back?" she repeats, blinking up at me. "I'm not sleeping here tonight. I have to work tomorrow at the shop."

"Fine, then I'm staying at yours. Or we'll pick up some clothes from your place after dinner and come back here."

"You know you are seriously bossy, right?" she prompts, rolling her eyes. "You never say 'Hey, what do you think about this?' or 'How do you feel about that?' It's always 'I'm paying' or 'We're doing blah, blah, blah,'" she mimics in a deep voice, shaking her head, and I fight back a smile. "It's really annoying."

"So you didn't enjoy sleeping in my bed?" I raise a brow.

She frowns. "I didn't say that."

"I'm guessing you also hated going out on the lake this morning."

"Don't be a jerk," she snaps, glaring at me.

"I'm not. I'm proving a point. You're telling me it's annoying when I'm bossy, yet you sure as fuck have been enjoying yourself."

"Don't cuss at me."

"Jesus," I growl, running my hand over the top of my head in frustration. "Are we seriously going to start fucking arguing about this shit right now?"

"No. Yes. I don't know!" she cries, throwing her arms in the air.

I know what she needs. Hell, I know what we both need, and I plan on giving it to both of us as soon as we get home from this fucking dinner tonight.

"I'm freaking out, and then there's you." She waves her hand out at me. "You look all hot and muscular, and I can't stop thinking about what happened this morning, which is making me want to jump you. And I know that wouldn't be good, because then we would be late, and everyone would know *exactly* why we were late. And then I would be embarrassed. So please, cut me some slack." She ends with her chest heaving and her eyes on mine.

"Come here."

"What?" She frowns, and I hold out my hand toward her.

"Come here."

"Why?"

"Trust me," I urge, and she places her hand in mine. Leading her to the kitchen, I turn her to face me then slowly slide my hands up her hips, bunching up the soft sweater as I go.

"What are you doing?" she pants, but I don't answer.

As soon as I have her dress up around her hips, I skim my hands down over her hips, feeling for her panties. Coming across the smooth material, I wrap them around my fingers and pull them down, lowering to my knees and muttering "step out" when they reach her ankles. Holding onto my shoulders, she does as I asked, and I lean in, placing a kiss to her stomach above her pubic bone. Hearing her pant and smelling her arousal causes my already hard cock to twitch and my hands to tighten into fists. I shove her panties into my pocket and wrap my hands back around her hips, lifting her to the counter and hearing her gasp as her ass hits the cool top.

"Lean back and spread your legs for me," I growl, fighting myself to stay calm. This will be a test of self-control if I've ever had one. The idea of eating her turns me on, and I know I'll want to fuck her. I know the second the taste of her hits my tongue I'm going to want to fuck her until neither of us can walk. Only I can't do that—not now anyway. But I can get her off and help her relax a little so she's not so on edge.

"I don't think...." she whispers, tightening her knees together, and I shake my head.

"Don't think, just do. Lean back and spread your legs for me," I demand, and her eyes widen and the tip of her pink tongue comes out to touch the edge of her lip.

Seeing that, I lose what little bit of self-control I was holding onto. Forcing her back to the counter, I grab her knees and spread them open. Dropping my eyes to her already glistening pussy, my hands fucking shake and my mouth waters. I trail one shaky finger up her inner thigh and move my eyes from the skin below my finger to her face, wanting to see her reaction to my touch. The moment my fingers slide through her folds and over her clit, her eyes slide shut and her head tips back, exposing the elegant slope of her throat as her back arches.

So fucking beautiful. So fucking perfect. All fucking mine.

"Sage," she breathes, her thighs visibly shaking as I take her in.

Hearing my name leave her mouth and seeing her reaction to my touch, I dive at her pussy, licking and sucking every inch of her. Using my shoulders, I keep her thighs spread wide and focus on her clit while plunging two fingers inside of her. Her moans and whimpers make my cock leak as I flick her with my tongue.

Feeling her pussy tighten around my fingers, I know she's close, and as much as I wish I could prolong her orgasm, I can't. If I keep going, I know this will no longer be about me getting her off. "Give it to me." My growled words against her clit send her over, and her body starts to shake as she comes on my tongue. I keep my fingers planted inside her as I stroke over her G-spot while she comes down from the orgasm, only pulling them away when her glazed eyes open on me. "You feeling better?" I ask.

Her eyes slide shut, and her head falls back as she lets out a puff of air and a laugh before covering her face. "I'm not sure I'm better, but after that orgasm, I think I'll be okay," she says, pulling her hands from her face and smiling at me.

Helping her sit up, I take hold of her face and kiss her until her nails are digging into my skin through my shirt. "You sleeping here?" I ask as soon as I pull my mouth from hers.

Her eyes flutter open. "Yes."

"Good." I drag her ass from the counter and help her right her dress then wash my face and hands.

"I need my panties."

"No you don't."

"Yes I do," she argues.

"You don't," I deny, moving her toward the front door.

"I'm not having dinner with your family wearing nothing but my dress."

"No one will know but you and me."

"Yeah, and then something freakish will happen and my ass will come out and everyone will see e-v-e-r-y-t-h-i-n-g."

"Nothing will happen, and sure as fuck no one will ever see your ass but me," I growl. Just the thought of someone, *anyone,* seeing her the way I have makes the uncomfortable feeling of jealousy roll through me. "Now come on or we're gonna be late." I hold open the door, and she huffs a little but moves past me, grabbing her coat and bag as she goes.

Shutting and locking the door behind us, I hit the key fob to set the alarm and move toward my Caddy, where Kim is already climbing into the passenger seat. I get in behind the wheel and start the engine as she pulls down the visor and starts applying a coat of red lipstick to her lips, making them look even fuller than they already are.

Fuck me, it's going to be a long fucking night.

Chapter 10

Kim

WALKING INTO THE restaurant hand-in-hand with Sage, we stop at the podium and wait for the hostess, who just walked off with a customer, to come back. "You okay?" he questions, and I look up at him, feeling my eyes get squinty. I asked him in the car if I could have my panties back, but he refused. So now my ass is out—not really, but it feels that way. Like, at any moment, someone is going to be all '*Oh my God, look at her ass. She isn't even wearing underwear!*'

"I would feel better if I had…." My words taper off when the hostess appears in front of us smiling, and I squeeze Sage's hand, digging my nails into his skin as I do.

"Table for two?" she asks, and Sage shakes his head.

"Mayson party," he replies, rubbing his thumb over my pulse.

"Awesome. God, there are a lot of you," she chirps happily. "Follow me." Looking up at Sage, I widen my eyes at him as the girl skips in front of us and winds us in and out of tables as she leads us to the back of the restaurant into a private room. "Here you go. Enjoy your dinner." She grins before disappearing out of sight.

Pulling my eyes from her retreating back, I turn to face the room and feel every inch of me freeze. Everyone is looking at us. Everyone. And I swear they all know I don't have on any flipping underwear under my damn dress.

"You're here!" Sophie squeaks, breaking into the silence and pushing back her chair. Coming toward us, she greets me with a hug, then Sage. After her, Nico hugs me but pats Sage's shoulder. Then it's pandemonium. Everyone is out of their seats and coming over to say hello or to offer their condolences.

By the time I have hugged every last person in the room, I feel spent, like I need a drink—a drink I can't have. Settling into my seat with Sage next to me, I'm thankful he's kept his hand in mine. I need it; I need his strength. The loss of Kelly is getting easier to deal with, but times like these, when everyone's attention is on me, I'm reminded of what happened and I feel uncomfortable. Honestly, I feel like I shouldn't be getting their 'I'm sorry for your loss' statements. Yes, Kelly is gone, but I lost her a long time ago. Really, I don't think I ever actually had her at all. Listening to everyone talk about what's happening in the family, work, or mundane things, I'm thankful when I hear Hope call to me from my other side.

"Kimmy, will you help me color my picture?" she asks, and I look down at her and smile. She looks adorable wearing the poufy blue dress I got her from the Disney Store that is the exact replica of Cinderella's from the movie.

"Of course I will," I agree quietly, letting go of Sage's hand as she climbs into my lap. Pulling her coloring book and crayons over, I rest my chin on her shoulder, and for a few minutes, I get lost in coloring a picture of a butterfly flying through a garden of flowers. I didn't even know how much the thoughtless action would help loosen me up, but by the time we're ready to order dinner, I'm relaxed and feeling much better.

"So Ellie was telling us that you girls are meeting with a banker to see if they approved you for your loan," Lilly says, and I swallow the bite of food I have in my mouth and take a sip of water before I answer her.

"We are. The bank has already completed the basic approval forms, and that all came out okay. So hopefully we will have some good news to share," I reply, looking at Ellie, who is grinning from ear-to-ear.

"I know it's in the bag." She shrugs, and I laugh.

"Have you girls thought of a name yet?" Sophie asks.

I look at her and shake my head while Ellie answers. "We're still looking for a name. We want something fun and original, but I think we're waiting to see what happens so we don't jinx ourselves."

"That's smart," November says, and then she mutters, "What about Mayson's Hair Salon?"

I don't frown even though I want to.

"Except Kim's not a Mayson," April says helpfully.

"Yet. She's not a Mayson *yet*," Sophie whispers.

"Here, here." November clinks her glass to Sophie's then Lilly's and Liz's.

My face gets hot, and I feel Sage's hand squeeze my knee. He wasn't lying. One minute, things are normal, and the next minute, not so much.

"I think you women need to slow down on the drinking," December says, rolling her eyes at her mom.

"Well, I know none of my girls are going to get married anytime soon, so I need to get in on the wedding planning somewhere. I was pretty good at it." November's eyes widen and sparkle. "Maybe I'll open my own business. November Weddings," she muses, and I wonder how much exactly she's had to drink.

"Babe, you're not doing that, and stop trying to marry off my girls," Asher grouches, and the men at the table chuckle while his wife glares at him.

"If I marry Kim, I'm just letting everyone here know that I'm taking her to the courthouse or to Vegas," Sage says.

I frown at him. "Pardon?"

"I'm not suffering through a wedding or wearing a tux."

"First of all, we have a long way to go before any of that happens. But when I get married, I will have a wedding. Whatever man I marry *will* wear a tux, and I'll be wearing a dress and holding flowers."

"You're not fucking marrying anyone else," he growls, squeezing my thigh. "And there will be no wedding. The dress and flowers are cool. You can have both those things in Vegas."

"I'm not getting married in Vegas," I snap, and then I look at Ash. "No offense."

"None taken. I don't even remember my wedding." She grins, and I return the expression, shaking my head.

"Vegas or the courthouse. Those are your options."

"Lord, he's as bad as you are," I hear Sophie say, and I look at the end of the table, where she is sitting next to Nico. He's smiling at Sage with what can only be described as a proud fatherly smile on his face.

"This argument is pointless," I mumble, ducking my head hoping if we stop talking about it now, my stomach that has filled with stupid butterflies at the idea of marrying Sage will calm the hell down.

Thank God, after that, the subject of mine and Sage's imaginary wedding is dropped and everyone starts talking about Talon and Bax. Both Sage's brothers have been living between Montana and Alaska for work, but in the next few months, they are moving home, so they're looking for land. While everyone is talking about that, I continue coloring with my favorite girl until dinner is over and it's time to leave the restaurant.

Getting in Sage's car an hour later, I'm more exhausted than I realized. So exhausted that I fall asleep with my head on Sage's shoulder and don't even remember him taking me home to my apartment, stripping me out of my clothes, or putting me into my bed before joining me there.

Hearing a buzzing sound, my eyes open and I see nothing but the hard male chest my cheek is pressed against. I blink, moving my hand that is lying across Sage's abs, and tip my head back to look at his sleeping face then frown when the buzzing that woke me up starts again. Debating how to get out of bed without waking him, I study him then let out a breath when his leg that is between mine cocks at the knee and his thigh moves deeper between mine.

Looking down at myself, my eyes widen. I'm naked, completely naked. I've always been a light sleeper, so the fact I'm naked and don't remember getting this way means I was out of it last night when he brought me home. Studying his skin pressed against mine, the tingle that has been a constant friend comes back to life full force.

"Dammit," he sighs when the buzzing starts back up, and I wonder if I should pretend to be asleep but I'm too slow. Before I can close my eyes, he's up on his elbow and looking down at me as he reaches over my chest and grabs his cell from my bedside table. "What?" he barks into the phone, making me jump from the sudden boom of sound. "Fuck." His eyes close briefly as he shakes his head. "Yeah, I'll be there. Give me an hour," he says before dropping the cell to the bed near my hip.

"Is everything okay?" I question softly, reaching down for the sheet to cover myself from his gaze that is traveling over every inch of my exposed skin. And there is a lot of it to see, since I'm still very much naked.

"I gotta go, which means I'm leaving you naked in bed. Pretty fucking sure that's the definition of not okay."

"Oh," I whisper, and he smiles, touching his mouth to mine before leaning back to look at me once more.

"What time are you meeting with the banker?"

"Two." I tip my head back to look at the clock and see it's not even eight. "Ellie and I both have clients before then, so we'll probably just walk over to the bank from the shop," I explain.

He nods, brushing a piece of hair from my forehead before tucking it behind my ear. "I'll be late tonight, so when you get done doing what you're doing, just head to my place."

"Sage."

"Please," he says quietly, and hearing the soft plea in his voice warms my heart.

"Fine," I agree, "but I might be late, too. I need to check in with Elizabeth to see if she wants me to watch the boys. She's been cool about it, but I feel like I'm taking advantage of her by not pitching in as much as I was."

"I'm sure she understands."

"She does, but still, it makes me uncomfortable. I don't like handouts."

"Baby, she's not giving you a fucking handout. She's your friend who cares about you. You need to stop thinking that people taking care of you makes you weak," he says, and my muscles get tight. I still haven't told him about my illness, and now I don't know how to tell him. Now I'm really fucking scared that the minute I do, he's going to run for the hills. "Stop overthinking." He taps my forehead, having no idea my stomach is suddenly a complete mess.

"I'll try," I agree, giving him what I hope is a convincing smile before asking, "What are you doing today?" I need to think about something, anything else.

"I'll be in Nashville. A client hired us to look into his wife a few months back, and he called Jax this morning, telling him she was going out today. So we need to follow her."

"Really? Is she... is she cheating on him?" I ask, and he shakes his head.

"She's a mom of four kids all under the age of six. We've followed her a few times in the past, and she normally grabs a coffee and takes it to the park, where she sits, doing nothing but staring off into the distance like a zombie."

"She's tired," I say quietly, and he nods, running his warm fingers along my jaw.

"Yeah, she's tired and he's always working, always out of town. So I'm sure when she gets the chance to take a minute for herself, she's clamoring for it. And he's taking her eagerness to get away as her fucking around on him."

"That's sad." I know that Elizabeth is always exhausted, but Jelikai always makes sure she has time to herself. He books her spa days or sends her to the salon. He's even booked her into a hotel for a night alone so she could just lie in bed and relax. "Maybe you can talk to him," I suggest as he rubs a thick chunk of my hair between his fingers.

"Tried to tell him what was happening after I followed her the first time, but he didn't want to hear it. He's set on the idea that she's cheating. He doesn't understand the stress of having kids, because he's never really around."

"He sounds like a dick."

"He is, but on the other hand, I make bank every time he calls to have her watched. And it's an easy gig, no drama, no need to watch my back. I'll take it. One day, she's either going to catch on to what he's doing or he's going to finally get it that his wife is struggling and needs help. Either way, they need to find a way to work on their shit and communicate. Otherwise, shit's gonna go up in smoke and they will have no one to blame but themselves. And when that happens, sadly the kids will be the only ones who suffer."

"I wish I could help her," I whisper.

His face softens. "That right there is the reason I couldn't move on."

"What?"

"Your soft spot, your kindness, and your need to make the people you don't even know feel better," he says, dropping his mouth to mine, which has opened to form a soft O. Then he leans back and runs his fingers along my forehead. "I gotta get up. You mind if I use your toothbrush?" he asks before I've even had a chance to recover from his sweet words or gentle touch.

At his question, I feel my face get soft and I shake my head. "No, you're welcome to it."

Smiling at my answer, he moves. But then he stops with his knees between mine, and I can feel the heavy, hard length of him come to rest against my lower belly and see his biceps flex as his fists go into the bed on either side of my head.

"Kiss me good. I need something to hold me over until tonight. You passed the fuck out before I even got my car started last night and didn't even make a peep when I carried you up here, took off your clothes, and put you into bed."

"I must have been tired," I whisper as his mouth drops closer to mine.

"Kiss me, Kim," he repeats his command, ignoring my excuse.

So I do.

I lean up and kiss him, but he's the one who makes it good. And then he makes it even better when he cups my breast and tweaks my nipple before getting out of bed and sauntering out of my room naked.

Pulling my eyes from his perfect ass, I fall to my back against the pillow and grin up at the closed skylight above me, taking a second to enjoy the feelings that have filled my stomach before I roll out of bed.

After putting on a pair of sleep shorts and a tank, I head to the kitchen and make him a fried egg, cheese, and turkey breakfast sandwich. I'm searching for one of my travel mugs that doesn't have flowers or some other girly thing on it when I see him wander naked from the bathroom and into my room. I grab the only cup I can find with a lid and quickly make him coffee that is done as soon as he comes out dressed a few minutes later.

"Here you go, for the road." I smile, handing the sandwich and coffee to him before I open the door.

Recognizing the look in his eyes when he sees what I've given him is better than any thank you. Or I think it is, until he drops the stuff to the counter and pulls me against him, planting a kiss on me that causes my toes to curl.

"Thanks, babe," he mutters against my lips, and I smile then melt against his chest once more when his hand wraps around me and he touches his forehead to mine. "See you tonight."

"Tonight," I agree as he lets me go.

Picking up his things, he heads down the stairs, and I watch him take a bite from the sandwich in his hand halfway down.

Yes, I'm most definitely falling for Sage Mayson, I think, closing the door when I hear the garage open.

Chapter 11

Kim

"I TOLD YOU so," Chris says after I tell him about what's been going on between Sage and me.

I ignore his words and focus on cutting his hair and not my fingers.

"Told who what?" Ellie asks from the sinks, where she's cleaning up after her last client. Looking at Chris through the mirror in front of us, I silently tell him to keep his mouth shut, because no one likes a know-it-all.

"Just told Kim something, and I reminded her I retained the right to say 'I told you so' when she realized I was right."

"Oh, like when she finally realized she and Sage are perfect together?" she asks, coming over while wiping her hands on a towel.

"Exactly." Chris swings his chair around to beam at her, causing me to almost cut off my finger. "They're meant to be together. Everyone can see it, can't they?"

"They are perfect together," Ellie agrees softly, holding my gaze, but then her expression shifts to worry. "Have you told him about...." Her words trail off, not that I need to hear them. I know exactly what she's referring to, and the thought causes my heart to squeeze painfully in my chest. I know realistically that I'm running out of time to tell him about my illness, but every second we spend together, the scarier the idea of confessing gets.

"Not yet."

"Fuck me," Chris growls, and I tip my head down to look into his disappointed eyes. "Kim, what the hell are you waiting for?"

"I...." I have no excuse except fear. The truth is like a big dark cloud that I can see off in the distance, but right now it's okay, because above me are blue skies and sunshine. Unfortunately, that cloud keeps getting closer, and I know when it's overhead I'm liable to drown in its downpour.

"You really should tell him," Ellie says, sounding as disappointed as the expression on Chris's face looks.

"I will. I'm waiting until the right time," I murmur.

"Dude, you've read as many romance books as I have. You know this is not going to end well if he finds out and you didn't talk to him about it first," Chris adds, shaking his head.

"Except this isn't a book. This is real life. I need to find a way to tell him that will ease any worries he may have so I don't end up—"

"Broken," Chris cuts me off, reaching out to take my hand. "I know you're still trying to protect yourself, but, baby girl, you need to do the right thing. You need to tell him, so you guys can move on from it and start on your happily ever after. You've been doing good. You haven't gotten sick since you met with your new doctor, and your last test results showed that your kidney function is holding steady. Those are good things, positive things." He is right. They are good things, but I'm still sick so it's actually *not* a good thing. "Please, for your sake, tell him."

"I will," I agree, leaving out the other words in my head. *I'll tell him when I'm brave enough to face his reaction.*

"Lord Jesus, I can see it in your eyes that you're not going to," he mutters, and I sigh. Having a best friend you've known practically your whole life is awesome on occasion, like when you're having a bad day and they know without asking to bring over ice cream and one of your favorite movies. Times like now, not so much.

"I'm going to tell him. I swear."

"I hope so, and don't think I missed your nose twitching, because I didn't."

"Whatever," I grumble, and he smiles at me and I smile back. "Now come on. Let me finish your hair. I've got a client coming in, and if you don't stop talking, I'm leaving you exactly like you are."

"You would never." He presses his hand to his heart.

"I will if you don't stop yapping."

"Fine, hurry up. I need to leave soon anyway. I have a date."

"Is Dale coming into town?" I ask, turning him around to face the mirror once more.

"No," he says, and I frown.

"Are you going to Florida?"

"No, I have a date with a guy I met at work."

"You have a date with a guy you met at work?" I repeat, staring at him and feeling my eyes widen.

"Yes."

"Who is he and why am I just now hearing about this?"

"His name is Fresco. I didn't tell you, because you have your own stuff going on. I didn't want to bother you with mine."

"Are you kidding me right now?" I ask, swinging the chair around to look at him.

"No."

"What the hell is going on with you and Dale?"

"We're not together. You know that. And I'm not feeling the whole long distance thing anymore."

"But you love him," I whisper, and his face changes ever so slightly, causing the mask he's obviously been keeping on for my sake to slip, showing me that he's hurting.

"I do love him, but me loving him isn't enough of a reason to keep my life on hold anymore. I want more than he's willing to give me. You know I want a husband and kids, and I know I won't find those things with Dale, so I'm moving on."

"Chris." I fall into him, wrapping my arms around his cape-covered shoulders. "I'm so sorry."

"Me, too, but this is life. Sometimes shit sucks for a while, and then later on, when you're feeling good and happy, you realize why you had to go through what you went through. You realize if you hadn't, you wouldn't have had a chance at that happiness you're feeling."

"Do you think this new guy will give you that happiness?" I ask, holding onto him.

His arms tighten around me. "I don't know, but I'm willing to find out."

"I want that for you," I tell him truthfully. I know how much he wants a family and kids, and I want that for him. Really, I just want him happy, however that comes about.

"Ditto, baby girl," he whispers, kissing the side of my head before letting me go and looking at me. "Now seriously, cut my hair. I've got places to be and shit to do, and if your next client comes in before you're done and you try to kick me out of your chair, I will throw a diva tantrum to end all diva tantrums."

"Oh, all right," I mutter, giving him a grin before I finish his hair. As he leaves, I make him promise to call to tell me every single detail about his date. Once he's gone, it's already 12:30, and luckily my next client shows up on time fifteen minutes later, so I'm able to get her wash, cut, and blow out done before it's time for Ellie and me to head over to the bank.

Standing with Ellie at the front of the bank, we share a nervous look. I know we've been pre-approved, but today we talk to the loan officers and find out exactly what will happen next.

"Hey, guys. They're ready for you. Follow me," Christy, the bank manager, says, leading us down the hall toward the back of the bank.

Feeling Ellie's hand find mine and give it a squeeze, I squeeze hers back before walking into a large office. There are two desks stationed in front of each other and a circular table on the other side of the room, with two women I know sitting on one side with three empty chairs across from them. Seeing the women, I smile. It's Selma and Sejla, Ellie's clients from the salon.

"I didn't know you guys were working on our loan." Ellie laughs, walking around the table to hug both girls.

"We didn't know either. Kirk was supposed to handle your case, but he's been out sick for a few days," Selma explains as she gives me a hug.

"Have a seat, girls. I think we may have some amazing news for you," Sejla says, motioning us to the empty chairs.

"You two are in good hands. If you need anything, let me know," Christy states before she gives us a smile and leaves.

Taking a seat, I watch Selma and Sejla work in sync, which isn't surprising, because they are twins. I imagine twins, who are as close as they are and spend as much time together as they do, would practically share the same brain.

"You guys have been approved for the loan," Sejla says with a smile, pushing a paper across the top of the desk toward us.

"You'll notice we were only able get you approved for your loan amount and an extra thirty thousand," Selma adds, pointing out the final figure with the tip of a highlighter before running over the number with the hot pink color. "We know it's not what you were asking for, but hopefully it will be enough to do some renovations. We're thinking that if you come back in a few months, you should be able to get the rest of the money if you still need it."

"Holy shit," I breathe, looking at Ellie's and my name in black lettering on the paper. "This is really happening."

"It's really happening," Ellie agrees, and I turn my head to look at her smiling face then she throws her arms around me.

"We're going to own our own salon," I say, hugging her, and she leans back to look at me.

"Yes, and it's going to be the best fucking salon in all of Tennessee by the time we're done with it."

"It is," I agree as she takes her seat once more.

"Have you thought of a new name, or are you keeping it the same?" Selma asks, looking at the two of us, and I shake my head. I still can't believe this is real. I don't think I'll be able to think about a name until my new reality hits me.

"Color Me Wild," Ellie says, and I swing my head in her direction.

"Color Me Crazy."

"Yes!" She laughs, throwing her head back. "Color Me Crazy, that is so perfect."

It is perfect, and this is really happening. Ellie and I are going to own our own shop. Holy shit! I want to call Sage and tell him my good news.

"All right, now that the exciting part is done, we need to sign papers," Sejla inserts as she pulls out a stack of papers from a folder.

"That can wait a second," Selma states, looking at me. "First, tell us what is happening with you and your guy."

Laughing at that, I tell her and Sejla about Sage and me, and by the time I'm done, they are both wearing smiles that match my own.

Sage

PULLING UP NEXT to Kim's car in front of my house, I park and head up the walkway, carrying the bottle of champagne I picked up on the way home. Kim called this afternoon, yelling into the phone that she and Ellie had gotten approval for the loan for the shop. As happy as I was for her news and the fact she called me before anyone, I couldn't really talk, so I told her we'd celebrate when I got home.

I unlock the door and push in and am instantly assaulted with the smell of garlic and something else I can't make out. Dropping my keys to the table, I head down the hall toward the scent, and the sound of Ed Sheeran playing in the background along with Kim's horrible singing over the top of it. Stopping at the threshold where the kitchen and hall meet, I stop to enjoy the show.

Kim is in the kitchen, standing in front of the stove with a wooden spatula to her mouth as she sings a sad song about a man losing his woman and wanting her to be happy, even if it's not with him. That man was obviously a fucking idiot, or he had never felt what I feel for Kim. I don't want her happy with anyone else; I want her happy with me. Call me selfish, but it is what it is.

Walking around the long peninsula that divides the kitchen from the living room, I come up behind her, realizing only then that her eyes have been closed. The second my hand comes to rest on her waist, she screams at the top of her lungs and spins around to face me with a hand to her chest.

"Easy," I say quietly as I watch her chest heave.

"You scared the crap out of me," she accuses.

"Sorry," I reply, watching her pull in a breath before letting it out slowly.

"It's okay. I just didn't hear you come in or even notice you. You're pretty damn light on your feet for such a big guy. That must be useful with your job," she mutters, and I laugh.

"It helps," I agree, dropping the bottle of champagne to the counter behind her before I pull her against me. "Congrats on the loan."

She smiles, but I only see it for a second before I drag her up my body and place my mouth on hers. Kissing her like a man starved, I lick and nibble at her mouth until I feel her nails dig into my skin through my shirt, and then I force myself to slow the kiss. Pulling back and looking down at her, it takes a second like it always does, but her eyes open to meet mine.

"You stopped," she complains, and I grin.

"You're cooking and I need a shower."

"Oh."

"What are you making?" I ask, looking over her shoulder into the pan behind her.

"Zucchini and pasta fried in olive oil and garlic."

"Sounds good," I lie, and she grins at me knowingly.

"The penne still need to cook, so if you want to shower, you have time."

"All right. When I get out, we'll open the champagne."

"I…" She bites her lip then shakes her head. "I don't drink." Frowning, I realize she doesn't, or at least I've never seen her drink. I've always assumed it was because she was driving. "I'll watch you drink it." She smiles, tipping her head to the side while pressing her hand against my chest. "You should go shower. I need to put the pasta in," she urges with a smile, but her expression is off, making me wonder what the hell that's about.

"You okay?"

"Yeah, why do you ask?"

"Nothing." I shake off the feeling that she's lying. "I'll be back in a few minutes."

"Don't rush." She gets up on her tiptoes, touching her lips to my jaw. "The food will keep."

With a jerk of my chin, I touch my fingers to her waist and leave her in the kitchen while I head down the hall. Pausing halfway to the bedroom, I turn to glance over my shoulder and see her pick up the bottle of champagne to look at it for a moment before she drops it to the counter. With a shake of her head, her shoulders droop forward.

What the fuck?

Spinning, I start back toward her to ask what the hell that reaction is about, but before I make it there, the doorbell goes off.

"I got it, babe," I say, walking past her when she turns around.

"Okay," she agrees, picking up a box of pasta from the counter and dumping the contents into a pot.

Heading down the hall, I move to the door and open it. I don't know who I'm expecting to see on the other side, but I'm sure as fuck not expecting my parents to be standing in my doorway, my dad carrying a bag and my mom holding flowers. "What are you guys doing here?"

"Apparently, we drove all the way out here to celebrate," Dad mutters.

"Stop being a jerk." Mom hits his chest.

"Baby, our son has his girl at his house. She just got good news. Do you really think he wants us here?"

"Yes," she snaps then her eyes come to me. "You want me here, right?"

Fuck me.

"Mom, you know you're always welcome."

"See? I'm always welcome," she says, turning her head to glare up at my dad.

"Our boy isn't going to tell you that you ain't allowed at his house, Sophie."

"Kim's family's not here, and I want her to know she has people close that are proud and excited for her. Can't you just entertain me for a few minutes?" Mom snaps as she moves past me into the house. Looking at my dad for help, he shakes his head.

"I'll try to get her out of here as soon as I can," he says, patting my shoulder as he follows my mom down the hall toward the kitchen.

Sighing, I close the door and follow behind them.

"Sage didn't tell me you guys were coming. I would have made more food if I had known." I hear Kim say as I walk into the kitchen to find her and my mom hugging.

"We didn't tell him. We just wanted to come by to say congrats. Lilly called to tell me this afternoon that you and Ellie got the loan," Mom chirps, giving Kim the flowers she brought in. "I also brought cake. Nothing says celebrating like chocolate cake."

"This is so nice. Thank you," Kim whispers, giving my mom another hug before giving my dad one. "Maybe I can just add a little more pasta to the water," she suggests as she starts to move toward the stove with the flowers.

"Not necessary, honey. We're not staying long," Dad inserts, and Kim looks up at him as my mom narrows her eyes.

"Are you sure?" Kim asks, setting the flowers on the counter, and I move to her side and wrap my hand around her hip.

"They have plans, babe," I say quietly, and Kim nods while I feel my mom's eyes burning into me.

"I'm taking Sophie out to dinner," Dad states, backing me up.

Mom places the cake on the island next to the flowers before she looks at him and asks, "Really, where are we going?"

"We'll figure it out on the road," he tells her, and her eyes squint a little.

"At least stay for the cake," Kim cuts in, and I fight back a groan.

"You don't mind?" Mom asks, looking at her, and Kim shakes her head.

"Of course not."

"Of course not." She smiles at my girl before looking at my dad and me triumphantly. "Did you hear that?"

Knowing it's useless to put up a fight, I press a kiss to the side of Kim's head and move to the cabinet, where I grab plates and forks while my mom opens the box the cake came in. After that, I spend the next hour and a half with Kim and my parents eating cake and drinking champagne. Really, my mom drinks the champagne by herself, so by the time she and my dad leave, she's half wasted and my dad has to carry her giggling out of the house.

Chapter 12

Kim

AFTER WASHING MY face, I grab the towel off the holder next to the sink and put it to my mouth. I'm nervous, so flipping nervous I can actually see the pulse in my neck thumping away. I know it's ridiculous to be nervous, seeing how I have been with Sage before and have fooled around a lot since then, but I'm still very, very anxious about the idea of being with him again.

Pulling in a breath through my nose, I drop the towel from my hands onto the counter and take a step back from the mirror to check myself out. I knew when Sage asked me to be here when he got home from work that I would be staying the night, so I made a quick run to Victoria's Secret when I left the salon. I told myself on the way to the store that I was just going to pick up a few things that needed to be replaced, but really, I wanted something sexy to wear to bed, something that would stop Sage from trying to slow things down when they started heating up. Looking at myself now, I'm pretty sure I succeeded in that endeavor.

The sheer black lace body suit looks good—no, amazing—against my golden skin. The front has a deep V that hits just above my belly button and the back high-cut legs shows off my ass. It has two slim straps that crisscross across my back, holding the straps in place. It's hot, super-hot. I just don't know if it's too much or if it screams *desperate*.

"Maybe I should just wear my shirt," I sigh, turning to look at myself over my shoulder and lifting up on my tiptoes to see my bottom.

"Kim," Sage calls, and I panic, falling forward into the door to make sure he doesn't come in, causing it to rattle loudly. "You okay?"

"Fine, fine," I cry out as I stand and attempt to spin around to grab the towel off the counter, but I'm too late. The door opens, and I barely have a chance to hold the face towel sideways in front of my chest.

"You... Jesus." He steps toward me, and I step back instinctively from the heated look in his eyes, noticing absently that all he's wearing is a pair of black boxers that are molded to his muscular thighs and his very large erection. "Drop the towel."

"I—"

"Drop it," he demands, cutting me off, and a shiver slides over me from the roots of my hair down to the tips of my toes.

Dropping the towel to the floor in front of me, his gaze licks over me and his eyes that were already dark heat up further.

"Christ." His bottom lip goes between his teeth as he reaches out to run one callused finger from my collarbone down the valley between my breasts to my belly button.

"I...." I don't even know what I was going to say, but anything that was going to come out of my mouth dies on my lips when his mouth captures mine.

Wrapping one hand around my waist, he pulls me flush against him while his other hand tangles in the hair at the back of my head. Gasping as his tongue sweeps into my mouth, his taste explodes on my tongue, causing a moan to climb up the back of my throat. I grab onto his shoulders as both his hands go to my ass and he lifts me up in one fell swoop. Wrapping my legs around his hips, I tip my head to the side to deepen the kiss as he walks us out of the bathroom toward the bed, where he drops down on top of me.

God, I will never tire of this. I will never get tired of his weight on top of me and his strength surrounding me. Really, I know I will never get tired of him.

"Sage," I breathe out as his mouth leaves mine to travel down over my jaw, my throat, and then my chest, where he drags the lacy material aside so he can pull one taut nipple between his lips. Feeling his teeth scrape over the hard tip, "Yes" leaves my lips, and my legs wrap tighter around his hips.

"Wet." His breath blows across my nipple as his fingers slide between my legs over the lace there, causing my hips to jerk.

"Yes," I agree. But I'm not just wet. I'm drenched, and he hasn't even really touched me yet. Kissing across my chest, he sucks my neglected nipple through the lace, sending a whole new sensation through my body, which causes my neck to arch and my nails to scrape across the smooth skin of his back. "Holy cow," I pant as his fingers run between my legs again and his teeth pull my nipple, causing a sharp burst of pleasure to shoot straight to my clit. "I need you," I say, and his mouth leaves my breast and his eyes meet mine. "Please."

At my plea, he leans back out of my grasp and flips me to my belly. "Up on your knees."

"Wh—" My words are cut off as he suddenly pulls me up to my knees, and then he's behind me and his mouth is on me. "Oh." My head drops to the bed, and my arms slide out in front of me as he feasts. There is no other way to describe what he's doing to me. His mouth is everywhere while his hands hold me open to the most exquisite torture of my life. Feeling a knot begin to form in the pit of my stomach, I moan and twist my head side-to-side, trying to fight it back. I want to come, but I know when I do it's going to wreck me.

"Let go," he demands against my pussy, and I shake my head. "Fucking let go," he growls, pinching my clit, and I do. I let go and my body rocks forward as one of the most intense orgasms of my life washes through me, sending me to the stars. Completely spent and seeing white lights dance behind my closed eyelids, I whimper when he flips me to my back. "Again," he says, burying his face between my legs once more. He licks me from top to bottom, and my legs tighten around his ears and my hands move to hold onto his head.

My clit is sensitive, too sensitive.

"Sage," I beg, but he ignores me, licking me again before circling my clit and pulling it into his mouth, flicking it with the tip of his tongue. My hips jerk and I try to get away, but he grabs my ass, pulling me deeper into his mouth. Oh, God, I didn't think it was possible, but I know that once again I'm going to come, and come hard. "Sage." My legs start to shake then he's there, over me and slamming into me so hard that my breath leaves on a whoosh and my orgasm that was building detonates, sending me screaming his name as I come, clutching him with every part of me.

"Fuck," he growls as his mouth lands on mine. Tasting myself on his tongue, I whimper against his.

Running my hands down the smooth skin of his back to his ass, I hold on to him, feeling his muscles contract every time he slams into me, and then he jerks my leg up over his arm. It changes the angle, causing him to hit something inside of me that I didn't even know existed. "I—"

"Do not fucking come until I tell you," he growls against my mouth as my muscles start to contract around his hard length.

"Sage...."

"We come together this time."

My legs start to shake and "Oh, God" leaves my mouth as I lean up, tucking my face against his chest.

"Look at me."

"Sage!"

"Look at me," he says, and my head falls back and my eyes meet his then close from the intensity in his gaze.

"Goddammit, Kim, open your eyes," he growls, slowing his thrusts, which causes the inferno that had been building inside me to turn into a slow burn.

"Keep your eyes on mine." He picks up the tempo and begins pounding into me harder as he holds my gaze. Dropping my leg from his arm, he leans forward and wraps his hand around my jaw as his thick length fills me. "This is us."

My eyes pull from his and I try to hide the fear that is suddenly overwhelming me. I should have told him. I should have told him before this, and now it's too late. He's once again clawed his way deep inside me, and I know I won't be able to get over the wounds from the loss of him this time.

"Look at me, baby." The edge in his tone has my eyes going to his. "Tell me that you feel this."

"I feel it." And I do, but now it's also accompanied by fear.

"It's going to be okay."

It's not.

Reaching between us, his thumb finds my clit, and my head arches back into the pillow as I contract around him, trying to pull him impossibly deeper.

"Perfect." He thumbs my clit, and that along with his cock filling me over and over has me once again on the edge. "Now." He takes my mouth on his quiet command and I fly over the edge, feeling his hips jerk as he loses himself inside me.

Panting for breath, I wrap my arms around him under his and my legs up higher on his hips as the aftermath of my orgasm sweeps through me like a tidal wave.

"Stay, please," I plea, tightening my hold on him when his hips shift like he's going to pull out of me, something I'm not even a little ready for.

"I'm not going anywhere," he whispers, but my limbs stay tight.

"Look at me, baby." I open my eyes that I didn't even know were closed and find him looking down at me. "You're beautiful. You're always beautiful, but when you come... Jesus, I don't think there is anything more extraordinary than the look you get in your eyes when you're about to come. But that's not what you gave me a second ago. I don't know what I saw, but I didn't like it."

"Sage—"

"Serious as shit, the first moment I saw you I thought for sure the universe was fucking with me. I think that's the moment I fell in love with you." Did he just say he loves me? "How? I do not fucking know. I didn't know who the fuck you were, but I swear to Christ, I knew there was something in you that had always belonged to me."

"Sage, I—"

"I'd never seen a woman as beautiful as you are, and now I know... not only are you beautiful here—" He runs his finger down the center of my face. "—I know you're beautiful here, too." He touches the skin over my heart. "That shit means everything to me, Kimberly. So whatever fucked up shit you have filtering around in your head right now, you need to let it go. I'm not going anywhere, and neither are you."

Oh, God, my throat burns as I swallow.

"Sa—" His mouth touches mine and he starts to move inside me once more, leaving me no chance to tell him that I feel the same way or about the secret I've been keeping from him.

Slowly waking from a deep sleep, I raise my arms up over my head and take a minute to enjoy the way every single inch of me feels beautifully used and sore. I've only felt like this once before, and it was after the first night I was with Sage. That night was good, but last night was a million times better. I don't know how many times he fucked me or made love to me, but it was a lot, and every single time, he made sure he got me off before taking care of himself.

And it was all fabulous.

Rolling to my side, I slowly open my eyes then blink when I see Sage with his eyes on me, dressed and sitting in a chair that he's pulled up close to the bed.

"Hey." I smile, getting up on an elbow. "What time is it?" I ask, looking from him to the clock on the side table, one of those old-time clocks with the bells on the top that ring loud when the alarm goes off. Seeing it's not even 7:00, my eyes go back to him, and it's then I register the look in his eyes, the odd energy pulsing through the room, and the fact he hasn't spoken a word to me since I woke up.

Dropping my eyes to the bed, I sit up, pulling the sheet with me as I go, and tuck it under my arms before looking at him once more. "Is everything okay? Di—" I freeze, and my stomach twists when I notice he's holding a transparent bright yellow bottle with a white twist-off top in his hands. One of my pill bottles.

One of my pill bottles. Oh, God.

"What are you doing with those?" I ask, and that's when his face changes and anger fills his features.

"I think I should be asking you what the fuck you're doing with these," he replies, shaking the bottle and causing the pills inside to rattle against each other. "Got something to tell me, Kimberly?"

"I...." I stop talking, not having the first clue of where to start.

"Got something to tell me?" he repeats loudly, and my heart constricts.

"Yes."

"Talk," he bites out, and I lean toward him with my hand out to touch him, but he sits back out of my reach. My hand balls into a fist that I drop to my side. "Tell me," he demands.

My heart pounds painfully against my ribcage and I study him, trying to find the words to make this better, the words to make him understand. "I'm sick."

"Yeah, I got that when I saw the fucking pharmacy in your makeup bag and did some research."

"My kidneys."

"I got that, too. What I want to fucking know is why the fuck you didn't tell me about this before." He shakes the pills again, the sound causing me to flinch.

"I was going to."

"Yeah, when?"

"I..." I shake my head, running my hand agitatedly through my hair. "When the time was right." I finally get out, and the energy beating against my skin goes scary.

"When the fuck would the time be right?" he roars, standing from the chair, and I get up on my knees in the bed.

"Please calm down," I whisper, and his eyes cut into mine, making me feel hollow.

"Calm down. You want me to calm down? Jesus, what the fuck, Kim?"

"Let me explain," I beg as tears burn up the back of my throat, making it hard to breathe.

"I don't want to fucking hear it," he roars, then his arm goes back and he throws the bottle of pills across the room, where it hits the wall with a loud thud, causing the cap to come off and pills to scatter like the pieces of my painfully beating heart across the floor. "You should have fucking talked to me." He shakes his head right before he's gone, storming through the bedroom door, and leaving me kneeling in the middle of his big bed, clutching the sheet to my chest as I breathe heavily.

Falling with my ass to my calves, my eyes close. I knew this was going to happen. I could have prevented it from happening, but I didn't, and now I'm left exactly how I knew I would be.

Shattered.

Feeling tears pool in my eyes, I shake my head. I can't cry, not yet. I need to get out of here before I have my breakdown. Falling to my side, I keep the sheet around me as I move and swing my legs over the side of the bed to put my feet to the floor. The moment I stand, my legs shake along with the rest of me.

"Keep it together, Kimberly," I whisper to myself as I go to my bag across the room on the floor, pick it up, and carry it to the bed. Hurrying, I throw on the first pieces of clothes I come across, a pair of loose sweats and a T-shirt from my college days. Dressed, I move around the room, picking up Sage's clothes from the last couple of days, which I take and put in the hamper. Then I find my nightie from last night, take it to the bathroom, and toss it in the trash under the sink.

Staring at my open makeup bag that I didn't get a chance to close up last night before Sage came in, my throat burns. My pills are all out of it and lining the counter like he had inspected each of them before he confronted me. I put everything back in the bag as I swallow over the knot forming in my throat, and I carry it to the bed to dump it in with my other stuff.

I spend the next ten minutes on my hands and knees picking up the pills that scattered across the wood floors, and once I'm pretty sure I've gotten all of them, I slip on my shoes, put my stuff on the floor, and strip the bed, folding the thick white duvet before taking the sheets to the laundry hamper in the closet.

Done, I give the room a once-over before I leave with my bag over my shoulder. I don't know if Sage left or not, but I'm not going to stick around to find out. Grabbing my keys off the island in the kitchen, I pull off his house key and drop it to the countertop, feeling that knot in my throat expand and tighten. I know I'm going to break at any second, and that pushes me to not walk but to run toward the door and out of the fairy tale house, where I had fallen in love with its owner.

Chapter 13

Kim

LISTENING TO THE phone ring and Sage's voice mail message click on, I close my eyes and pull the phone away from my ear.

"Honey," Mom calls, and I hang up, drop the phone to my lap, and look at her.

"Yeah?"

"You okay?" she asks, stepping into my room—or what used to be my room. My first year away at college, she'd kept the space exactly as I left it. My second year, she added a treadmill to the corner of the room. And by the time I graduated college, she'd added boxes, a sewing table, and a work desk.

"I'm okay," I lie.

She shakes her head. "Do you want to eat something?"

"No." My stomach rolls at the idea of food and I pull my quilt up around my waist.

"You really should eat."

"I know. I'm just not hungry right now," I say, and her face softens as she walks across the pink rug covering the floor toward where I'm sitting in the middle of my day bed before taking a seat next to me.

Running her hand down the hair at the side of my head, she pulls it back over my shoulder. "Things will be okay. Give him some time. He'll come around."

Nodding, I don't agree out loud. I can't. I left Tennessee on a whim, and now I'm wishing I hadn't. I should have waited Sage out. I should have let him cool down then talked to him. Instead, I ran away to my parents' house like a coward. I was so caught up in everything I was feeling and protecting myself that I didn't think about what Sage must have felt when he found out about my illness and how upset he was by the news. I didn't think about anything except running away from him.

"Have you tried calling him?"

"His phone is going to voice mail," I whisper, closing my eyes. I've called three times since I realized me leaving was a mistake. Every single time, his phone has gone right to voice mail, which means he's turned it off and doesn't want to hear from me.

"Don't cry, honey."

"I'm not," I lie again, wiping the proof of my lie from my cheeks.

She laughs softly while she wraps her arms around me and drags me to rest against her chest. "Even as a kid, you were stubborn." She pulls in a breath while running her hand down my hair. "Always so hard-headed." I hear the nostalgic tone in her voice, and my arms tighten around her middle as I bury my face against her. "Your dad and I learned early on to let you make mistakes. You wouldn't learn any other way. We could tell you fire was hot and that it could hurt you until we were blue in the face, but until you felt the heat from the flames yourself, you didn't believe us."

"Because I'm an idiot."

"No." She leans back, taking hold of my face, and I watch tears pool in her eyes. "You're not an idiot. You're one of the most amazing women I know. You're smart, loving, loyal, and inspiring. You make me want to be a better person. From the very first moment I held you in my arms, you made me want to be a better person, and your determination to do things your way is one of the things I admire about you."

"Mom." I close my eyes then open them back up when she gives me a gentle shake.

"If he doesn't find a way to accept you as you are, then he's not worthy of you," she says quietly, and I nod then close my eyes again as she leans in, pressing her lips to my forehead. "I'll bring you some soup. You need to eat and take your pills."

"Okay."

"Okay." She kisses my cheek before she stands and leaves the room, coming back a few minutes later with a bowl of hot soup.

After eating as much as I can stomach and taking my pills, I climb under my covers and call Sage one last time, feeling my heart clench in my chest when he doesn't answer and I once again get his voice mail.

"I'm sorry," I whisper before I hang up and drop my phone to the bed.

Tucking my hands under my cheek, it takes a while, but eventually I cry myself to sleep.

Sage

OPENING THE FRONT door, I head down the hall, past the kitchen, and straight to the bedroom. As I flip on the light, my jaw clenches when I see the room is picked up, the sheets off the bed, and the duvet folded neatly across the end of the bare mattress. Moving to the closet, I grab my duffle off the top shelf and drop it to the floor.

An hour ago, I got a voice mail from Jax telling me that Kim left town. He said Ellie called him earlier in the afternoon to tell him that Kim was taking off, that she stopped by the shop on her way to the airport to let her and Frankie know she was leaving and needed a few days off to go see her parents.

When I got that message, my anger that had dissipated throughout the day came back. Jax knew I had been out of cell range all day, but he didn't know Kim and I fought. He thought something happened to one of her parents, so he'd been trying to get a hold of me. Unfortunately, I had taken off to the mountains to think, which left me without phone service, and my delay in getting any calls all afternoon meant Kim was able to leave town without me knowing.

As much as I could understand her reason for leaving, I'm still pissed she did. Yes, we fought. Yes, I lost my shit. But Jesus, I just found out the woman I'm in love with is sick. Not just sick, but seriously fucking sick. And she didn't fucking tell me about it.

When I saw her pills and realized what was going on, I couldn't think straight. I should have left her in bed, gone to clear my head, and then talked to her when I was calm. But I didn't do what I should have done. The same fear I felt when I was told she was dead came back tenfold, making it impossible for me to be calm.

Dropping enough clothes for two days into my bag, I pull off my shirt, taking it to the laundry hamper, and see the sheets from the bed when I shove it in. I ignore the clench in my gut as I grab a clean tee off the shelf and put it on, then leave the closet and walk across the room to the bathroom.

Spotting her nightie in the trash under the sink when I grab my overnight kit, my teeth grind. If she thinks me washing the sheets and her trashing her nightie will erase things for her or for me, she's lost her damn mind. I waited too fucking long for my shot, and I'm not going to let her run off and build up walls. Not this time.

I'm done fucking around.

Heading back to the closet, I grab my duffle from the floor and leave, shutting off the lights as I go. My flight leaves in two hours, and I should have plenty of time to make it to the airport as long as there's no traffic on the highway. I pull my cell out of my front pocket and stop in the kitchen to get Chris's number from the eraser board on the fridge, and that's when I spot a key laying on the counter. Leaving the key where it is, I punch Chris's number into my cell and head for the door, calling him as I get in my car.

"Hello," he answers on the second ring, and my fingers tighten around my cell. I don't know if he'll be willing to help me out. He's so close to Kim. He's been her shoulder to lean on and her protector for a long time, and if he knows how shit went down this morning, there's a good chance he'll tell me to fuck off.

"I need you to text me Kim's parents' address."

"You're going after her?" he questions, sounding relieved as I start up the engine and back out then switch to drive and take off.

"Yeah."

"Thank fuck. I told the stupid woman not to leave, but when the hell does she ever fucking listen to me?" he mutters, and I shake my head then tighten my hand on the steering wheel when he continues. "She wanted to tell you. Sh—"

"She didn't," I cut him off. "She should have fucking told me, but she didn't. I came across her goddamn pills this morning by chance. I had no idea what the hell they were for, so I looked them up online. That's how I found out. Not by her telling me, but by fucking sitting in my bathroom at five in the morning, googling the shit on my phone."

"I'm sorry, man," he says quietly as I flip on my turn signal and pull onto the main road off my lane.

"Me, too."

"But you're still going after her, right?" he asks, sounding worried now.

"I told you I was. This isn't going to end us, and if I have my way, nothing ever will," I state, and the phone goes quiet for a long moment before he clears his throat.

"You love her."

"I love her," I confirm, thinking that doesn't come close to how I feel about her.

"I swear I'm going to kick her ass when you get her back to town," he growls, and for the first time since this morning, I smile.

"I'll let you know when that is," I say, pulling onto the highway. "Don't tell her I'm on my way. I don't want her to take off before I can make it to her parents' house."

"I won't."

"Text me the address. My flight leaves in a little under two hours."

"I'll text you. Let me know if you need anything else."

"Thanks." I hang up. Leaning back, I shove my cell back in my pocket and drive, making it to the airport just in time to catch my flight.

Arriving in Miami at a little after 2:00 p.m., I make my way through the airport with my bag over my shoulder toward the rental car pickup, thinking I should have driven. Between the wait at the airport, flight time, extra time in the air because of a storm on the ground, and the two hours it will take me to get to Kim's parents' house, I could have been to her, or at least close, by now.

Turning my cell off airplane mode as I walk, I put my phone to my ear to listen to the three voice mails I got while I was in the air. Two from my mom, the first telling me that she loves me and the second telling me I'm an ass and I better make things right with Kim and bring her home. I expect the third message to be her apologizing for being harsh, but it's not her. It's Kim whispering she's sorry.

Hearing the hurt in her voice, I rub the back of my neck and quicken my steps. As much as I want to call to tell her everything will be okay, I don't. What I need to say needs to be said face-to-face, no more hiding, no more bullshit. I've been taking it easy and going slow for her, but that shit is done. Now that I know about her illness, I will never take a moment with her for granted, and I sure as fuck won't allow her to, either.

Knocking on her parents' door two and a half hours later, I wait for someone to answer. I should have grabbed her dad's numbers off the fridge before I left, but I didn't think about it at the time. Clenching my hands as the porch light comes on, I take a step back, not sure what to expect.

"Took you long enough," her dad, Donald, says in greeting as he opens the door to me, and my brows draw together. "I knew you'd show up. Though, I did expect you a few hours ago, to be honest." He steps back, letting me inside and closing the door behind me.

"I was in the mountains. I didn't have phone service, so I had no idea she'd taken off until a few hours ago," I tell him, and he nods.

"Figured it had to be something. When she showed up, I knew that if you were the man I thought you were, you'd be here to set her head straight." He pats my shoulder. "Glad to see I was right about you," he states, and my muscles that had coiled on the drive here relaxed.

I wasn't sure what kind of situation I would be walking into, but I knew one way or another I would be talking to Kim, and it's a relief to know I won't be fighting with her parents to get to her.

"Thank God." At those quiet words, I turn my head and watch Kim's mom, Pattie, come toward me with her arms open. Giving me a hug, she leans back, patting my cheek and sighing. "I told her everything would be okay," she says, and then her eyes narrow slightly, reminding me a lot of my mom. "Everything is okay, right?" she questions, studying me.

I nod. "It will be."

"Good." She shakes her head. "She's been a mess since she got here. I probably shouldn't tell you that, but it's the truth. So if you go in there and she tries to play it cool, don't let her fool you."

"I won't."

"All right, go on then. Her room is at the end of the hall on the left."

"Thanks." I lift my chin to both her parents before heading down the hall. Reaching the room, I pause with my hand on the handle and pull in a deep breath. I turn the knob, but before I have a chance to push in, the door is pulled from my grasp.

"You're here," Kim squawks, right before she's throwing herself at me and wrapping her arms around my neck. Mine instinctively wrap around her middle, hauling her tighter against me as she sobs. "I'm so sorry."

Picking her up, I carry her farther into the room and kick the door closed behind me before searching through the dark for the bed. Seeing it across the room, I move us there then settle her sideways on my lap.

"Calm down," I whisper, and she cries harder, clutching me as she apologizes over and over again, which kills me. I'm the one who should be apologizing for losing my shit, being a dick, and taking off. "Please, baby, calm down," I beg as her tears rip me open one-by-one.

"I should have told you. I should have told you, but I didn't. I... I was a-afraid that you would... wouldn't be able to handle it a-an... and that you would leave me," she says between sobs, and my stomach turns.

I did exactly what she thought I would do. I flipped out then took off. I didn't tell her that we would talk about it when I had a chance to calm down, so she didn't know I wasn't leaving her.

"I'm sorry, baby, I shouldn't have left things like I did. I just needed to clear my head," I tell her, tucking my face into her neck and breathing in her warm scent.

"I... I tried to call you."

"I went to the mountains, so I didn't have service. I wasn't leaving you. I just needed to think for a bit."

"I'm an idiot."

"You're not." I rub her back, and thankfully after a few minutes, her sobs quiet down. "I need to see you," I tell her quietly, and she leans away from me. A second later, soft light fills the room, and her tear-stained face looks up at me. Using my thumb, I wipe away the tears from under her eyes and study her beautiful face. "I was scared," I admit, and her body jolts like she's shocked by that statement. "So, fucking scared." I run my fingers across her soft cheek, catching a tear before it falls. "I can't imagine a world without you in it."

"I'm not going anywhere," she whispers, lifting her hand to my jaw. My eyes close and my forehead drops to rest against hers as my arms tighten around her, the thought of losing her too much for me to handle.

"Marry me."

The words are out before I can catch them, but now that I've said them out loud, I know that's exactly what I want. I want her to be my wife. I want to wake up with her every morning and go to bed with her every night. I want to spend the rest of my life making her happy.

"What?" she breathes.

I pull back to look into her eyes, and repeat, "Marry me."

"We—"

"I don't care how long we've been together," I cut her off, knowing exactly what she was going to say. "I know I want a life with you. I know now, just like I knew the moment I met you, that you were made for me."

"Sage." Her eyes close and her head shakes.

"Just say yes. I won't give up until you say yes."

"You're serious." She opens her eyes, studying mine, and I hold her gaze letting her see the truth there.

"Never been more serious about anything in my life."

"I'm not dying. I'm sick, but I have a long life ahead of me," she says softly, and I pull her closer.

"Then say you'll live your long life with me," I urge, and her bottom lip goes between her teeth. "I love you, Kimberly, from the moment we met, and since then, I've fallen deeper in love with you. Tell me you don't feel the same. Tell me from the second we met you haven't felt this pull between us, like our lives have always been intertwined in some way. Tell me we're not meant to be together."

"I…" She swallows, closing her eyes. "I love you, too. I just… I don't want you to want to marry me or to be with me just because you think my time is limited."

"Everyone's time is limited, baby," I say, gently taking her face in my hands. "No one knows when their time on earth will come to an end. I could die tomorrow, but if that happens, I want to know I died meaning something to you."

"You mean everything to me."

"Then tell me you'll marry me."

"God, you are really serious. You're crazy."

"Say you'll marry me, Kimberly. Tell me you'll be my wife."

"I'm not getting married in Vegas or at the courthouse," she whispers, and my heart leaps in my chest.

Taking her mouth once more, I roll her to her back and pull away slightly to look down at her. "Is that a yes?"

"God, I'm seriously as crazy as you are." She closes her eyes then opens them back up, wrapping her hand around the side of my neck. "Yes."

"Thank fuck." I kiss her deeply but pull back before things can get out of hand. "Your parents are down the hall," I remind her quietly when she looks up at me disappointedly, and then her eyes close.

"Right." She swallows, lying back on the bed. I curl her into my side, noticing the early morning sun filtering in through the closed blinds. Running my fingers down her side, I smile as she cuddles deeper into my chest. "I have a request," she says quietly, and my hand pauses on her hip.

"What is it?"

"Next time you're mad at me, can you take time to cool down before we talk? You..." She pauses then moves, getting up on an elbow to look at me. "That's the second time you've gotten mad at me and flipped out without giving me a chance to explain."

"I'm sorry, baby," I reply, hating that she's right.

"Me, too." She shrugs, running her fingers across jaw. "I hate that I didn't tell you before and you had to find out the way you did."

"It's done. We're moving on."

"Yeah," she agrees, resting her head back against my pec. "Your mom and mine are going to fight like crazy. You know that, right?" she asks, breaking into the quiet after a few minutes.

"Why?" I dip my head down to look at her, and she tips hers back to meet my gaze.

"My mom has been secretly planning my wedding since I was sixteen when she took me prom dress shopping at a bridal shop. Judging by the way your mom acted at dinner, she is the same way, or she's got ideas of how she wants things to be."

"We'll go to Vegas and make it easy on them."

"I already said I'm not going to Vegas."

"I'm not giving up on the idea. How long do you think it will take you to plan this wedding anyway?"

"It will be *our* wedding," she mutters, tweaking my nipple, and I clamp my hand over hers, feeling her cheek move as she smiles. "I don't know how long it will take. Probably a year or so."

"Pardon?"

"A year, maybe a little longer," she reiterates, looking at me.

"I'm not waiting a fucking year to marry you."

"We'll see."

Rolling to my side, I get up on an elbow and look down at her. "I'm not waiting a year," I repeat.

"I want my mom and dad to have this. It's important to me that they get these times with me. I'm it for them. There are no other kids for them to marry off. I know my dad will want to walk me down the aisle, and my mom will want to help me find a dress and plan the wedding."

She's right; it's only her. I have five brothers and sisters. If I don't have a wedding, my parents will be able to get that from one of my siblings. But for Kim's parents, it's only her, and as much as I want her to be tied to me, I want her to be happy and her parents to be able to share that with her. They deserve that, and so does she.

"All right," I agree reluctantly, and her face softens. "I'll try to be patient, but I can't make any promises."

"Thank you." She leans up, brushing her mouth against mine, and then that brush turns into her whimpering into my mouth as her tongue toys with mine and my hand finds her breast.

"We're staying in a hotel tonight," I growl as soon as I pull my mouth from hers.

"What?" She blinks her eyes open to look at me.

"I can't make love to you here, and I really want to make love to you," I say, pressing my hard-on into her hip, and her mouth forms a soft O. "Exactly. So tonight, we'll stay in a hotel. That way I can take you whenever and however I want."

"Okay," she concurs, then she yawns and I follow hers with one of my own.

"But right now, let's sleep," I say quietly, moving her back into my arms.

She tucks her body down my side with her head in the crook of my arm, and I listen to her yawn again right before her quiet snoring fills the room. Smiling at the sound, I kiss the top of her head then lie here until long after she's fallen asleep, thinking, *Fucking finally.*

Chapter 14

Sage

SITTING ON THE side of the bed, I rub my hands down my face then turn and let my eyes wander over Kim when she shifts behind me. Carefully sliding a piece of hair off her forehead behind her ear, my heart squeezes in my chest when she moves toward my touch, even in sleep.

Last night, we didn't talk about her illness. Honestly, I'm scared as fuck to find out what it all means. The idea of losing her isn't something I want to even consider, but I need to know what's in store for her and for us. Meaning: I'm going to have to get over my shit and talk to her about it. I know she said she has a long life ahead of her, but what will that life entail?

Pulling in a deep breath, I stand from the bed and grab my duffle from the floor on the way to the bathroom attached to the room. I close the door quietly behind me and open my bag to put on a pair of shorts and a tee then quickly take care of business, brushing my teeth before leaving the bedroom. Stepping out into the hall, I walk slowly toward the kitchen. I didn't get a good look at the house last night when I came in. Even when I went out to get my bag, I did it quickly, but seeing it now, I can tell both Don and Pattie are proud of their daughter.

Covering the wall in the hallway are pictures of Kim and her parents, Kim with family and friends, and others with just Kim by herself. I stop to look at one of them more closely and smile. Kim looks like she's probably ten years old, and she's smiling so brightly I can actually feel her happiness through the picture. Leaning in to get a better look at the grainy black-and-white image, I notice the older woman in the photo with her isn't kissing her cheek like I thought she was. She's whispering in Kim's ear as Kim stirs something in a mixing bowl.

"That was my mom." Turning to look at Donald when he speaks, I find him standing a few feet away with sorrow-filled eyes. "She died not long after that photo was taken. Kim was her baby, and her only grandchild."

"I'm sorry."

"Long time ago." He takes a step closer. "But the pain of losing a parent always cuts deep. It didn't help that after we lost my mom, we lost my dad. He died two weeks after her from heart failure. Really, I think he couldn't live in this world without the woman he loved," he confides, coming toward me then pointing at another picture; this one of an older gentleman, with Kim sitting on his lap holding a newspaper open and smiling up at him as he smiles down at her. "My parents were against Pattie and me adopting," he says, catching me off guard.

I look at the man in the photo, trying to see if I missed something, but all I see is happiness in his eyes as he smiles down at a five-year-old Kim.

"They thought that if Pattie and I were meant to have a child, we would have a child. They grew up in a different time. Things like infertility and adoption weren't talked about." He shakes his head then a smile twitches his lips. "That all changed the moment we came home with Kim wrapped tight in a pink blanket with only her chubby little face out. The second they saw her, she became a piece of them. She was their world, and no one could tell them different."

"I'm glad she had that and felt that from them, and you guys."

"Me, too." He lets out a breath then looks at the photos once more before meeting my gaze. "We need to talk. How about we get a cup of coffee then head out back by the pool where it's quiet?" he suggests, and I lift my chin then follow him down the hall, through a sitting room with two well used recliners and a TV, and into a large, updated, eat-in kitchen. On the opposite side, there are sliding glass doors that look out over a small patch of grass and the pool.

Getting a cup of coffee, I follow him out the back door and around the side of the house to a covered patio, where I take a seat across from him on one of the wicker chairs around a short glass table. Looking around, I can't imagine growing up here. Houses are lined up one after another, front-to-back, and even with the wrought iron fence that surrounds the yard, there is still no real sense of privacy.

Pulling my attention from the yard when Donald clears his throat, I notice he's set a small black box on the table between us. "Are you going to marry my girl?" he asks.

I sit forward in my chair and set my cup of coffee on the table before I answer. "I am." My elbows drop to my knees and I lean in, dropping my voice. "I hope we have your blessing. If not, I'm sorry, but I'm still going to marry her," I state, and he smiles before hiding it by taking a sip of coffee.

"You have my blessing, but I want a favor," he inserts, and I hold his stare. "I know it's a lot to ask a man like you, but I'm going to ask all the same." Keeping my eyes on his, I wait for him to speak, and then watch as he reaches forward to nudge the black box toward me. "That was my mom's. I don't have a son to pass it down to, and honestly, even if I did, what's in that box has always been Kim's. Please, open it."

Picking up the small velvet box, I flip the lid and study the ring inside. It's beautiful and unusual, not something you would find at a jewelry store today. The band is made of thick white gold filigree work, and it has one large deep blue sapphire stone set into the middle of the ring, with much smaller diamond chips around the outside.

"What's this?" I pull my eyes from the ring, wondering what to say to him.

"Kim loved that ring. When she was growing up, my mom used to tell her stories about the women in our family who once wore that ring, and through each of those stories, she fell a little more in love with it. She made me promise her that one day, when she got married, that ring would be hers. I know it goes against tradition, but—"

"I'll give her the ring," I rumble, trying to keep the emotion out of my voice. "It means something to you, and it means something to her. I'll give it to her."

"Pattie and I got lucky," he says, and my head jerks back. But he leans forward, getting close and wrapping his hand around the back of my neck the way my dad does when he wants me to hear what he's saying—really hear what he's saying to me. "All any parent wants for their child is happiness. You're a good man, the kind of man who will take care of her, the kind who will find a way to make her happy and keep her that way. She found that in you, which means we can live the rest of our days not worrying about the type of man she will end up with. Because we already know he's exactly the kind of man we would have chosen for her. That's rare, which means we're lucky."

Holding his eyes, feeling those words wash over me, I nod then lean in and touch my forehead to his. Him telling me that I'm good enough for his daughter, good enough for his family, means everything to me, and I will work hard every day for the rest of my life to make sure I never let him or Pattie down.

"Thank you," I murmur, and his hand squeezes before he lets me go. I sit back, closing the lid on the box and putting it in my pocket.

"I was looking for you two. Did you guys want breakfast?" Pattie asks, coming around the corner, and I pick up my coffee and stand when Donald does.

"Are you making eggs benedict?" Donald asks, kissing the side of her head.

"Is that a request for me to make eggs benedict?" She raises a brow.

"It's Kim's favorite." Donald smiles down at her, shrugging.

"It's *your* favorite." She smacks his chest. "Don't you think I've caught onto that trick by now?" She shakes her head at him then looks at me. "Is Kim up?"

"She wasn't, but I'm heading that way now."

"Tell her I need her help making breakfast."

"Will do," I agree before I head inside, dropping my empty cup in the sink. I move toward the bedroom and open the door, finding Kim up and sitting on the side of the bed. She's looking at her phone, with her fingers moving quickly over the screen.

"Morning." She lifts her head and smiles at me as I shut the door, and then her phone dings and her eyes drop back down to it. Shaking her head at whatever she's reading, she starts typing once more.

"What's up?" I ask.

"Chris is mad at me." Taking a seat next to her, I rest my lips to her bare shoulder, watching her type and having no clue what the hell the two of them are talking about, because none of it makes sense to me. Something about a horse and carriage and an ugly, pink, poufy dress. "Have you been up a while?" she asks when she stops typing once more and her eyes come to me over her shoulder.

"Not long, but your mom said she needs your help making breakfast."

"Is she making eggs benedict?"

"She is. Your dad said it's your favorite."

"It's *his* favorite, but because it's so bad for him, my mom only makes it when I'm home." She smiles, but then her phone dings again and she sighs, ignoring it. "I told Chris that everything worked out, but he's still pissed I didn't listen to him when he told me not to leave town."

"You shouldn't have left town," I agree, and she pouts her bottom lip. Dropping my eyes to her mouth, I lean forward, kiss the pout away, and then pick her up, moving her to straddle my lap.

"Sage," she whimpers, pressing her tits into my chest as I smooth my hands up the warm skin of her back under her tank. As my tongue slips into her mouth, I slide one hand around her waist to cup her breast. "Oh," she breathes as I skim my thumb over her erect nipple. Her hips grind hard into mine, and I fight back a curse. "Ignore it," she pants against my mouth as her phone starts to ding in rapid succession.

"Perfect." I cup both her breasts and she rocks against me, moaning into my mouth. But then she whimpers when I pull back as her phone starts ringing. Seeing it's Chris calling, I pick it up and put it to my ear. "You're gonna have to fight with Kim when she gets back to town," I growl in frustration.

"Right," he mutters, and then continues, "but let her know that next time, she's out of the running for my best woman."

"I'll let her know," I agree before hanging up and pulling Kim's mouth back down toward mine. Then I stand with her wrapped around me as I hold onto her ass.

"What did he say?" she asks, kissing and licking my neck as I toss her phone to the bed behind me.

"He said next time, you're out of the running to be his best woman."

"I'm so sure," she hisses, lifting her mouth from my skin. "No one else would be able to deal with him."

"You two can sort that out when you get back." I nip her bottom lip then set her on the vanity in the bathroom.

"You're right." Her eyes darken and her hands push my shirt up my chest then over my head. "When are we going back?"

"I leave tomorrow."

"You have to leave tomorrow?" She frowns, looking up at me, and I rest my hand around the side of her neck and lower my face toward hers.

"I have to get back to work, so I need to catch a flight tomorrow evening. I know it's not a long visit, but this trip wasn't planned, baby."

"Right." She nods, tightening her legs around my hips. "I'll change my fight and go back with you." Studying her for a long moment, I wonder how selfish I should be. Part of me wants to take her back with me, but I know her parents miss her and they don't get to see her often enough.

"You should stay and finish your visit."

"I'm ready to go home." Her hands on the back of my neck pull my face down toward hers.

"Home," I murmur. Liking the sound of that, I brush my lips over hers, seeing her face soften. "When we get back, I'll talk to the guys and we'll get you moved out of your place and into the lake house."

"But—"

"No buts, baby." I give her neck a squeeze and use my other hand to pull her hips tighter against mine. "We're starting our life together. I don't want to hear you think it's too soon for you to move in with me."

"I wasn't going to say that," she grumbles, dropping her head back.

I smile. "Yeah? Then what were you going to say?"

"I don't know," she lies, and my smile turns into a grin.

Running my thumb under her chin, I touch my mouth to hers then pull back, keeping our eyes locked. "I'm willing to wait for you to take my last name. But I won't wait on this. I want you with me, in my bed, under my roof, and in my life in every way possible."

"Okay," she whispers.

"Okay," I state, and I kiss her forehead then take her mouth before I force her to release me so she can get ready.

Kim

"CHRIST," SAGE RUMBLES as I pull my dress off over my head and drop it to the sand at my feet, leaving me in nothing but my bikini.

Moving my eyes over his shirtless torso, I feel my mouth go dry. He's always beautiful, but with the warm Florida sun shining down on him and the ocean behind him, making his eyes stand out even more, he's gorgeous.

He told me when we were having breakfast with my parents that he had never been to the beach, so I made a decision to rectify that. I told my parents I was sorry for cutting my trip short but that Sage and I were going to head to Miami to spend the day at the beach before catching our flight back to Tennessee tomorrow afternoon. My mom was bummed, but she promised she would talk Dad into coming to Tennessee in a few weeks, and my dad was surprisingly okay with the new change of plans.

"Do you really expect me to keep my hands off you?" Sage asks, breaking into my thoughts, and I realize then that he's no longer a few feet away. He's in front of me, with his fingers curved possessively around my hip and his eyes burning into every inch of my exposed skin.

"There are a lot of people here," I point out, and his fingers dig in as his eyes move to look around us before coming back to mine. "So you don't have to keep your hands off me. You just have to keep things PG." His eyes narrow like he's not happy about that idea. Knowing that if I'm not careful, things will get out of hand between us, I take his hand. "Come on." I lead him down to the water and smile as the ocean skims across my feet, only to shriek a moment later when he scoops me up in his arms and carries me out into the waves until he's waist-deep. "Sage!"

"What?" He grins, sliding me down his chest, and my legs wrap around his hips as my arms lock around his shoulders. "I don't need everyone seeing my hard-on, so you're going to help me hide it."

"I'm not sure me being wrapped around you is going to help with that," I tell him truthfully as my core pulses at the feel of his erection against my clit. I've been on edge since the moment he showed up at my parents', and every second with him is making my need for him grow.

"Then I guess we'll be out here a while." He kisses me, and my head tips to the side to deepen it. I press closer against him, as close as I can get, as his tongue tangles with mine. He tastes like the ocean, sun, and Sage, and I realize instantly it's a taste I don't just like. It's something I love and want much, *much* more of. Feeling him pull back, I blink my eyes open. "I love you."

"I love you, too," I whisper, moving my fingers up the column of his throat to the underside of his jaw, watching his face go softer than I've ever seen it. "What?" I ask, but he doesn't answer. He takes my hand in his, and then my whole world stops and tears fill my eyes as he slides the most beautiful ring I've ever seen onto my finger.

"Baby," he whispers, pulling me closer, and a sob I can't control climbs up my throat. Dropping my head to his shoulder, I hold on to him with every part of me.

"H... how?" I finally get out, and his hand moves to wrap around the back of my neck, holding me tight.

"Your dad gave it to me."

Leaning back, I take hold of his face then look at my hand resting against his jaw and the ring sitting on my finger. A ring that was, at one time, my MeMe's ring. She used to tell me stories about the ring when I was little, but my favorite one was always how she and my papa got together and ended up married.

They only went out two times before they got engaged, and not long after that, he left to go fight in World War II. She promised him before he left that she would wait for him to return and would never take the ring off. Even after friends and family told her that he would probably never come home, she kept her promises. She told me she knew that as long as she was wearing his ring that he would find his way back to her. Thankfully, she had been right. A year and a half after he left, he showed up on her doorstep and they got married right away. They stayed married and happy until they passed away within a few weeks of each other. They loved each other from the moment they met, and I knew even as a little girl how very special and rare that was.

"Tell me you're happy, baby."

My eyes meet his and I shake my head, trying to fight back the tears burning up the back of my throat. "I'm happy." I rest my forehead to his and run my fingers along his cheek. "Thank you for giving this to me. Thank you for giving me everything."

"If I could give you the world, I would."

"I don't need the world. All I need is you." I kiss him, but he takes over, making it deeper and wetter, only to pull back smiling a moment later when someone yells "Get a room!" in our direction, making me laugh.

"Maybe we should get out of the water," he suggests, carrying me back to the sand, where we sprawl out on the blanket I brought. Pulling my sunglasses out of my hair, I put them on then grab my bottle of water. I take a drink as Sage grabs his bag and pulls out his phone that's ringing.

"It's my mom," he mutters, kissing my shoulder, and I watch him put the cell to his ear then feel my eyes widen when the first words out of his mouth are, "It's all good, Mom. Swear. She even agreed to marry me."

"Oh my God! You did not just tell her like that," I hiss as I hear Sophie shout out in glee.

"Baby, she's gonna find out," he mutters, and I shake my head then

181

grab my phone and dial my own mom. The last thing I need is her finding out from someone else—that someone else being Chris—that Sage and I are getting married.

"Hey, honey. Is everything okay?" she asks as soon as she answers, and I bite my bottom lip, not sure how to go about telling her the news. I know she adores Sage, but I also know Sage and I haven't been together long. "Honey?"

"Sage asked me to marry him," I blurt, and then turn to glare at Sage when he chuckles.

"Oh, baby girl...." She goes quiet, and I hear her move as she tells my dad my news. "We are so happy for you."

"Are you?"

"Yes. Why are *you* not happy?" she asks, and I hear the concern in her voice and close my eyes.

"I'm so happy it's scary," I tell her honestly, feeling Sage's lips rest against my temple and his arm wrap around me.

"That's the best kind of happy, honey. Hold on to that."

"I will," I promise, leaning into Sage as I stare out at the ocean and the setting sun.

"We'll come visit soon and get to planning. I can't imagine Sage is going to give us much time to plan a wedding," she mutters, and I smile as tears fill my eyes.

"I love you, Mom. Thank you for everything, and I mean *everything*," I whisper then clear my throat. "Tell Dad I love him."

"I will," she agrees. "Love you. We'll talk soon."

"'Kay."

I hang up and drop my cell, listening to Sage as he finishes up his call with his mom, smiling as he mutters, "You're gonna have to sort all that out with Kim and her mom. I'm not getting into it." Turning my smile toward him, he shakes his head then kisses my nose. "Yeah, love you guys, too. Talk to you when we're back." He pulls the phone from his ear and drops it to the blanket at his hip. "Mom and Dad want us at dinner when we get back."

"Sure," I agree quietly, and his eyes roam over me and heat in a way that makes my skin tingle.

"Are you ready to go back to the hotel?"

"Have you seen enough of the beach?"

"Yeah," he rumbles, and I breathe a sigh of relief then whimper when the backs of his fingers brush lightly across my nipple through my bikini top. "But I haven't seen enough of this, and I'm looking forward to exploring every inch."

"Sage...."

"Let's get packed up, baby." His mouth touches mine, then his tongue touches my bottom lip before he stands, pulling me with him.

Shaking with want, I hurry along with him and get us packed up. We rush to the car and back to the hotel, where he spends the rest of the night exploring me, and I return the favor.

Chapter 15

Sage

"H URRY," KIM MOANS against my ear as I drop our bags to the floor. Kicking the front door closed behind us, I carry her into the house and down the hall past the kitchen and into the bedroom.

Our flight home was torture; even after spending last night and most of this morning inside of her, it still wasn't enough. Pressing her back to the wall just inside the bedroom, I take her mouth, kissing her deeper while I slide my hand into the front of her jeans, finding her already wet and ready for me. I groan as I circle her clit then grit my teeth as her hips jerk, causing her pussy to bump the tip of my cock.

"Sage," she breathes, and I lean back, keeping my fingers on her clit.

"This is all your fault. You're the one who insisted we couldn't fuck in the bathroom on the plane," I tell her, capturing her waist with one hand before moving it up her side to rest under her breast.

"Yeah, because it would have been impossible and gross," she pants, tugging at my tee. She slides it and her hands up my abs and pecs to my shoulders before stripping it off over my head.

"We could have made it work," I say, and her hips jerk again, making my cock twitch.

"I need you inside of me."

"No, I want to enjoy this for a minute." Her head falls back with a thud against the wall as her eyes slide closed. I pull down the front of her shirt and run my thumb over her nipple while watching as she rides my fingers.

Gorgeous.

"Please… I need you," she whispers, and I pull her from the wall and lead her across the room toward the bed then settle her on her feet in front of me. As soon as her feet touch the floor, she drops to her knees, running her hands up my thighs and over my cock through my jeans. Meeting my gaze her hands slide up, and then her fingers move along the waist of my jeans, releasing the button before sliding the material down over my hips.

Realizing our height difference in this position, I move and take a seat on the side of the bed, making room for her between my legs.

"Perfect," she whispers, wrapping her hand around me. Her eyes stay locked with mine and her mouth opens over the head of my cock, sucking just the tip as she flicks her tongue along the underside.

"Christ." My hands wrap into her hair and I pull it away from her face so I can watch her take me down her throat. Feeling her moan around me, my head falls back as she uses her hand in sync with her mouth, twisting and pulling while sliding her mouth up and down my length. Tightening my hold on her hair, I look down at her, finding her lust-filled eyes on mine. "Stop," I growl, but she doesn't. She takes me deeper, so deep I bump the back of her throat. "Fuck." I pull her head back, forcing her to release me with a pop.

"I wasn't done."

"You were." I tilt her head to the side and take her mouth in a hard kiss before nipping her bottom lip. "Lose your shirt and bra," I growl, and she leans back just far enough to tug her tee off over her head, and then her hands move behind her back to unhook her bra, letting it fall from her shoulders. Taking her in, I pull her up to her feet to stand in front of me.

I move my mouth down her neck to her bare shoulder, licking and nibbling my way down and across her chest before pulling first one nipple then the other into my mouth. I wrap my hands around her hips and slowly slide her jeans down her legs, letting the material pool at her feet. Lifting her in my arms, I twist and drop her to the bed behind me then stand, taking a step back to watch her writhe under my stare.

Kicking off my shoes and jeans, I wrap my hand around my cock and stroke while she watches, her tongue coming out to touch her plump bottom lip as my cock leaks. "Open your legs for me," I command.

She hesitates only a second before her legs spread, and I see the lips of her pussy glistening with arousal. Putting my knees on the bed, I crawl up between her thighs and she arches against me and wraps her hand around my cock, stroking once before I pull her hand away. "Honey, please," she moans as I pull her arms up over her head, wrapping them around the headboard.

"Hold on and don't let go," I demand, and her eyes heat as her fingers tighten so much her knuckles turn white.

Dropping my mouth to hers, I kiss her in approval then lick my way down her body, between her breast and over her stomach. Her hips lift when I kiss her pubic bone, and then she whimpers as I slide two fingers through her folds.

Drenched.

Holding her thighs open, I run my tongue up her center and groan, lifting her higher into my mouth and circling her clit.

"Sage," she pants as her back arches off the bed. Focusing on the tight bundle of nerves, I lift my eyes and watch her head thrash side-to-side and her chest rise and fall rapidly.

Beautiful.

Filling her with two fingers, I pull her clit into my mouth and flick my tongue over it, hearing her cry out. As her pussy starts to contract and suck my fingers deeper, I work her over until she comes shouting my name, and then gentle my strokes as she comes down from her orgasm. Kissing my way up her body, I adjust her hips then bury myself deep in one stroke.

"Don't move." I slide my cock slowly out then back into her wet heat, feeling her walls contract on every downward thrust, sending me deeper.

"Sage, please." Her nails scrape down my back, and I bite back a curse as my balls draw tight.

Placing my forehead against hers I take a few deep breaths, trying to control the sudden urge to come as her pussy tightens once more. Leaning back once I've gained control over myself, I slide my hands down the back of her thighs to her knees then grab her ankles and pull them around my hips.

"Hold me tight. Lock your ankles," I demand, and her feet hook behind my back as her arms tighten around my sides. Dropping forward, I put my fist to the bed on either side of her head and glide in and out of her, loving the way her pussy tightens on each outstroke.

"Yes," she breathes, circling her hips to meet each thrust. I know I'm going to come if I don't change positions, and I'm not ready for this to be over. Not yet.

I roll us until my back hits the bed, and her hand lands on my chest as her wild eyes meet mine. "Fuck me," I demand, rocking her against me, and her head falls back, causing her hair to run across the top of my thighs. Fuck, this position isn't any better for my situation. Seeing her sitting on my lap, full of my cock, her breasts swaying in front of my face, makes my balls draw up even more. Leaning up, I hear her gasp as I slide impossibly deeper, bumping her cervix.

Wrapping my hand around the back of her neck, I pull her mouth down to mine as I use my free hand around her hip to rock her into me. "Just like that," I urge, and her hips dip and roll as her hands travel up my chest to my shoulders, which she uses as leverage to bring herself down hard while my hips slam up to meet her.

"Sage!"

"Me, too," I hiss against her mouth as her pussy starts to pulse around my cock, pulling my orgasm from me. As I fuck up into her, her mouth drops to my neck and she moans against my skin. I groan against hers as I hold her down against me, coming hard. Resting my forehead to her chest, I listen to her breathing even out, and mine does the same.

"Maybe after I've had you a few million times, I won't want to come the second I'm inside you," I say, hearing her laugh and feeling that sound slide through her and into my skin. Placing a kiss to her collarbone, I look at her beautiful face, wild hair, and eyes shining with happiness, and I shake my head while my cock twitches. "Then again, maybe not," I admit, and she touches her smiling mouth to mine. Locking my arms around her, I roll us to our sides, keeping us connected as I settle her against me.

"Are you hungry?" she asks after a few minutes, and I smile, sifting my fingers through the hair at the side of her head.

"Are you asking because you're hungry?"

"I'm not really hungry, but all I had to eat today was an orange at the airport. I need to eat something so I can take my pills," she says, and I instantly pull out of her then roll off the bed, dragging her with me as I go.

"Sage…?"

"Come on. Let's get you some food. Are your pills in your purse or your luggage?" I question, starting to leave the room, and she latches onto my arm, holding me in place.

"I'm okay."

"You're not okay," I growl, picking up my shirt from the floor, attempting to put it over her head, only to have her bat my hands away. She takes a step back and plants her hands on her hips.

"I've been dealing with this for a long time and know what I need to do to take care of myself. So please, don't start going all weird on me. I don't need that or want it."

"Baby—"

"No, don't 'baby' me, Sage Mayson. I need you to hear me when I tell you this. I'm okay, and the minute I stop being okay, I'll tell you."

"Will you?" I ask, crossing my arms over my chest, and her body jolts back and her eyes fill with anger and frustration. *Fuck.*

"You...." She pulls her eyes from me then jerks her hand through her hair while looking around. Spotting whatever it is she's looking for, she moves across the room and picks up her shirt. She starts to put it on, but I grab her around her waist from behind before she can.

"Let me go."

"Never." My hold on her tightens as I lead her across the room to the bed and fall into it with her in my arms.

"Sage!"

"I shouldn't have asked that."

"No, you shouldn't have." She wiggles, trying to break my hold.

"I'm sorry, baby, but I have no fucking idea how bad this is or what you need from me."

"I need you to let me go," she growls, trying to pull free.

"Anything but that. Now talk to me," I prompt, turning her in my arms to face me. As soon as we're front-to-front, I tighten my arms around her and toss my leg over both of hers.

"You are so annoying!" she screams, trying to shove free, but I don't let go or loosen up.

"Talk to me," I demand, giving her a shake, and her eyes fly up to meet mine then narrow, showing just how pissed off she is.

"If I were bigger, I swear to God I would kick you in your balls."

"Then you'd be kissing them better, baby, so it's a good thing you're not bigger," I mutter, and she glares.

"Put your balls near my mouth and I'm biting them off." She snaps her teeth together.

I try not to laugh, but I still feel a smile twitch my lips. I've never seen her like this, and it's both adorable and hot as fuck. Not the part about biting off my balls, but the rest. "Talk to me."

"Fine," she pants, narrowing her eyes on me when she realizes she's stuck. "My kidney disease is at a stage three right now. I still have about fifty-eight percent function in my kidneys, which isn't great, but since I got a new doctor and started my new diet, my function has improved. The last time I went in for lab work, my numbers were even better, putting me at a functioning rate of sixty-one percent."

Her body slowly starts to relax against mine as she continues. "For a while, I wasn't doing so well because of stress and my diet, but I'm better. I will never be one hundred percent. There is no cure for what I have, but right now, I'm all right. And I will keep fighting and working at being all right. If my numbers start to go down again, I will get on a transplant list and go from there."

"How did it happen?" I ask, and she closes her eyes briefly.

"The doctors think that it was my biological mom's drug use that was the cause of it. She was addicted to crack when she got pregnant with me and Kelly, and didn't stop using until the day she gave birth to us."

"What the fuck?"

"She was an addict," she whispers, dropping her eyes from mine. "Kelly and I were both addicted when we were born. We had to stay in the hospital for three weeks after we were delivered while we were both carefully monitored and weaned off the drugs the hospital gave us so that we didn't suffer from withdrawals."

"And they let your birth mom keep Kelly?"

"The system is messed up," she replies quietly, tipping her head back to look at me. "She told the doctors and the social workers that she wanted to change and they believed her, so they set up my adoption and got her the help she needed in order for her to take Kelly home with her. My parents were there for the three weeks I was in the hospital. They said after she made the decision to give me up, she never saw me again."

"Baby." I tuck her head under my chin and hold on to her as tightly as I can, wishing I could absorb her pain, and go back in time and change things for her.

"I never knew I was adopted until I got diagnosed with kidney disease. That was when I found out about Kelly and my birth mom."

"What?" I hiss in disbelief, and her head shakes while her fingers dig into my skin. "I thought you knew you were adopted."

"I didn't. If I hadn't gotten sick, I doubt I would know now. My parents freaked when I was diagnosed. They were worried I'd need a transplant and have a hard time finding a match, so they told me everything. Until then, I had no idea. I grew up being told I looked like my mom and dad. I thought they were my birth parents."

"Christ." My eyes close and my arms spasm around her.

"I was so mad at them for a long time for lying and never telling me the truth. I felt like my whole life was a lie. I couldn't understand how they could keep something like that from me."

"I'm sorry, baby. Jesus, I'm so fucking sorry."

"It's okay."

"It's not. It's not okay they didn't tell you."

"I get it now. I know now that they were trying to protect themselves and me from getting hurt, but it still sucked finding out the way I did. And it was worse that Kelly thought I was trying to use her."

"She didn't think that."

"She did. She hated me because of it, because I didn't contact her until I found out I was sick."

"She didn't hate you. She was mad at the world for the hand she was dealt, but she also didn't do anything to change that or make it better. She could have changed her path, but she didn't want to."

"Our mom—"

"Your birth mom is a cunt," I cut her off with a squeeze. "But Kelly wasn't a child. She was an adult making her own decisions. Just because you grow up one way doesn't mean you can't make a better life for yourself. Every single person has the ability to change the course of their life, no matter who they are, how they grew up, or what they've done in their past."

"You're right," she whispers, and I roll her to her back and look down at her.

"Are we okay now?" I question, and her eyes soften and her hands slide up my chest to my shoulders.

"We're okay," she says quietly, and I drop my forehead to hers, resting it there.

"All I want is to protect you." I move my thumb and cover her lips when it looks like she's going to talk. "I know that's impossible in this situation. This isn't something or someone I can protect you from. But I can do my best to take care of you, so let me do that. Even if it's just making sure you eat or sleep, I need to know I'm doing my job." I run the back of my fingers down her cheek and neck.

"Okay." She smiles softly, sliding her hand up my neck and jaw and curving her fingers around the side of my head. "In that case, I'm hungry."

"What do you want to eat?" I ask, and she tips her head to the side before she grins.

"A salmon taco salad sounds good. Are you in the mood for an obnoxiously large burrito?"

"No, but I'm sure I can find something else to order." I kiss her nose and pull her out of bed then take her to the shower.

Later, I put her in the car and take her out to dinner. While we're there, I send a text to my sister, Nalia, telling her I love her and support her in her decision to get to know our birth mom even if I still don't understand her reasoning.

Chapter 16

Kim

RINGING THE BELL and hearing Elizabeth yell, "Come in," I pull in a breath as I turn the knob and open the door. I'm nervous. I hate letting people down, and I feel like me moving out of my place and not being around is definitely letting Elizabeth and Jelikai down.

Five days ago, Sage and I got back from Florida, and yesterday, he left for Alabama for the week with Jax for some job. I hate that he had to leave so soon after we got home, but with him gone, I know I can take care of a few things I've been putting off, like telling Elizabeth I'm moving out, closing on the shop, and getting things worked out with Ellie there.

"Why did you ring the bell?" Elizabeth asks, looking down at me from the upstairs platform as I shut the door.

"Sorry, I didn't think."

"I'm doing laundry. Feel like keeping me company?" She smiles, tipping her head to the side.

"Yeah." I drop my bag on the entryway table and head up the stairs, following behind her into the laundry room at the end of the hall.

"How are things and how was your visit with your parents?"

"Things are good and the visit was nice," I say, picking up one of the boys' T-shirts, folding it, and adding it to one of the piles. "I..." I pick up another, folding and using it as an excuse not to look at her, because I don't want to see the disappointment in her eyes. "I have some news."

"You're moving and getting married," she states, and my eyes fly up to meet hers, knowing mine are wide with surprise. "Honey, this is a small, small town, and you just took Sage Mayson off the market. *Permanently.* Everyone—and I mean everyone—knows about it." She laughs, and I shake my head then still when she reaches out, taking my hand. "This is beautiful," she murmurs, moving the engagement ring on my finger from side to side studying it.

"Thank you," I whisper, wrapping my fingers around hers, and her eyes meet mine and soften.

"Are you happy?"

"Yes."

"Then so am I."

"You're not mad at me?"

"God, no. The only way I'd be mad at you is if you didn't flipping move in with that man. Believe me, I love my husband and my boys, but if Sage Mayson showed up at my door and asked me to move in with him, I might consider it for a half a second longer than I should before I turned him down." She laughs and I giggle. "The boys will still want to see you."

"I'm not moving far," I say as an answer to that, and she nods. "Thank you for everything you've done and for being my friend. You and Jelikai have been so amazing to me." I give her a hug and she squeezes me back.

"You're a part of our family. So remember that when you leave and know you can always come back."

"Thanks." Tears prickle the back of my eyes, but I fight them back, tightening my hold before I let her go. Then I spend the rest of the afternoon hanging out with her until the boys get home from school. We all go out to dinner, where I promise the boys they can come to the lake house when the weather gets warm enough to go kayaking with

Sage and me.

"PINK AND GLITTER!" Hope shouts at the top of her lungs, and I look at her mom and laugh.

"I'm not sure about pink and glitter for paint colors, honey," Ellie says, and Hope's face falls.

"I like it," I say, and Ellie's eyes come to me and widen with surprise while Hope claps in glee.

"I know the idea of painting the salon pink and glittery is a little over the top, but it could work. We could do the walls hot pink, with thick white glitter stripes. Then we could get those cool mirrors we were looking at, the squiggly ones, and put them above each station, and change out the chairs to the white and chrome ones we found."

"Hmm." Ellie taps her chin with her finger while Hope stands up on her chair, waiting for her mom's reaction. "If we do that, we can then do the front of the salon white with bright accent colors. We love this couch," she says, running her hand over the purple material. "So it could stay, and we could just add a few pops of pink and other bright colors with pillows and art."

"That would look amazing," I agree, and Hope tackles me, wrapping her arms around my neck. I hug her back then kiss her cheek before she settles on the floor between Ellie and me, where she goes back to coloring.

"Jax and Sage said they'd get the guys together to paint and to do the construction. So we will save a little money that way, meaning we can open up the front wall the way we wanted and add a couple more chairs," Ellie thinks aloud.

"I love it." I smile, and she grins back. "This is really happening, isn't it?" I ask, and she reaches over to take my hand, giving it a squeeze before letting go.

"It is. We close tomorrow, and when that happens, this place will be ours," she replies, looking around, and I follow her gaze around the salon, thinking that I really do love this place. Frankie helped me settle into life here, and if it wasn't for him, I don't know what I would have done.

"I'm sad Frankie's leaving," I say quietly.

Ellie's smile disappears. "It's not going to be the same without him."

"No, it won't be," I whisper as tears start to clog my throat.

"You bitches better not be crying," Frankie calls, coming out from the back of the shop.

I wipe away the tear that had fallen down my cheek and shake my head before tipping it back to look up at him. "No one's crying."

"Good, I can't deal with crying." He kisses the side of my head then leans over, doing the same to Ellie before stepping back. "You girls know I'll be back from time to time to check on things and you two. Plus, I expect you to come down to Florida to visit, and do it often."

"We will." Ellie smiles, and Hope yawns, turning toward me and climbing onto my lap before resting her head against my chest.

"I'll see you guys tomorrow at the closing," Frankie tells us, giving us each another hug before leaving through the door.

"We should probably call it a night," Ellie whispers, looking at Hope, and I glance down, finding her eyes closed.

I smile. "Yeah, it's been a long day," I agree, kissing the top of Hope's head before handing her off to Ellie when she stands.

"Are you staying at the lake or in town?" Ellie asks as I gather our stuff and put it away behind the front desk.

"Probably in town tonight. That way, I can head to the hospital in the morning and go visit with June and hopefully see the baby," I say, referring to Sage's cousin and my friend, who's pregnant. This morning, she was admitted to the hospital after she started having contractions, but she still hasn't had the baby. The last time I called to check on her, she was still only dilated to a four, but her husband refused to let them kick her out, which didn't surprise me at all. Evan is part crazy and completely in love with his wife, and he's freaked out that she's now two weeks past her due date.

"Since Jax and Sage are both gone, do you want to stay with Hope and me for the night? Then tomorrow we can all head over to see her together," Ellie suggests, and Hope perks up, twisting her head toward me.

"You can stay in my princess bed with me." Hope smiles at me sleepily, and I grin at her and run my fingers down her cheek.

"I'd love that, but I need to run home to get some clothes first," I reply, picking up my bag and Ellie's, carrying them toward the door behind her.

"Cool, we'll figure out dinner when you get to the house."

"Sounds good," I agree, opening the door and letting her out before turning and locking it behind us. Helping her into the car, I get in mine then head home.

I pick up some clothes then head right back across town, where I spend two hours hanging out with Hope and Ellie before we get the call telling us to come to the hospital, because June finally had Tia.

"She's perfect," I whisper, looking down at the baby in my arms then at her momma, who is sitting up in bed looking as beautiful as ever. Her husband is cuddled up next to her with his big bulky arm around her shoulders.

"She is, isn't she?" Evan asks.

I grin at him as June elbows him in the ribs, rolling her eyes at his arrogance. "Absolutely," I murmur, pulling my eyes from them to look at the sleeping baby girl in my arms. Evan has a right to be arrogant. Tia is perfect; she is one of the cutest newborns I've ever seen.

Running one finger down her soft cheek, my heart gets tight as I wonder if I will ever have this with Sage. I want a family with him, but I'm not sure it will ever happen unless we adopt since it's not very safe for me to get—

Oh, shit.

My heart stops, and then starts to pound in my chest as my palms start to sweat. I haven't had my period since Sage and I got back together.

Oh, God.

I haven't had my period since Sage and I got back together!

My stomach rolls at the realization.

"You okay?" June asks, and I lift my eyes to hers and nod dumbly then hand Tia over to November when she reaches out to take her from me.

"Are you sure? You look like you just saw a ghost," April says, and December nods in agreement while May and July all study me, looking concerned.

"I'm fine," I whisper then clear my throat and look at June, plastering a smile on my face. "I'm so happy for you."

"Thank you." June smiles, and then her eyes go to the door as people start to come into the room.

My heart lifts when I see Sage come in behind his sisters, mom and dad, and Ashlyn, Dillon, and Jax. Giving everyone a quick hello, I move right to him and into his arms, where I rest my head against his chest.

"Hey, baby." He kisses my hair then drops his mouth to my ear. "I tried to call you to let you know Jax and I were on our way back to town, but you didn't pick up," he says as my arms tighten around him.

"Sorry, I put my phone on silent when we got to the hospital."

"You okay?"

Am I okay? I have no idea, but I don't say that. I know he worries, so I don't want to give him something else to worry about unless it's necessary.

"I'm okay. I've just missed you." I tip my head back, and his hand wraps around the side of my head and his thumb smooths over my cheek as he studies me with soft eyes.

"Missed you, too." He kisses my forehead and my nose before brushing his lips across mine softly, touching his tongue to my bottom lip. Pulling back, he grins and I smile at him. Leading me across the room, he gives June a hug and Evan a pat on the back before taking Tia from November. She growls in annoyance that she's once again giving up her granddaughter.

Watching him with Tia, tears burn the back of my eyes. I don't know what I will do if I'm pregnant, but I know if I am, I will do whatever is necessary for Sage to hold his child like he's holding his niece.

"Okay, give me my daughter." June reaches out to him a few seconds later when Tia starts to wake up, and he laughs then carefully places her back in her mom's arms. Tucking me back against his side, he turns us around, and the moment he does, everyone is there giving us hugs and quiet congrats on getting engaged.

"Your ring is gorgeous," Willow whispers, taking my hand.

"When are you getting married?" Harmony asks, stepping closer and away from Harlen who's been holding her possessively since he walked into the room much to the dismay of Nico who's been glowering the whole time.

"I don't know. Probably a year or so. It depends on how long it takes to plan the wedding," I reply, and everyone starts to laugh.

"Good luck with getting him to wait a year," April inserts, and Sophie, who is standing next to me, narrows her eyes on her son, making me smile.

Yesterday, Sophie called me to get my mom's number, and twenty minutes after that, my mom called to tell me that Sophie called her to ask when she would be in town so she could take Mom out to show her a few venues. So I know she wants a wedding as much as my mother and I do.

"Okay, everyone out," Evan calls, breaking into the moment, and all eyes go to him as he gets off the bed, tucking a thick white blanket around June, who is asleep with Tia resting against her chest.

"But—" November starts.

Before she can say more, Asher cuts her off by wrapping his arm around her and dropping his face toward hers. "You can visit tomorrow."

"But I was going to stay the night," she tells him, and his head goes back.

"No, you weren't," he mutters, and she frowns up at him then moves her eyes to Evan.

"You're not staying. You can come back tomorrow," Evan confirms, shaking his head in denial, and her narrowed eyes move between both men.

"Damn bossy men," she huffs, stomping toward the door. "You guys are annoying." She leaves and Asher chuckles, giving Evan a pat on his shoulder.

Fighting my own laughter, I say a quiet goodbye to Evan, not wanting to wake June or the baby, and leave the room with everyone else.

I stop Sage with a tug of his hand holding mine once we get outside. "My car is at Ellie's."

"We'll get it tomorrow. It'll be safe at Jax's."

"I need my bag from their house. Then I need to stop at the drugstore," I tell him.

He frowns, taking a step toward me, dropping his voice while wrapping his hand around my hip. "Are you okay?"

"I'm fine. I just need to make a stop," I say, not sure if I'm lying about being fine, because I'm totally freaking out on the inside.

"All right, we'll stop, grab your bag, and then head to the pharmacy."

"Right," I concur, figuring I can leave him in the car and run into the drugstore on my own.

Lucky for me, the gods were feeling generous, because he was going to come inside with me but got a call right as we pulled up to the store. While he took his call, I was able to go in and quickly buy a couple tests and a few random bits from the aisles I walked down. I hid the test at the bottom of my bag, telling myself I wasn't really keeping anything from him; I was just waiting until I had something to say before I brought the situation to his attention.

Not Pregnant.

Seeing those two words, my chest hurts. I know it's for the best, but between last night and this morning, I had gotten used to the idea of being pregnant and what that would mean. Tossing the test in the trash under the sink, I wash my hands while fighting back the tears suddenly blurring my vision. It wouldn't have been good if I were pregnant. I know that realistically. But hope can sometimes be a dangerous thing.

I shake my head and leave the bathroom, heading for the kitchen, where I make myself a cup of tea. Then I take it out to the sunroom, where Sage and I had been lounging in one of the hammocks until a few minutes ago, when I went inside to take the test. Seeing his eyes are closed, I set my cup of tea on the floor then fall-slash-roll into the hammock next to him, resuming my position with his arm around me, my head against his pec and my thigh over his hip.

"I'm not pregnant," I whisper, and his abs under my hand tense. I feel his chin tip down, but I don't look up at him.

"Pardon?"

"I… I realized yesterday that I hadn't had my period since we got together, and I thought…" I let my words taper off as my eyes close. "It doesn't matter. I'm not."

"That's why you wanted to stop at the drugstore last night," he accuses, and it's my turn to tense.

"Yeah."

"Why didn't you tell me?"

"I didn't want you to freak out and go all weird on me the way you tend to do when anything happens."

"I don't go weird." His arm tightens. "I love you. I worry."

"I didn't want you to worry until there was something to worry about."

"Look at me," he rumbles as the energy around us changes. My eyes fly up to meet his, and I swallow at the intense look in his eyes. "You do not get to do that."

"What?"

"It's my job to protect you. You do not get to keep shit from me under the pretense that you're trying to protect me. That is not okay with me."

"But—"

"No buts," he cuts me off. "I love you. I love that you want to do that for me, but no. Next time you have something like that happen, you tell me straight up. You do not wait until after the fact to talk to me."

"I—"

"No. Tell me you get me."

"Okay, I get you," I agree, and he shakes his head before cupping my jaw.

"You wanted the test you bought to be positive, right?" he asks, and my shoulders tense along with the rest of my body.

"I...." I shrug, unable to form words.

"I know you did. I can see it in your eyes and hear the disappoint-ment still lingering in your voice. I can't say I'm not happy you aren't pregnant, baby," he says, and my heart cracks. I start to bolt from him, but his arms tighten and he continues talking. "I know from what I've read that pregnancy at your stage could be complicated for not only the child you're carrying, but for you, too. And I do not want that." His lips rest against my forehead as he whispers there. "What I want is that long life you promised me."

"You read up about it?" I breathe, and his fingers move to my chin and he lifts until my eyes meet his soft ones.

He turns toward me, resting his leg over mine as he sifts his fingers through my hair. "You're not the only one who wants a family, Kimberly. I want children with you. I just know we will probably have to adopt or get a surrogate to carry that child for us. I will never put you at risk. Never."

"You've really thought about this."

"After I fucked up with you, I spent a lot of time thinking about the things I'd do if given a second chance. I've definitely thought about our future and what that future would entail."

"Oh my God. You're going to make me cry," I whisper, right before I start to cry and bury my face against his chest, swearing I hear him laugh. But I ignore that, because it will annoy me. Instead, I focus on the fact this amazing man is mine.

"When the time is right, we'll talk about babies and figure out what we should do."

"Okay," I agree as his hand moves down my spine then back up, wrapping around the back of my neck.

"I'd give you the world," he says quietly, and even though those words are spoken softly, I can still hear and feel the depth of emotion they contain.

I know he would. If he could give me the world, he would do it. But like I said before, I don't need the world.

All I need is him.

Chapter 17

Sage

"BABE, WE WERE supposed to leave fifteen minutes ago," I shout, walking back into the bedroom, where I left Kim over an hour ago to get showered and ready.

"Don't you dare start with me. Us being late is your fault. You should have kept your hands to yourself and let me get into the shower earlier... alone!" she shouts the last word back and I smile, thinking about what I did to her in that shower as I walk around the corner into the bathroom.

Seeing her standing in front of the vanity applying mascara, her upper half bent over the sink with her ass in the air while wearing nothing but a pair of high cut sheer panties, my cock twitches. I cannot fucking believe that tomorrow she will be my wife. Between her, her mom, and my mom, aunts, and cousins, they got our wedding planned in nine months instead of a year, which worked for me, because I was starting to get impatient. Her living with me has been good—no, better than good—but it hasn't been enough. I want her tied tight to me so that nothing will ever separate us.

Stepping up behind her, I wrap my hand around her waist, pressing my hips into her ass.

"Don't," she hisses as my hand slides around her stomach.

"Don't what, baby?"

"Don't look at me like that," she says, then her eyes flare and her pupils dilate as my hand slides down.

My fingers slip into her panties between her legs and through her folds. "How am I looking at you?" I circle her clit, and her ass presses back into my erection while her eyes hold mine in the mirror. "Tell me?" I pinch her clit, causing her hips to jerk back and her neck to arch.

"Like you want to devour me."

"I like the idea of devouring you."

"We are going to be so late," she pants, trying to stand, but before she can, I slide my free hand up her back and hold her in place bent over in front of me while I work her over.

"Hold onto the edge of the sink," I murmur, and her wild eyes meet mine as she does as I asked. Pulling my hand out of her panties, I take a step back and slide the silky material down her legs. "Bend over a little more," I instruct, while smoothing my hands over her ass cheeks. Complying, she bends at the waist, causing her ass to tilt even farther and me to get a glimpse of the swollen lips of her pussy from behind. Getting down on my knees, I spread her open and blow across her wet sex.

"Sage."

"Shhh, I want to eat in silence." I lick through her folds, listening to her moan deep in her throat. I love the way she tastes, but I love the way she lights up every fucking time I get my mouth on her more. Keeping her open, I lick and suck every inch of her pussy but her clit.

"Sage." She twists at the waist and grabs onto the top of my head.

Smiling, I give in and pull her clit into my mouth. The second I do, she goes up on her tiptoes trying to get away, but I keep a tight hold on her ass, so tight I know she will have marks from my fingers. Sucking her clit into my mouth, I flick my tongue over the tight bundle of nerves until the sound of her coming bounces off the walls in the bathroom. She falls forward, her forehead resting against the top of the vanity, and I stand, keeping one hand around her waist while I use the other to free myself from my slacks.

Wrapping my hand around my painfully hard cock, I press the swollen head against her slit then slide into her slowly, inch-by-inch, feeling her walls tighten, and ripple. Her head flies back, causing her mass of hair to hit my chest.

"Sage," she breathes again. My mouth goes to her shoulder and I nip there, listening to her moan as I pull out and slide back in.

Lifting my head to look at her in the mirror, I watch my hands slide across her creamy skin, one down to her clit, the other up to her breast, cupping and squeezing her roughly. "Take me there," I growl, and she does. She fucks back onto me, matching me stroke for stroke until my spine tingles and her pussy pulses around my cock, sending me over with her.

"I can't move," she whispers as I lift her up with my arm around her middle, and rest my chin against her shoulder, catching her smile. "I don't even know if I will be able to walk."

"I'll carry you." I tip my head to the side and kiss her neck, and then my cell rings and I groan against her skin.

"We're probably in trouble for being late." She laughs then whimpers as I carefully pull out of her and turn her in my arms.

Taking her face in my hands, I kiss her wet, deep, and hard then pull back, muttering, "I don't give a fuck" as my phone stops ringing, only to start back up again a second later.

"That can't be good," she says, I don't agree even though she's right. I bend down, jerk up my pants, and grab my phone.

Seeing my dad is calling, I put my cell to my ear. "What's up?"

"If you're on your way, don't stop. And if you're not, keep Kim home," he tells me, and my muscles get tight.

"Why?" I bark, causing Kim, who is pressed against me, to jump.

"Ginny just showed up."

"Come again?" I growl, but I know Kim heard, because her eyes lock with mine while pain and anger fill them.

"She's here at the restaurant. She's drunk. Bax and Talon are trying to get her to leave, but she's refusing and keeps saying she needs to talk to Kim."

"Fuck."

"I'll call and give you an update," he says, and Kim, who I had been trying to hold onto, pulls from my arms and runs out of the bathroom. Clicking off my phone, I follow her across the bedroom and into the closet, where she's yanking on a pair of panties similar to the ones she had on earlier before grabbing a dress off the back of the door.

"We're going," she says as she pulls the dress down over her head.

Shaking my head, I cross my arms over my chest and plant my feet apart, blocking her exit. "We're not," I tell her softly, and her eyes meet mine.

"We are, and either you're taking me, or I'm going by myself." Seeing the pain in her eyes, mine close against it. "Please," she whispers, wrapping her hand around my forearm, and my eyes open.

Fuck, I do not want her around that woman, but I can see she needs this. A war rages inside of me, a battle between keeping her safe and giving her what she needs.

"Please," she repeats, and my hands clench into fists.

"Fuck." I uncross my arms and pull her tightly against me. "You stay with me, right next to me, and if shit goes south or if I feel like you're in danger, you do as I say when I say it."

"She's not dangerous."

"Has she hurt you before?" I question, and her face answers for her. She might not have hurt her physically, but she has hurt her emotionally. "Right, like I said before, you stay with me and do what I say."

"Okay," she agrees, and I give her a nod then a quick kiss before I move back to the bathroom. Meeting her in the kitchen a few minutes later, I curse under my breath and vow that bitch will not ruin our rehearsal dinner. I know tonight is important to Kim. She looks beautiful wearing the simple white sleeveless dress she has on. It hits her just above the knee and high around her neck with silver and gold beads around her throat, and taupe-colored platform heels on her feet.

"You sure about this?" I ask when she looks at me.

"Yes."

Placing my hand against her lower back, I lead her out of the house to my car and help her in before slamming the door and jogging around the hood. As soon as I'm in and buckled with the engine running, I look over at her, taking her hand. "No matter what happens, she is not allowed to hurt you."

"She's never harmed me, honey," she says quietly, and I shake my head.

"I'm not talking physically, baby. I'm talking about emotionally. I was there when you met her. I saw the pain she left you with when she didn't give you what you needed her to," I explain, and her hand spasms in mine. "I'm giving you this because you need it, but you need to prepare yourself for whatever she is going to say to you. You can hear her out, and you can say whatever it is you need to say to her, but when she's gone, you let that shit go and we continue moving on with our lives the way we have been."

"I promise," she agrees, and I bring her hand up to my lips, kissing her fingers before placing her hand on my thigh and maneuvering us away from the house, down the driveway, and into town.

Pulling into the parking lot of the restaurant thirty minutes later, I park in an empty space while Kim's grip on me tightens. I know she saw the same thing I just did. Ginny sitting on the ground outside the entrance to the restaurant, with my family and hers gathered around her in a semicircle. "Are you ready for this?"

"Yes," she answers immediately. Unhooking her belt, I pull her into my lap. I don't want her to do this; it's going against every instinct I have to let her. "After this, she doesn't get anything else," she assures, and I nod, pulling her face toward mine to kiss her. I then open my door and step out with her in my arms.

Letting her feet touch the ground, I study her in the dim streetlight for a moment before releasing her, taking her hand, and shutting my door. Walking through the parking lot toward the entrance, I can hear the murmur of voices and the sound of a woman crying. When we hit the edge of the building, Kim's steps slow as we see everyone's eyes come to us.

"Honey," Pattie says, walking quickly toward us. "You guys shouldn't be here."

"It's our rehearsal dinner. So yes, we should be here," Kim corrects her mom before looking at Ginny, who is staring up at her with tears in her eyes. "You shouldn't be here, though."

"You're my daughter," Ginny replies as she puts her hands to the cement to heft herself up off the ground. Instantly, I pull Kim closer, but it's not necessary. Talon, Bax, Jax, Evan, Wes, and Cobi all push forward, blocking the older woman from getting close.

"I'm not your daughter. You gave birth to me, but you're not my mom. You never wanted to be my mom," Kim says quietly, and anger flashes in Ginny's eyes as she looks from Kim to the people gathered around her.

"You think you're too good for me. Just like your sister, you think you're too fucking good for me," she hisses, and Kim's body tenses at the mention of Kelly.

"I wish…" Kim closes her eyes then opens them back up, dropping her voice. "I wish Kelly had thought she was too good for you. I wish the second she had the chance that she would have left you and never looked back."

"You bitch." Ginny lunges, and I pull Kim behind me as Jax and Talon catch her by her arms. "Fuck you!" she screams.

"Why are you here? How did you even know about tonight?" I ask, and her eyes come to me.

"Her gay friend told me," she hisses, and I look at Chris, who is standing with his boyfriend, looking completely freaked out as he takes in the scene.

"What?" Kim whispers, looking over at Chris, who is now pale.

"I… I called to her to ask for the ashes. I wanted to give them to you. I told her you were getting married and that… fuck…." He jerks his hand through his hair.

"Chris," Kim whispers, and his eyes meet hers and fill with tears.

"I swear I didn't know she'd do this. She was just supposed to come and meet me. I wanted you to have them."

"It's okay."

"It's not." He shakes his head.

"You will never have any piece of her," Ginny yells, and Kim's body jolts. "You don't deserve to have a piece of her, so fuck you." She points at Kim then she swings her hand around, pointing at everyone else. "Fuck all of you."

"Are the cops on the way?" Talon asks, looking at my dad, and I see him nod before watching Ginny's eyes get wide.

"You called the cops on me?"

"You're wasted. You drove here wasted. No fucking way am I gonna let you get behind the wheel of a car in the state you're in," Dad mutters, and she starts to fight, but with six giant dudes holding her, she is barely struggling when the cops pull in and put her in cuffs.

"Well, now that's done, how about we go celebrate?" my mom suggests with a smile fifteen minutes later as the cops load a still screaming Ginny into the backseat of the squad car.

"Seriously, babe?" my dad scolds with a grin twitching his lips.

"What?" My mom frowns at him.

"Nothing," he mutters, pulling her in to kiss the side of her head.

Leading Kim away from everyone, I wait until we're out of earshot then tug her into my front and rest my hand around the side of her neck, dipping my face close to hers. "You okay?"

As she pulls in a breath, her head tips back and her hands move to rest against my chest. "I'm okay."

"You sure?"

"Yeah, I think I needed that. I used to wonder why Kelly cared about her so much and why she kept going back. I thought maybe I was missing something or that I was missing out on something," she confesses, dropping her forehead to my chest. "I'm glad I know now there is nothing for me to mourn. She's just a person. Yes, she gave birth to me, but she will never be a part of my life, and I will never be a part of hers."

"Baby." I kiss the top of her head, keeping my arms tight.

"It's for the best," she adds, then she lifts her head and looks around my shoulder when footsteps get close. I know who it is without looking, so I kiss the side of her head and let her go to her friend.

"I'm so sorry," Chris says, and I can hear the stress in his voice as Kim steps forward to hug him. As much as I want to be pissed at him for what went down, I can't be. He didn't know the bitch would make a scene, and he was trying to do something for my woman.

"It's okay," Kim whispers, patting his back as he cries.

Thankfully, by the time we make it into the restaurant, the drama for the evening has come to an end and we're able to do nothing but celebrate with our friends and family.

LYING IN BED with Kim asleep against me, I stare up at the night sky as my mind replays what went down with Ginny and the pain I kept seeing in Chris's eyes throughout dinner. Even with Kim telling him that it was okay, he was still a mess. "Fuck." I rub a hand down my face then carefully get out of bed and get dressed.

"Baby, I'll be back," I say as I take a seat on the side of the bed touching her hip, and her sleepy eyes blink open to meet mine.

"What? What time is it?" she asks.

I look at the clock then mutter, "It's 12:15."

"Where are you going at 12:15 at night? On the night before we are supposed to get married?" she asks, getting up on her elbow.

"I need to take care of something," I answer vaguely, and her body gets tight.

"Should I be worried?" she asks, wrapping her hand around my jaw and smoothing her thumb over my bottom lip.

"No."

"Promise?"

"Promise. Sleep. I'll be back."

"Okay," she whispers, leaning up and touching her mouth to mine, then dropping her head back to the pillow. "Be safe."

"Always." I kiss her once more then leave the room, closing the door as I go.

Heading out of the house, I set the alarm then get in my car and take off toward town. When I pull up in front of Chris's house forty minutes later, I shut down the engine and hop out, slamming the door behind me. Walking up his front porch, I pound on his door twice and wait for him to answer.

"Hey." He pulls the door open. "Is Kim—"

"Not here about Kim. Get dressed. You're coming with me."

"What?" His eyes get big and fill with panic. "Where are we going?"

"Alabama," I tell him, and the panic slides out as realization filters in.

"I'll be right back." He runs off, and I shake my head, feeling a smile curve my lips. Two hours later, we break into Ginny's house. Three hours after that, I climb back into bed with Kim, who only wakes enough to turn in my arms and cuddle close.

Kim

STANDING AT THE end of the aisle with my arm tucked into my dad's, I look around and tears blur my vision. The hall is beautiful, more beautiful than I could have imagined, with nothing but white tulle and bright pops of red and orange flowers everywhere that match my bouquet.

Touching one finger to the pendent around my neck, my throat closes up. A few hours ago, when I was getting ready before I had my makeup done, Chris came in to see me and gave it to me. At first, I thought it was just a beautiful necklace. I didn't know what the significance was. But then he explained that inside the pendent was a little bit of my sister's ashes.

I didn't ask him how he got them. I knew. After he told me that, I cried, because even if Kelly and I didn't have the best relationship, I want to believe that she would have wanted to be here with me today. So being able to carry her with me meant a lot.

"Don't cry," Dad mutters, handing me a handkerchief out of his pocket.

Turning my head his way, I smile. "I'm trying not to."

"Well don't, 'cause I don't want to cry," he says, and my heart gets warm as his eyes water. "You make a beautiful bride."

"Thank you, Dad."

"I love you. One of the best things that ever happened in my life was you," he whispers, kissing the side of my head, and I bite the inside of my cheek so I don't cry.

"I love you, too."

"I know," he mutters, and then the music starts up and he squeezes me in with his arm. As we make our way through the chairs lined up on each side of the aisle, my heart lodges in my throat.

I had imagined a million times what it would feel like to walk to-ward Sage on our wedding day, but I had no idea I would feel so complete. Watching his eyes heat and darken as they move over me in my wedding dress, and seeing the love and possessiveness in his gaze almost brings me to my knees. I love him. I love him more than I ever thought I could possibly love another person.

Seeing him step close, my eyes stay locked on him as he takes me from my dad, and then I'm in his arms, right where I'm meant to be. As we stare at each other, speaking our vows and holding on to each other tight, I know everything that has happened to me in my life led me to him.

"You may now kiss the bride," the pastor says, and my husband's hands hold my face gently as he kisses me, and the moment he pulls back, Monopoly money rains down on us, making me laugh.

"I love you, Kimberly Mayson," my husband tells me.

"I love you, too," I whisper, and then I wrap my hands around the back of his neck and pull him down for another kiss, hearing a cheer go up in the crowd.

Epilogue

Kim

Two years later

"HARDER." MY HEAD falls forward to the mattress and my hands slide out in front of me across the bed. "Please."

"Fuck," Sage growls, bending over me, and then his arm is under my breasts, lifting me up. With my back to his front, his free hand slides down over my stomach, zeroing in on my clit.

"Yes!" My hips rock into his fingers on my clit while his cock fills me over and over. "I'm going to come."

"Kiss me," he demands. Turning my head so he can capture my mouth with his, I feel his tongue slide between my parted lips. Oh, God, my body shakes as I come. Thrusting his hips once... twice more, he plants himself deep inside me, following me with his own orgasm.

"I'm going to be so late," I pant, trying to catch my breath.

He laughs. "Chris will get over it. Last month, he was two hours late showing up to dinner."

"True," I agree, and then whimper as he pulls out of me and smacks my ass hard enough to sting.

"You shouldn't be walking around in a towel, baby. That kind of easy access isn't something I can turn down."

"Whatever," I mutter, rolling to my back and pulling the sheet up my body feeling myself drift off to sleep.

"Kimberly?"

"Hmm?"

"You need to get up."

"You just gave me three orgasms. I'm taking a second to get myself together," I tell him, keeping my eyes closed.

"All right." He kisses my forehead then my lips, and then I hear the shower turn on. Ten minutes later, I finally pull myself out of bed and get cleaned up and dressed so I can meet Chris for his fitting.

"Um… do you think the white horses may be a little much?" I ask Chris, looking up from his wedding planning folder in my hand, and his head spins around as his eyes pin me in place.

"Are you asking me if I think my fairy tale wedding is too much?" he asks, sounding appalled, and I bite my lip.

"You rented two white horses," I state.

He rolls his eyes at me then mutters, "How else are we going to get to the venue?"

"I don't know. Maybe by car or a limo, like normal people?" I suggest, and he stares down at me like I've grown a third eye.

"Normal people? I don't even know what that means." He waves me off then stands still so the seamstress can get back to pinning his tux once more.

"Have you ever even ridden a horse before? Because I never have, and I'd rather not die on your wedding day," I mutter, taking a seat on the bench facing him.

"Don't be dramatic. How hard could it be?"

"So I take that as you've never ridden a horse before either." I sigh. "I do not see this ending well," I say, and the seamstress nods in agreement.

Chris looks between us like we're the crazy ones and his idea isn't outlandish or crazy as hell. "I'm getting married in a castle. I can't just pull up in a limo."

"I give up. I see you're not going to be deterred from having things your way." I shake my head at him.

Since the first time Fresco and Chris went out on a date, they have been together and completely inseparable. And three months ago, Fresco asked Chris to marry him. Since then, Chris has been planning his fairy tale wedding. A wedding that includes a real-life castle, two white horses, and twelve doves that will be released at the end of the ceremony. All a little over the top for my taste, but this is his wedding, not mine. And since I got my way and had the wedding of my dreams to Sage, I can't be mad at my friend for wanting his fairy tale wedding his way.

"Enough talk about the wedding. How are things with the adoption coming along?" he asks, and I feel my face get soft and a smile touch my lips.

"It's good. We just finished up the first step and went live on their website, so now we wait and see what happens and hopefully get chosen," I reply quietly, and his eyes fill with tears.

I know he's happy for me. For two years, I've been able to maintain my kidney function and haven't had any problems. Around the time Chris got engaged, Sage and I decided it was time for us to get serious about having a baby, so we started to look into adoption agencies. After we found one we both liked, we did all the necessary paperwork—which there was a lot of—including background checks, credit checks, visits with social workers, and physicals.

We are both excited about the prospect of becoming parents, but the last few years with just him and I have been nice. It's given us a chance to get to know each other—really get to know each other—and travel around a bit, which has been awesome. It's also given me time to focus on the salon, which is doing amazing. Business has been booming, and most days, there is a waitlist to get your hair done at Color Me Crazy.

"What did I tell you?" Chris asks, and I come out of my head, finding him looking at me softly.

"What did you tell me?" I whisper, and his face gets even softer.

"That life sometimes sucks for a while, but when you're feeling good and happy, you'll realize why you had to go through what you went through. You realize if you hadn't, you wouldn't have had a chance at the happiness you're feeling."

"You were right."

"I'm always right, not that you listen to me," he snarks.

I laugh at that then stand and walk across the room, where I carefully hug him so I don't get pricked by one of the many pins sticking out of him. "I love you."

"You, too, baby girl. From the bottom of my heart."

"Ditto," I whisper, and then I quickly wipe the tears off my cheek and look back at him. "I still think your fairy tale wedding is crazy, and I don't know how Fresco puts up with you."

"Fresco loves me."

"He does. I'm glad you found him and your happiness," I whisper.

"Ditto," he whispers back, kissing the top of my head before letting me go.

THREE MONTHS LATER, when I ride alongside him on a white horse toward the castle, and then stand by him as he marries his Prince Charming, all I think about is how crazy and amazing my best friend is and how only he could pull off a wedding like the one he had.

Sage

Six months later

HEARING A LOUD scream, I shut down the treadmill, turn, and hop off, and then let out a grunt as Kim runs into me at full speed. "What the fuck?"

"It's time," she pants, looking up at me.

I frown. "What?"

Shaking her head frantically while gasping for breath, she points the screen of her phone up toward me. "It's time. We're having a baby!"

"Jesus."

"Yeah."

"Christ," I mutter, moving her with me toward the door then through the house, past the living room, and down the hall to the bedroom.

"What are you doing?" she shrieks as I head for the bathroom while she heads for the closet.

"I need a shower."

"You can't shower. We're having a baby!" she shrieks at the top of her lungs.

"Baby, take a breath for me and calm down. You're not even dressed." I point out, and she looks down at the thin nightgown she has on. "You need to change, and since you've had us packed for weeks now, there's nothing else to do. As soon as I'm out of the shower, I'll get our shit in my ride and we can hit the road."

"I guess you're right," she says, and then her eyes fill with tears. Seeing those tears, I close the distance between us and pull her against me as she whispers, "We're having a baby."

Fuck me. I want to remind her that things can still go south, but I don't. I hold on to her, say a fucking prayer that things work out, and then kiss the top of her head.

"Go get dressed. As soon as I'm done getting ready, we'll leave and call our families on the way."

"Okay," she whispers, and then she leans up on her tiptoes and I tip my head down, kissing her once before letting her go. I move to the shower, coming out and finding she's gotten all of our bags, including the baby's, and is waiting for me at the front door.

Eight hours later, I hold on to her hand as we walk through the door of the hospital and head toward the nurses' station. It's now six in the evening, and we got word two hours ago that our son had been born.

Feeling Kim's hand shake in mine, I stop us and give her fingers a squeeze so she'll look at me. "Whatever happens, I promise everything will be okay," I tell her, and her worried eyes meet mine as she nods once before looking at the older woman approaching us.

"Mr. and Mrs. Mayson I presume," she greets us.

"Yes, hi," Kim says quietly, as she stops in front of us.

"It's nice to meet you both." She shakes our hands. "I'm Bethany, the social worker here at the hospital. If you'll follow me, I'll get you two checked into the hospital and your room, and then we'll introduce you to your son."

"Um... how's Ima?" Kim asks about the birth mom as we hand over IDs and sign in. At Kim's question, Bethany turns to face us. "She's okay, but she's chosen not to have any contact with the baby since delivery."

"What?" Kim whispers, squeezing my hand.

Ima and the agency told us about the birth plan weeks ago. The plan was that Ima would spend as much time as she could with the baby until she had to leave the hospital, so this news is a punch to the gut.

"These situations are always difficult, and sometimes the birth parents find it easier to deal with things if they don't have one-on-one bonding with the child after the birth," she explains quietly. My heart squeezes, not only for my son, who has been alone since the moment he was born, but for the mother of my child, who is somewhere in the hospital, fighting through what I can only imagine is excruciating pain.

"She may change her mind, but then again, she may not."

"Okay," Kim says, and I know she's just as worried about this new change of plan as I am.

Holding on to Kim after we get checked in, we head down a long hall, past an empty nursery, and into a simple room with a bathroom attached, a hospital bed, a chair, and a TV on the wall. "Wait here and I will be right back," Bethany says, leaving the room.

"I'm worried," Kim whispers, looking up at me as soon as she's gone.

I turn her in my arms, resting my hands around her waist. "It will be okay."

"I know. I... Ima just seemed so sure about wanting to spend time with him. What do you think it means that she changed her mind?"

"I don't know but I do know that it will be okay, baby. One step at a time," I tell her, and then the door is opened and Bethany walks in pushing a cart in front of her. Seeing the small bundle of blankets in the middle of the clear plastic bassinet, my heart beats hard against my ribcage.

"Mr. and Mrs. Mayson, I'd like to introduce you to your son."

Swallowing down the lump that has lodged itself in my throat, I stand with my wife in my arms as she picks up our son and brings him to her chest. "He's perfect," she whispers, and I hear the tears in her voice. Curling her closer, I study our boy, Nash, and grin when he pouts out his lips.

"He's probably hungry. The nurse was on her way to get you some supplies, so she should be here soon. You guys can move with him around Labor and Delivery as long as you have on your bands I gave you, but he can't leave the hospital until you guys get checked out. And before that, all the paperwork with the birth mother needs to be completed. As I said before, Ima may at some point want to visit with him, but as of right now, he will be staying in here with you two. So plan for the nurses and doctors to be in and out throughout the night and the next few days to check on him."

"Thank you," Kim tells her quietly.

"I pray that everything works out for you guys. You make a beautiful family. Congratulations." She smiles at us as the nurse comes into the room. "This is Minnie. She will be your nurse for the night," she introduces us to the nurse, who looks like a bulldog but is so soft-spoken I have to lean in to hear her as she tells us hello. "You guys are in good hands. If you need anything at all, my number is on the board," Bethany says, motioning to a whiteboard in the room in front of the bed.

"Thank you."

"Anytime." She smiles before she leaves.

Once she's gone, Minnie goes over the feeding and nighttime schedule with us. Then it's all a blur of diaper changes, bottles, and countless doctors and nurses.

We spend the next two days in the hospital with Nash, only seeing Ima once before she is released to go home. During that short visit, she chose not to hold Nash. I could tell she was settled in her decision to give him up for adoption, but she was still hurting and trying to cope with that pain the only way she knew how.

The day after Ima was released, so were we, and I rented us a house close to the hospital, where we waited for our lawyer to call and give us the all-clear to go home. Four days later, we got that call and we headed home with our son.

Kim

One week later

HEARING NASH CRY, I blink my tired eyes open. "Sleep baby, I got him," Sage whispers, touching his lips to my forehead then lips before he slides out of bed. Rolling to my side, I watch him walk across the room to the bassinet and pick up his boy and rest him against his chest with one hand on his back and one on his bottom. Seeing him hold our son so carefully, my heart warms in my chest. "How about you and I get a bottle and watch some TV?" he suggests, and I smile at that then watch the two of them leave the room thinking no fairy tale has ever been better than this.

Three weeks later

WALKING OUT OF the kitchen and into the living room with a fresh bottle for Nash, I smile when Nalia's eyes meet mine. "I think he's getting cuter by the day," she tells me, looking down at my son, who is now wide awake and looking up at his auntie. The week after we got home, Nalia called and asked if she could come visit for a couple weeks to spend time with her nephew. Sage and I both immediately agreed. It's been awesome having her around, and I know her being here is good for Sage. He misses his sister; everyone misses her, and we're all glad she's back for a while, even if it's just temporary.

"He does get cuter by the day, doesn't he?" I hand over the bottle to her, and she adjusts him in her arms, settles him against her chest, and then pops the bottle in his mouth like a pro.

"Totally. I sent my mom a couple pictures," she says absently, and then her eyes fly up to meet mine as her face pales. "I—"

"It's okay. I get it. I mean, I don't get it, because I don't have any kind of relationship with my birth mother, but I get why you want that."

"Sage—"

"He's dealing with it," I cut her off then drop my voice. "Your brother loves you, and even though he doesn't want to have a relationship with her, he respects that you do."

"I wish he would talk to her and get to know her the way I have."

"Don't count on that happening," I say, and sadness fills her eyes, making me feel guilty. But I've talked to my husband about this, and he is very firm in his decision. "Who knows what the future has in store for them, honey? But you can't force that on him if he's not ready."

"You're right, and on the plus side, since he's been with you, he's gotten better about talking to me about her. So maybe one day, right?"

"Right," I agree, and then I look down at my boy and feel my face get soft when I see he's already asleep.

I don't know what kind of relationship Nash and Ima will have in the future, but I know she loved him beyond measure. And as he's growing up, that's exactly what Sage and I will tell him.

Sage

One year later

"DADA, DADA, DADA," Nash sings as he waddles around the living room in a T-shirt and diaper, through the hundreds of toys that have gotten scattered across the floor since he got up this morning.

Pulling my eyes from my boy, I look at my wife, who is curled into the corner of the couch asleep, and I smile. She's tired; it was a long night and an early morning. Since Nash started teething, his schedule has gotten jacked. Last night, he was up until three in the morning. The good thing about it is he's happy when he's up. The bad thing is neither of us gets much sleep.

Moving across the floor on my hands and knees toward my son, I watch his eyes light up as he grins. Crawling toward him slowly, he laughs then runs off with me chasing after him. I listen to his laughter fill the room and grin as I catch him and toss him up in the air, making him giggle and babble away. Holding him against my chest, I kiss the side of his head then let him go when he wiggles, wanting down.

As I lean back against the couch, I stretch my legs out in front of me and cross my ankles. Our wedding picture on the mantel catches my attention, and I smile as I study it. The photo wasn't taken by a professional. My mom just so happened to take the perfect picture on her cell phone. In the photo, Kim and I are standing front-to-front, me looking down on her smiling, her head thrown back in laughter as a million dollars in Monopoly money flutters to the ground around us. She didn't know I had that planned, so when it happened, her reaction was priceless.

"Mama, Mama, Mama," Nash sings, and I feel Kim's hand on my shoulder then her lips at the top of my head.

Turning to look into her tired eyes, I feel my face get soft. "You should go lie down in bed, baby."

"And miss a second of this?" She shakes her head, and Nash waddles over, holding out his arms for her to pick him up. Cuddling him close to her chest, her eyes soften on mine. "I never want to miss a second of this."

Fuck, but I love my wife and our son, and I'm thankful every fucking day for the second chance I was given.

Until Harmony

"**H**ARLEN," I SHOUT as I hurry in my heels across the hospital parking lot, watching him kick up the stand on his bike and plant both his booted feet to the asphalt.

His eyes meet mine over his shoulder and just like the first time our eyes locked, my lower belly pulls tight and my blood sings through my veins.

God, he's gorgeous, but not in the traditional sense. He's too scary-looking to be pretty. His eyes too dark and his jaw too hard, the scruff there making him look almost dangerous. The kind of danger you want to see if you can tame. Only I doubt Harlen is the kind of man you tame.

"Hey." I smile once I'm close, feeling my skin warm as his eyes wander over me and he lifts his chin. Taking that for a scary guy hello, I grin. I remember that from a few weeks ago when I took him home from my cousin June's house.

He didn't say much then either, just grunted a few times but mostly he looked at me like I was a mix between amusing and crazy.

"Were you here to see the doctor?"

"Not sure why else I would be at the hospital, darlin'," he mutters.

"They take semen drawings all hours of the day," I mutter back, then watch as his lips twitch into an amused grin, which turns that tightness in my belly to something else, something I like even more.

"What did the doctor say?" I ask after a moment of enjoying his expression.

"It's all good. Stitches are out."

"Good," I say softly, reaching out to touch his muscular tattooed arm. His eyes drop to my hand resting on him then lift to meet mine and fill with something that makes me feel off-balance and dizzy. Dropping my hand away quickly, I take a step back. "I'm glad you're doing okay," I say, and he lifts his chin once more.

"Why are you here?"

"I had an interview for an RN position that opened up."

"Did you get the job?"

"I did." I smile in happiness. I've wanted to move home for a while now so getting the job at the hospital in town means I can now do that without having to lean on my parents.

"Feel like celebrating?" he asks, and my stomach does a flip at the idea of celebrating with him.

"Yes," I say without thinking, and he starts up his bike.

"Hop on."

"Hop on?" I repeat as he hands me his helmet.

"Yeah, hop on."

Acknowledgments

First I have to give thanks to God, because without him none of this would be possible. Second I want to thank my husband. I love you now and always—thank you for believing in me even when I don't believe in myself. To my beautiful son, you bringing such joy into my life, and I'm so honored to be your mom.

To every blog and reader, thank you for taking the time to read and share my books. There would never be enough ink in the world to acknowledge you all, but I will forever be grateful to each and every one of you.

I started this writing journey after I fell in love with reading, like thousands of authors before me. I wanted to give people a place to escape where the stories were funny, sweet, and hot and left you feeling good. I have loved sharing my stories with you all, loved that I have helped people escape the real world, even for a moment.

I started writing for me and will continue writing for you.

XOXO Aurora

Other Books by Aurora Rose Reynolds

The Until Series

Until November

Until Trevor

Until Lilly

Until Nico

Second Chance Holiday

Underground Kings Series

Assumption

Obligation

Distraction

Until Her Series

Until July

Until June

Until Ashlyn

Until Harmony (Coming Soon)

Until Him Series

Until Jax

Until Sage

Shooting Stars Series

Fighting to Breathe

Wide-Open Spaces

One last Wish (Coming Soon)

Alpha Law CA ROSE

Justified

Liability

Verdict (Coming Soon)

Finders Keepers

Fluke my life series

Running into love (Coming Soon)

About The Author

Aurora Rose Reynolds is a *New York Times* and *USA Today* bestselling author whose wildly popular series include Until, Until Him, Until Her, and Underground Kings.

Her writing career started in an attempt to get the outrageously alpha men who resided in her head to leave her alone and has blossomed into an opportunity to share her stories with readers all over the world.

For more information on Reynolds's latest books or to connect with her, contact her on Facebook at

facebook.com/AuthorAuroraRoseReynolds

on Twitter

@Auroraroser

or via e-mail at

Auroraroser@gmail.com

To order signed books and find out the latest news, visit her at

www.AuroraRoseReynolds.com

or

goodreads.com/author/show/7215619.Aurora_Rose_Reynolds

Made in the USA
Las Vegas, NV
08 February 2025